MW01611314

Other Comments about *Mame's Spirit*

Mame's Spirit conjures the power of Black women in the Mississippi Delta which I experienced in SNCC in the 60s. The spirit of women was the backbone of the freedom movement. Dr. Demczuk traces this spirit from Africa to America and back again, demanding justice long overdue. Read, remember and rejoice.
—**Dr. Frank Smith**, SNCC leader and founder of the African American Civil War Museum & Memorial.

Mame's Spirit helps to raise this vital question: How should we atone, reconcile or rectify the brutality of racism and caste that have damaged and continue to harm generations of humanity? The story of King Leopold and the Congo is an especially troubling case. This book represents one fictional answer and helps introduce this central topic that all of us will one day have to confront if we ever want to heal and transform the legacy of hate, human bondage and their pivotal role in the wealth building of the Western world.
—**Brenda Jones**, Author, *Queens of Resistance: Maxine Waters, Elizabeth Warren, Alexandria Octavia-Cortez and Nancy Pelosi*

A MUST READ, especially with the current climate demanding a more factual explanation over the colonial invasion of West Africa and racial reckoning worldwide. I see a film coming out of this story. We need more "truth-telling" in cinema now!
—**Robin N. Hamilton**, Documentary Filmmaker.

Dr. Demczuk and CMZ are savants for facts and enlighten the public to a very dark history. The narrative unfurls in a thought-provoking yet entertaining method.
—**Josh Lasky,** Author, *Every Step is a Gift.*

One of the most required narratives for the ever-evolving contemporary conversation about colonialism. Dr. Bernie Demczuk and CMZ Blackwell and walk a fine line of mystery and predetermined order as a result of a very dark secret of Africa's past.
—**Marcia Davis,** Supervising Editor of Race and Identity, *NPR*

I believe *Mame's Spirit* should be categorized as a "Real-fi" as it blends multiple realities and Afro-futurist possibilities of what the outcome could be if one became obsessed with one of history's most covered-up atrocities.
—**Essence Revealed,** Author, *STRIP: A Stripper's 20 Life Winning Lessons*

Mame's Spirit is an exceptionally told story with plot twists and rich characters that fascinates readers. Dr. Demczuk and CMZ weave a poignant and timely tapestry of true history that brings the story of human resilience to life.
—**John and Oumou McCarthy**, Author, *Filmmaker, and Baseball Coach.*

I hold this narrative close to my heart. Reparations and Romance should be discussed in the context of land stolen, which steals the heart out of Africa and her people. *Mame's Spirit* brings land home, and her truth will lead not run from history.
—**Aleya Frasier,** Argo-Ecologist, *Teacher and Farmer.*

If I were alive, I would recommend this novel as a must-read. Dr. Demczuk eloquently and compellingly brings light to a tragic period of inhumane proportions while CMZ drives home the point in the Afterword. I'll be back.
—**Mark Twain,** Author, *King Leopold's Soliloquy.*

One of the most required reads on the ever-evolving contemporary conversation on colonialism. Bernard and CMZ tell a deep story of personal and political intrigue and expose the lies of European colonialism forcefully. I felt like I was reading Franz Fanon.
—**LaNora Clark-Williams,** Author, *Muse*

"I am a champion of Bernard's past and *future* passion and expression for reparations. I highly recommend absorbing *Mame's Spirit* then forwarding to all contemporaries and their students. I can't wait to meet CMZ Blackwell."
—**Beverly Hunt,** Herbalist.

Mame's Spirit:
Reparations and Romance

Bernard Demczuk

with
CMZ Blackwell, Muse
www.mamespirit.com
@BernieInDC

ISBN: 978-1-7367247-2-9

Publisher:
Robert G.L. Newkirk III
RGLN3, LLC
www.rgln3.com

Editor:
Alice Heiserman
Write Books Right
www.writebooksright.com

Dedications

To my mom, **Berdena Jane Demczuk,** who joined her ancestors at ninety-one. She was a Rosie-the-Riveter in WW II at Bethlehem Steel Mill in Baltimore and a tough union organizer. Thank you for teaching me your arrogant Wonder-Woman attitude and for kicking my ass non-stop. To my dad, **Bernard Peter Demczuk,** who joined his ancestors at age seventy-one. He was a sailor in the South Pacific in WW II, an assembly-line factory worker, born in Turner Station, Maryland, a good union man who never scolded, yelled, or hit me; he was always helping to fix someone's car in our community. To my son's mom, **Jennifer Dee Mumford,** thank you for helping raise our beautiful son and showing him how smart and tough Black women are in a cruel world that devalues Black women.

And most importantly, to my son, **Che Marley Demczuk** — you display the best of the best above. You are smart to discard our weaknesses yet embrace our strengths. You are a kind and gentle person. Your natural brilliance taught me much, like, when those fastballs came in high and inside. Some knocked you back; some knocked you down, but you got back up, stayed in the box, and kept swinging as you continue to do today. You are my hero! I dedicate this novel to you, my son, Che, and ask that you continue to be kind, work hard, and stay honest. I learn so much from you. Thank you.

Acknowledgments

"To lose the way that is the way to know the way."
— Zanzibar Proverb.

I thank many people. They each deserve an essay of thanks. Without my friends and critics, *Mame's Spirit* would not be wandering around bookshelves or in the hands of those sipping wine in cafes, discussed in coffee shops, proudly being checked out in libraries, and gracing bookstores in Treme, Mississippi, and many other places, including at NYU's bookstore.

Along with the book, I anticipate hearing debates about methods to achieve reparations. When I began, I had no idea that this theme would become a novel, nor did I understand the extent of the horror that I would discover in the Heart of Darkness. But Africa, and those below, are helping me find my way. First, to my editors: Alice Heiserman, Larry Rubin, and Marcia Davis—their hard-hitting edits and ideas to move the story forward made the novel a reality. A special thanks to my friend and critic, Brenda Jones, who told me that my first draft should be deleted, trashed, and I should start over. Crushed, I started over. Thank you, Brenda. Alice Heiserman, you are so special as an editor because you are so patient. I wouldn't have tolerated me as you did. Alice believed in the story. So smart. Thank you, many times, over.

Special thanks to the Artists-in-Residents at GivernyWest

on the Choptank who read the early manuscript and offered ideas and criticism: Beverly Hunt, Aleya Fraser, LaNora Clark Williams, Robin N. Hamilton, Essence Revealed, John McCarthy, Josh Lasky, and Brenda Jones.

Most importantly, all are artists and authors in their own right, providing inspiration and guidance throughout the novel's five-year development. GivernyWest on the Choptank is fortunate to host a Guest Gardening Program yearly to maintain and manicure the sixteen gardens at GivernyWest. Thank you, guest gardeners: John and Oumou McCarthy, Nizam Ali, Jyotika, Tariq Ali, Jason Cross, Kimberly Young, Michael and Wendi Moy-Akin, Tiffany Greaves, Stephanie Drake, Josh Lasky, and Kate McMahon. You helped keep my gardens growing for inspiration and joy. Chef Oumou fed us well with her extraordinary authentic Senegalese cuisine. Thank you!

Thank you to *Mame's Spirit* legal advisor, Tiffany Greaves, Esq. She has, thus far, kept me out of jail. Your expert advice moved the novel and website to fruition, and your spirit is Mame's. My publisher and website wizard, Robert G. L. Newkirk, III, thank you, RGLN3! Your brilliance and bullish behavior keep the website and production churning to new heights as a working document, offering valuable information on the Democratic Republic of the Congo, the reparations movement, and West African spirituality. The website, **mamespirit.com**, is intended to be a living, growing, and always relevant document for students, scholars, and those curious about the spirit of African women, the true progenitors of us all, and our ongoing quest for social justice and racial equity.

We say "Mother Africa" for a reason. Robert has captured this truth by designing the website. You can take the African out of Africa, but you cannot take Africa out of the African. Listen to Black women. They know the way.

To friends wide and far in L.A.: film director Charles Burnett, Joanne Morris, Val Peacock, and Robin N. Clark. And to those struggling artists in Treme; Clarksdale, Mississippi; Brooklyn; Harlem; and Paris who offered input on the storyline and cover design of the novel: John McCarthy; Robin N. Hamilton; LaNora Clark-Williams; Josh Lasky; Beverly Hunt; Tiffany Greaves; Jamal Holtz; Stephanie Drake; Nizam Ali; Wendi Moy-Akin; Mike Akin; Leonette Henderson; Bubba O'Keefe; the family of Billy, Madge, and Mary Jane Howell; Colleen Buyers; Julia Browne; Tiffany Boyle; Doug Levin; Val Peacock; and Robin Marcus, —thank you! We went through eleven cover designs, and you made it what it is.

Capri and Willair St. Vil and our group of yearly trekkers to Haiti bring joy and material support to the Marius Levy Institute students in Le Cap Haitian. These friends were good enough to leave me alone while writing the novel on the seductive beach at Cormier Beach Resort. Many thanks to the staff and management there, especially owner Jean-Francois Bernard, for running one of the world's most artistic resorts.

To my Ben's Chili Bowl family, thank you for giving me a place and space to be creative, relaxed, and productive. Special appreciation to our matriarch, Virginia Ali, the quintessential hostess of our Nation's Capital and her sons, Nizam, Kamal, and Haider and their families Jyotika, Tariq, Sonya, Suraya, and Jaleel, and Vida Ali. Thank you!

To Jennifer Mumford and my son, Che Marley Demczuk, you gave me the space and support to think, write, and struggle through the writing and publishing process. To my mom, Berdena Demczuk, who passed while the novel ended its ordeal of being written. Mom, your strength, hard-headedness and wonder-womanhood arrogance are where I got my drive to create this story. To family members, including brother Steven and his daughters Gabriela and Nicole Demczuk and their mom Geltrouda, thank you for always being there for family.

To CMZ Blackwell, you are my source of inspiration. But first, I want to thank LaNora Clark-Williams, my muse from the North, for introducing me to you in the South. *Mame's Spirit* could not have been written nor the website designed without CMZ, whose Afterword provides a fitting coda to this novel. CMZ is rooted in the Mississippi Delta soil awash with ten thousand years of an overflowing river. From that soil, that hot sun, that terrible toil and the tears of Choctaws and Chickasaws that soaked the dirt fertile, you gave me the spirit to cry and write. You were with me every step of the way in heart, mind, soul, sleep, anger, and love. Thank you CMZ!

—Bernard "Bernie" Demczuk, August 2021

GivernyWest on the Choptank, Easton, Maryland,

Contents

Prologue: In the Beginning—1890: Boyeka Village, the Congo Free State

Tswambe lay face down on the ground at the beginning of the horror, covered with cow dung a few feet from his hut. He hoped the soldiers would think him a corpse, like his brother Dembia beside him. Tswambe's arm flopped on Dembia's back. The other seven kinfolks near him lay where they dropped when the Force Publique soldiers shot them because their family did not meet their quotas for collecting rubber.

A few feet away lay the corpse of his young, beautiful wife, Oumou. The soldiers had pulled her out of their hut. He could hear them laughing and her crying out as they raped her. She screamed; then they shot her. The soldiers laughed.

He desperately wanted to scream, to sob with overwhelming grief, but he tried to lie motionless. It was painfully difficult. He had to twist his lips to one side to be partially above the dung so he could breathe through his mouth. He listened while the soldiers began to hack down his home with their machetes, whacking his mud-lined walls and the roof he constructed of palm fronds and stems.

The soldiers had no patience to finish the job and walked

among the bodies, hacking off right hands with razor-sharp bush machetes to prove to the White captain they had not wasted expensive ammunition. The number of bullets used had to match the number of people killed, and the hands were the proof of the killing.

The soldiers were drunk and didn't notice that Tswambe slightly twitched when they harvested his hand. He had grown up with these men. He knew that the more hands they presented to their Belgium officers, the quicker they might be discharged from the Force Publique, King Leopold II's private army. They had already cut off the right hand of one of his children, who was screaming in pain in his partially destroyed hut.

Welcome to the Congo, 1890, a rubber-collecting camp along the Congo River about 186 miles north of Boma in the Kilanga village. The slightly sweet smell of latex from the rubber trees permeates the air along with other forest aromas. Groups of bonobos play under the trees. Wild orchids grace the lush diversity. Yellow, red, and purple flowery vines encrust the treetops. Rainbows arise from the sunlit spray from the waterfalls rushing down steep hillsides covered in luxuriant banana and mango trees. The beauty of the landscape contrasts with the barbaric horror of the soldiers' maiming.

La Force Publique lay claim to this land of plenty and beauty, violating God's peaceful presence by chopping the hands off of the children of parents who collected rubber too slowly or by killing their parents. Where is the

Catholic's *Jesus of Mercy* now? Is the Jesus of the Belgian pope represented by the Society of Missionaries of Africa, known as the White Fathers, human? Is this Jesus, the reincarnation of the devil? Force Publique soldiers dangle gold crosses of Christianity around their shiny jet-black necks, sweating from the exertion of killing their countrymen, countrywomen, and children, forever silencing their laughter.

In the far corner of the village, a dozen drunken soldiers slaughter the village's prized cow, slicing the back of its neck with machete hacks. Its blood spurts two feet high. This cow supplied milk to many of the children. This evening it will be medium-rare steak, ribs, and chops for the hungry, happy brutes. They'll drink the cow's blood like shots of single-malt scotch in a festival of music, machetes, and violence. This is King Leopold II's Free State of the Congo, 1890. "The horror, the horror".

Chapter 1

Greenwich Village, Coffee Shop Encounters

Strolling down 7ᵗʰ Avenue South, Ayo James absorbs Greenwich Village through all her senses. Ayo smells chestnuts roasting, urine drying in odd corners between buildings, and an occasional whiff of pot. The honking and screeching of traffic and drivers cursing each other in many languages make her smile. She feels the New York City air of early spring.

She thinks about how much she loves being where she is. Glancing at FAO Schwarz, she remembers that a bodega used to be there, and she feels guilty about enjoying being on a street that pushed out all but the very rich. She is so absorbed in her thoughts when her shoulder bumps into a middle-aged, portly woman. The woman has a pearl necklace and carries a Prada handbag.

"Watch out, nig..." the woman snarls but stops before finishing the word because she is surrounded by New Yorkers who might attack her for her virulent racism.

Ayo's first instinct is to whip out her badge, but she stops herself because she is conscious of being surrounded by New Yorkers and doesn't want to land in the *Daily News*, even as an anti-racist hero. Instead, she quickly apologizes and tugs down her purple NYU sweatshirt to ensure it covers her gun. Instead of making eye contact with the woman, she looks over her shoulder and spots Zuri, her best friend from college, heading into the Birch Coffee Shop across 7th.

"Zuri! Zuri Henri!" Ayo hasn't seen her in ages. She ignored whatever the White woman was about to say and was almost run over while bounding across the street against the light. Ayo pushes open the door and enters Birch's.

"Girl, where you been?" Ayo asks, hugging Zuri.

"Wassup, Ayo? It's been way too many years."

They chit-chat while purchasing their coffees and grab one of the coffee shop's few tables.

"You ever see Sharita?" Ayo asks.

"Yeah, last year. Sharita's now *Doctor* Sharita Jacobson. She got her doctorate in Black studies at Howard and now teaches at the University of DC. Big time prof."

"Did she marry that sweet guy named…what was his name?"

"Robert," Zuri responds.

"No, not Robert. Robbie. That lovely guy with a sweet smile, Robbie."

"Yep, she sure did. I need to find me a 'Robbie.'"

"How about Jennifer Munston," Ayo asks?

"That girl married an Italian stallion and moved to Tuscany—just like she said she would. She always loved the exotic. And Italian men are exotic and hot!"

"I wish we could get our whole gang back together," Ayo says. "We were some badass sistas. I still see some of the group, including Aisha and Kayla."

"Tell me when you see them again. I'll be there. Meanwhile, let's go to Jennifer's place. Have a reunion in Tuscany. An all-girls trek to Italy!"

"Yeah, right! So, you still seeing that jerk, Andre?"

Zuri almost spits out her coffee. "Oh, he's long gone. I'm not seeing anyone. Too busy. I'm a journalist, and my specialty is finance. Right now, I'm writing a series about the economics of women in Africa; how they're blocked from getting credit and can't get into programs that teach entrepreneurship—stuff like that."

Ayo notes that Zuri is wearing a very professional-looking yellow linen dress suit that beautifully sets off her Brown skin. She was tall and athletic, like Ayo herself. In college, Ayo recalled their long late-night discussions about solving the world's problems. "You majored in international relations, didn't you? Go on, tell me more about what you're up to?"

Zuri was eager to go on. "You remembered. Yes, my major was international relations, but my real interest was in

Africa and the Congo—the DRC—the Democratic Republic of the Congo. I'm actually on a lunch break from a meeting I'm covering about the progress women are making in the DRC. Remember how I told you that the women in Africa would rise up? Well, for years now, women in Africa have been demanding their rightful place."

"Yes," Ayo nods. "I remember when you talked about the woman warrior, Mame? She totally inspired me."

Ayo notes the passion in Zuri's eyes as her friend continues. "For fifteen years, Mame fought King Leopold-the-fucking-Second. That bastard personally owned the Congo and enslaved the people there, mostly Pygmies, forcing them off their land to collect rubber. During his reign, the last part of the nineteenth century, the Belgian aristocracy made a fortune—billions! But in the process, half the population of the Congo died, nearly ten million people.

"But Mame helped hundreds of people escape slavery and set up their own Maroon villages. If that woman could take on Leopold almost by her lonesome, then watch out when the women of the Congo get together! But enough about me. What about you? What've you been doing? Did you make it to law school? Doing anything with your French lit?"

Ayo sighs. "Law school—maybe someday, not now. French literature—I still read a lot and go to Provence as often as I can. But hold onto your latté, Zuri. I'm a cop."

7

"You're kidding!"

In answer, Ayo takes out her wallet and shows Zuri her gold NYPD badge. She lifts her sweatshirt to display the holster on her waist with a Glock 19-millimeter special.

"Oh shit!" Zuri squeals, pounding the table. "You're a cop! A real Black woman warrior. Isn't it dangerous?"

Ayo flashes a self-satisfied smile. "Sometimes. Actually, I'm a detective. I feel like I'm doing good. I'm part law-and-order warrior and part social worker. Hey, what about your brother? Jacques, right? You were always talking about him, but I never met him."

"It's funny you should ask," Zuri says, showing Ayo Jacques's picture on her smartphone. "He'll be here any minute. He knows everything there is to know about the Congo, and he's gonna give me background info to help me better understand what they're talking about at the meeting I'm covering."

Ayo studies the picture of Jacques, noting his slightly dimpled chin and penetrating eyes. His smile is both intimate and radiant. She couldn't stop herself. "Does he have a girlfriend?" Zuri raises her eyebrow.

"Let's just say he's not starved for female companionship. But he wants his women to be like Mame — strong and sure of themselves. Want to meet him? I have to warn you — he's very intense, especially about the Congo, and he likes to lecture people. Now and again, you'll have to remind him to get real."

8

As if on cue, Jacques walks into the cafe. Zuri excitedly says, "There's my brother. Jacques, Jacques, *ici, ici, par ici, allez.*" She waves her hand, smiles at her brother, speaking to him in French.

Suddenly, the tall, trim Jacques is at their table. He looks effortless in jeans, a sports jacket, and crocodile loafers— with a charming smile and a cappuccino in hand that matches the color of his skin. His photo did not lie. He is mighty fine; Ayo notes approvingly.

Zuri introduces them. "I'm happy to meet any friend of Zuri's," he says very formally, shaking Ayo's hand while staring intently into her cavernous brown eyes.

"We were just talking about you, and now, here you are."

Jacques looks at Ayo, studying her and, with a slight smile, explains, "I believe the spirits of our ancestors intervene when needed. Others call it serendipity or magic," Jacques continues, his smile growing larger.

Ayo has no idea what he means, but it doesn't matter. She quickly becomes entranced by his sonorous voice filled with promises that Ayo had heard before but somehow, intuitively, felt this time is different.

Jacques beams at Ayo as he joins the women at the table. He senses Ayo's lean form under her loose-fitting sweatshirt and momentarily pictures her naked, but being a new-age man simply deepens his smile. He likes her flawless, dark complexion and her short natural hair accented with cowrie shells. Even seated, her tight jeans

9

show off her muscular, shapely legs, her flat belly, and the firm curve of her hips. He is eager for more. And somehow, he knows that with this woman, there is something more profound to look forward to than just horizontal exercise.

Ayo beams back, wondering if the allure of Jacques's smile is a truthful advertisement for the rest of him. It strikes her that she is unaccountably interested in more than this guy's body, though that looks mighty fine to her. She likes the fact that he is taller than she is and in good shape.

Zuri starts to ask Jacques about something that a Congolese professor, Kwasie Sharita Bambassi-M'Ziri, said at the conference — that women were still suffering from the oppression of Belgian colonialism and that Belgium owed them reparations — but she sees Jacques is intently drinking Ayo in. "Well, just look at the time!" Zuri says with a smile. "I better get back to the meeting. You guys stay. Jacques, I'll call you later with my questions because you were late again, brother!" Zuri hits her brother on the shoulder with a quick zinger because he rarely shows up on time. "Ayo, it was great seeing you again. I'm calling you tomorrow!" They both look in Zuri's direction as she leaves. Glancing at them over her shoulder, she knew they only half heard her.

"So, Jacques, what do you do?" Ayo asks, breaking the ice.

"I'm with the Africa-Europe Parity Group, mostly, we work for UNESCO." Jacques can't help getting lost in Ayo's eyes, but he manages to sound slightly aloof. "I have

10

a law degree, but I don't use it much. Mostly, I work on development projects in French-speaking Africa." As he looks into Ayo's eyes, he desperately wants to open himself up to her to see if they can touch each other.

"I was born to this work. Whenever I hear African drums, my heart seems to beat in time with them. I was born and raised in Tremé. You ever been to New Orleans?"

Ayo's eyes widen. She emits a deep sigh. "I think Tremé's one of the most special places on Earth."

"You know about Tremé? Few people do. My family has lived in Tremé since 1808 after they fled the revolution in Haiti. We still own a big Victorian home on Esplanade Avenue in a beautiful chichi neighborhood. Before Haiti, my great-greats were in the Congo. Do you speak French?"

"Oui, je parle Français," Ayo responds. Continuing in French, "I've studied French most of my life. I often think in French. French allows me to express my thoughts more than English does. I often dream in French."

Jacques feels warmth spread over his body. He thinks this woman gets better and better. He feels a different rapport with her—more than just an erotic attraction. He wants to open up and explain who he is to her. He continues, "I went to a fancy Jesuit High School in New Orleans and was a half-decent athlete on the basketball and wrestling teams. With that and my grades, I had a choice of any college I wanted. Zuri and I both chose NYU. We love the Village and NYU's study-abroad programs, especially the

11

French ones."

"You're Catholic?" Ayo asks. "Zuri never mentioned it."

"We're not real Catholics. We follow the old religion. We believe that if we're open to the spirits of our ancestors, they look over us."

Ayo realizes that this second mention of the ancestor business must be a pet theme of his. Jacques begins to sound as if he were drifting away somewhere. "Every year, we have family reunions in Armstrong Park. We hire music students from Dillard and Xavier to play African drums.

"Didn't the slave masters ban drumming?" Ayo asks.

"That's what makes it extra satisfying. The slavers banned drumming, but they couldn't stop it. Between the 1740s and 1860s, freed and enslaved Africans gathered in the corner of the Congo Square around Armstrong Park during their Sunday free time. They affirmed each other and their cultures by singing and dancing while selling and bartering their goods and services. They rejoiced in family time together."

Not pausing to allow Ayo to comment, he rushes on. "The same thing happened in the Congo. The Congolese sustained their community—even though they or their forebearers were ripped from their native villages. Their drumming undermined the masters' control of their slaves. Drumming gave voice to countless Africans ripped from their homeland and stripped of their culture. The sounds of drums helped in the organization of slave revolts.

"Anyway, the drummers my family hired for our reunions wore African clothes—dashikis with Kente, Ankara, and Adinkra prints. They formed drumming circles." Jacques starts drumming out a beat on the table with his index fingers. "I was mesmerized by the colors of their dashikis: red, yellow, gold, blue, green, brown, and black, swaying as they beat out rhythms. The sounds and colors merged. That's the space I enter when I have to escape from bullshit, excuse my language. I close my eyes and go back to that time. When I hear African drumming, I feel transported, and my pulse quickens," he says from wherever his mind had taken him. He becomes absorbed in beating a more complicated rhythm on the table with his fingers.

"Armstrong Park is named for Louis Armstrong," Ayo explains, to say something to bring Jacques back to her. "I took trumpet one year in high school, but I didn't have the discipline to stay with it."

For a moment, Jacques is back at the table. He smiles directly at Ayo. "My soul was formed by growing up in Tremé," he explains. "I'm glad that you can relate to that area."

Then he drifts away again, this time mounting a lecture platform instead of going into himself. "Armstrong Park encompasses land still called Congo Square—separating the French Quarter from Tremé, one of the oldest free

13

Black neighborhoods in America. In Tremé, free and enslaved Blacks thrived, even at the height of Louisiana's sugar cane slavery era with its cruelty and terror. In the eighteenth and early nineteenth centuries, Tremé was one of the few places where free Blacks and even African slaves were allowed to own property.

"Today, Tremé is a vibrant community. The music, myths, legends, and even voodoo that are part of our African heritage are kept alive here. When the community rebuilt after Katrina, people went to great lengths to maintain its uniqueness."

Ayo is interested in what Jacques says, but his formal tone doesn't match where they are in the crowded, noisy Birch café. People stand around, eyeing their table, eager to grab it when they leave. This guy's pedantic and pompous, Ayo thinks. But she is drawn in, fascinated despite herself. Maybe it's those eyes and that enigmatic smile. His eyes are not brown; they are grayish-green — unique for a Black man.

Still, on his podium, Jacques expounds, "Today, when I go to Africa, I always seek out the drummers. Drumming is the spiritual heart of villages. It invokes the ancestors to intervene in the lives of the living."

Jacques suddenly stops. He doesn't want to lose Ayo and the chance to know more about this beautiful woman wearing an NYU sweatshirt.

"I'm doing all the talking," he says. "Force of habit. I'm

sorry for going on so long. You must know all this anyway."

Ayo smiles demurely. "I know a little," she says, "but please tell me more." She really means it.

She enjoys hearing me talk, Jacques almost says out loud. This is a first. "Would you like something more to go along with the coffee?" he asks. "Maybe some chocolate? I always crave chocolate."

"No, thanks, I have to keep my fighting form."

"Well, tell me about yourself," Jacques says.

"I have my bachelor's degree from NYU, where I met your sister and an NYU master's in public administration. My fluent French sent me to New Orleans on a summer project in my sophomore year to study Gens de Couleur Libres, (free people of color). I spent lots of time in Tremé and along the Esplanade in the Musée Les Gens de Couleur Libres. What beautiful architecture! The French Creole scene has fascinated me since I first read a biography of Franz Fanon, the French West Indian psychiatrist and political philosopher concerned with the psychopathology of colonialism."

Jacques sits wide-mouthed, listening to Ayo speak to the heart of his deepest interests. He thinks, Wow! Who is this extraordinary woman? No one has ever known about my history and culture better.

Ayo drops her voice and says, "But, tell me more about

your work. When did you know for real what you wanted to do with your life?"

Jacques refocuses. "Well, there was this time when I was nine years old…."

Ayo looks at her watch. "I love listening to you, Monsieur Jacques, but let's save that for another time. Here's my card. My personal cell number is there, too."

Before Jacques can say anything, Ayo bends down, kisses him on the cheek, and walks away, giving Jacques the chance to assess her from a different angle. She's one smart lady, Jacques thinks to himself. She allowed me to see she was a little nervous meeting me, which was very sweet. But she knows exactly how to handle a guy. Build him up, then split, so he'll be left wanting more. She knows what she's doing. I like that.

He intensely watches her leave the cafe. Ayo walks like she's in charge. Her back straight, her head high as she exits through the glass door, holding it open for the next customer. He follows her walking across the front of the wide cafe window, striding down the sidewalk her tight jeans, firm breasts, and upright torso cutting a path of confidence, even arrogance as her natural Black hair blends in with the frenetic street scene of New Yorkers on the move.

She swaggers down the sidewalk. Her intellect and education equip her with the power of outthinking any person who comes her way. She is a real New Yorker.

Finally, he looks down and reads her card: "Ayo James, Detective, NYPD, 6th Precinct. Homicide."

Conflicting emotions overwhelm him. As a Black man, he has an uneasy feeling about the police, but he thinks I must see her again. She is the one sent by my ancestors. Besides, I've never met an NYPD cop who speaks French, let alone a Black woman homicide detective.

That evening, Jacques talks with his sister, Zuri, who reassures him of Ayo's special qualities, which he already understood.

After talking with Zuri, he phones Ayo. They talk for more than an hour. But he can't remember — and doesn't care — what they talked about. They plan to get together on Friday. He thinks she tells him that she likes to work out, jog, and lift weights. He realizes he's getting slack about his gym membership.

Chapter 2

1998 — Tremé, New Orleans, Drumming in Congo Square

Just before Jacques met Zuri and Ayo, he had the following conversation with his mother.

"I'm not sure why, but I'm not feeling like myself. Things seem gray. I just needed to talk with you to get your perspective," he explained on the phone.

"I'm glad you've called. It's been nasty weather here and perhaps the same where you are. That's always a downer, but maybe something else is going on. How are you feeling physically?"

Jacques admitted that he was a bit rundown, but his mother sensed that something else was off with her son — she could hear and feel the weariness in his soul — and she probed a bit.

Jacques admitted that he had no serious love interest in his life. His mother was surprised. Jacques usually had women chasing after him. Even from a young age, girls seemed attracted to him, and this magnetism always accompanied him.

"Honey, I'm sure someone will come along and capture

your heart. You have to be open to it. Love is a mysterious thing. Maybe you talk too much. You know you love to talk. Do more listening. You will be happier. Open up more. Let someone in, just a little.

"I remember when I met your father. I went to a jazz club with a man I was seeing. One of the musicians smiled at me, and even from his small stage to where we were sitting, his eyes pierced mine. When my date got up to go to the bathroom, the musician came over, gave me his card, and asked me to call him. Normally, I wouldn't do that kind of thing, but I felt a special connection with him. I sort of let him in. That guy was your dad.

"I put his card in my purse, and I called him the next day."

"We talked for hours on the phone, and I knew that he was someone I wanted to get to know. I couldn't wait to see him. Because of his strange hours, our first date was in the afternoon, and he was almost late for his next performance because we couldn't stop talking. He invited me to join him at the club, but because I was teaching and had to be up early the next day, I couldn't meet him, but I was at his performance when the weekend came. After he was finished, we talked for hours, closed down the club, and wandered the now quiet streets of Treme and Marigny. The rest is history. We married a few months later, and then you were born."

"But I guess I've told you all this before. The point is that your time will come. Some special woman will dance right into your life, and the gray you're feeling will be gone."

19

"I hope so," Jacques said. "I feel like what's missing from my life is the kind of love that you had with Dad. Hearing your story reminded me of how much I have missed him after his heart attack. I recall his fellow musicians accompanying the casket as we went into the 'The City of the Dead' and found his particular resting place in the "The Musician's Tomb." I've often wanted to talk with him to ask him things."

With a big sigh, Jacques said, "I'm so grateful that you're around, Mom, and that we can talk."

"Jacques, honey, you know I'll always be there for you. Your father, too. You have to access him through your thoughts and spirits. Your father and the other ancestors are waiting to hear from you—to guide you."

"Yes, I know. I just tend to forget," Jacques lamented.

"Jacques, I'll always be there for you. I've tried to be a role model for you and Zuri. When I was teaching, I was one of the first Black teachers at the newly integrated elementary school. I made sure that my students were in the top-rated class for their grade. I gained a special reputation, and I simply looked at my class, and they stopped their talking and restless behavior. They believed that I had eyes in the back of my head because I knew what was going on even with my back turned when I was writing on the board. They assigned some of the toughest kids to my classes, and I loved them all. I often visited their parents and learned about their home life so I could better help their children adjust and succeed."

"I know you succeeded with them and with us," Jacques said.

"Before you were born, I went out on strike in 1978 and had my picture in the paper. Here I was, a tall Black woman, who, I must say, looked mighty good. I carried a picket sign and marched, and we won our demands.

"Do you remember coming to school with me when you were older? The kids idolized you. As my son, you had a special status. Some of the girls had crushes on you. I'm glad that you're now touring schools and lecturing about the Congo and Black heritage. Your dedication to speaking up for Black history and culture makes me so very proud. But I admit, like all mothers, I worry about you. I worry about your intensity; I fear that someday your passions might overcome your good sense.

"Do you understand what I'm saying? Perhaps at the next family gathering, you can learn a chant or get a special token to keep with you to help calm your nerves."

"A mojo, like dad used to carry?" asked Jacques.

"Yes, exactly. A mojo. It seemed to work for your dad."

"Thanks, Mom. You've helped. I feel better just talking to you. Zuri wants to meet with me on a new piece she's writing on the Congo. When did you talk to her last?"

"Just yesterday. Zuri told me she was meeting you. You both have fun. All my love to you both. We'll talk again

21

soon."

"You bet," Jacques said.

****

Before her date with Jacques, Ayo calls her friend, Aisha. "Guess who I bumped into today?"

"First, tell me how you're doing," Aisha insists. "Then we can chat. I've wanted to catch up with you, but you're always so busy."

"I'm doing great. And you?"

"Yeah, I'm struggling with my dissertation, but it's coming along. Eventually, I'll forget all the long hours I've invested in it—all the writing and rewriting and praying that my professors will accept it. Now, tell me your news."

"I was walking down 7th, and there was Zuri. I haven't seen her for two years. She wants to get together with us soon."

"That would be wonderful, but I rarely have time to go to the bathroom, let alone go out. I can't wait till I'm done with this thesis. But, for you and Zuri, I'll carve out some time. What's Zuri doing?"

"She's still a journalist working on African commerce issues. She looks great. She's kept her figure, and her eyes have a new glow. Remember how she talked about her brother, well he happened to be meeting her and I met him. He's a dreamboat. He's tall and intriguing, and we're going out tomorrow. I'm pretty excited."

"Hey, great. Have a good time. Let me know how it works out. I've got to get back to the books. Hugs to you."

"Okay Ai, hugs back."

That evening Jacques arrives at Ayo's apartment. It's a Friday; the weather is superb, a slight breeze spreads the smells of the city throughout its streets. At her apartment—57 Christopher Street near 7th Avenue and West 4th Street, the high-rise next to the Stonewall Bar—Ayo gets ready for Jacques to pick her up. Ayo consciously chooses a red sheath dress—red to signal passion, excitement, and energy. She dons her three-inch heels, which make her see eye-to-eye with Jacques. Ayo looks at her figure in the mirror and is pleased. After re-adjusting the cowrie shells in her hair, she smiles as she realizes she hasn't dressed for a man in a long time.

Jacques picks her up at her front door, observing her red dress, delighted that she made an effort just for him. Jacques is dressed quite preppy. He wears a dark blue blazer with tan buttons that matched his tan Van Heusen button-down shirt with an open collar. His shoes, too, match his shirt. Leather deck shoes, light brown. He looks like he just walked out of a *GQ* magazine. Ayo is pleased. They walk to Mimi's on Sullivan Street for an intimate, romantic, and very French dinner. As they sit on a velvety couch, Ayo feels Jacques's nervous energy. They begin with bluefin tuna appetizers and choose an entrée of veal tartare and lobster from the handwritten menu, which they share.

Ayo selects a slightly chilled French pinot noir, and Jacques, with a big smile, mentions he prefers Santa Barbara pinots. Ayo says, "Well, of course. That's because the pinot grape comes from France, but the climate in Santa Barbara County is even more perfect for it than France." Jacques loves that she knows her wines.

Ayo reassures him that she wants to hear the story he started about when he was nine.

As they sip their pinot noir, Jacques describes his annual family gatherings. "Since I was nine, every year, our family gets together. Nearly one-hundred Henri family members, most from Louisiana but some now living across the United States, gather in Armstrong Park. They set out card tables covered with red-and-white-checkered French tablecloths. Everyone sits either on folding chairs or quilts spread out on the lawn and cobble-stone plaza, along with food baskets, coolers, and boom-boxes. A few older men and women always slump over in their portable lounge chairs, fast asleep.

"My mom would strategically place everything under the shade of large southern oak trees, which offer some relief from the hot New Orleans sun. I remember the humidity that clung to everyone like a huge, damp blanket. I can almost feel it now. But you know the area and must remember the intensity of summer there."

Ayo sighs, looks at Jacques, and says, "Yes, I remember it

very well. Everyone grumbles about the heat, but all that heavy air takes the energy out of people, forcing them to be casual and be together. And you know what it does to your hair!"

Jacques, almost on cue, continues, "People fan themselves with paper church fans, more in an attempt to do something about the heat and humidity than actually to overcome it. The fans come from nearby St. Augustine Catholic Church. The church was founded in 1841 for Catholic free persons of color. Generation after generation of Henries have attended the church since its beginnings.

"I recall you told me that you had studied the Code Noir. I've had to explain to some of the audiences that this Code is why many Blacks in New Orleans are Catholic. Code Noir defined the circumstances of slavery in the French colonial empire, restricted the activities of free Negroes, and forbade them practicing any religion other than Roman Catholicism, but, of course, you knew all that," Jacques adds with a big grin.

Ayo nodded, not wanting to interrupt the lush description of the family gathering. She senses how important the family is to Jacques. "Of course, their church attendance didn't mean that they had abandoned the beliefs of their forebearers in Haiti and the Congo. Most of my kinfolk didn't see the difference between Catholicism and animism—that was in our DNA. We are steeped in the belief that every living thing, from trees to animals, to people, has a soul and that each different type of soul has

25

a god to look after us.

"Catholicism called these gods *saints*; the Africans called them *loas* and think of them as guardians and call on them during voodoo practices."

"So, what's the difference between saints and loas?" Ayo asked.

"Not as much as you might expect. A few websites compare them. Based on your studying of the *Code Noir*, you know Catholics believed that the slave had a soul. So, supposedly," Jacques said, shuddering a bit, "it was harder for the French to maim Blacks at will. Life in the Congo, Haiti, and New Orleans had been long controlled by Catholic slave masters who imposed their religion on Black people—free and enslaved.

"But you also know that. Very quickly, the people figured out that they could maintain their old beliefs inside while *acting* as a Catholic outside. Functioning with this dual perspective was a good way to protect themselves from being punished. Don't we all have an outer persona and an inner core that we rarely expose to others?" Jacques asks, looking deeply into Ayo's eyes.

"Certainly, I know that I do," Ayo responds. "Dubois's double-consciousness. I have my professional being as a member of the New York Police Department, but inside, I'm very Black! When there's a police killing of a Black person, I cringe and hope that it wasn't a case of racism, but I feel that I can work from within the department and effect change. At least, I hope so."

"But what about your inner beliefs? Do you feel there's a spirit in all living things?"

"I guess I was brought up more traditionally," Ayo admits, "but I'm eager to learn about this ancestral spirituality you've mentioned a few times."

"Our family gatherings bring together our relatives and our ancestors each year. Near the family reunion's main assembly area is a large bronze frieze of bamboula dancers called 'The Gathering.' Looking at that statue, I always felt that our family had chosen the right spot for our annual reunions, even though Armstrong Park swallowed up the Congo Square of my youth."

"What's the significance of the frieze?" Ayo questioned.

Jacques leaned in toward her and said, "A bamboula is but one type of drum made from a rum barrel with animal skin stretched over it. Bamboulas were used in voodoo rituals and incantations. A dance accompanied the drum, which has a deep sensual sound. Maybe sometime I'll show you my drum collection," Jacques offered.

Ayo nodded, "I'd like that."

"Anyway, drumming was a vital part of these family gatherings along with popular soul and neo-soul music. A strong female presence came out from the boom-boxes. When I was nine, my friends and I danced enthusiastically to the beat of the drums. We ran around and chased each

27

other, enjoying seeing our cousins."

"Do you still dance?" Ayo asked. "I love dancing."

"Dancing is one of my favorite activities," he responded, grinning at her. "We'll have to go dancing sometime. I love to dance and feel the rhythm envelop me."

Like a magnet drawn, Jacques returns to his narrative. "But after the dancing came the storytelling. In Tremé, it was the best part of the event. As evening approached, breezes stirred the oak branches, and the hot day cooled down.

"An older woman, one of my cousins, dressed in African robes, rang a bell, once, twice, many times over. '*Venez ici, Venez ici. Rassembler, Rassembler, toutes suite!* Come here. Gather round me,' she called out to the young people, waving her arms at the children assembling in front of her. She was a large, very Black woman with a big voice and big hair. She was the family *griot*, a keeper of our family history. She always wore brightly colored African fashions and demonstrated her dramatic French to anyone who would listen. When she spoke, she waved her arms and body with each phrase.

"'Children, my beautiful children, settle down, *assayez vous, ecoutez,* listen carefully,' she entreated us. 'You are from great African kingdoms in the Congo.' She peered into each of our eyes and said in a voice that went right through me, 'Know thy history, know thyself. Be proud of your glorious history and culture.' She told us stories about the dozens of different cultures that the Congo had nurtured for centuries. Her stories described the battles for freedom that the Congolese people — our relatives — fought against the French and the Belgians. I especially liked her stories about runaway slaves who established their own communities, Maroon villages."

"I've heard of Maroons. Who are they?" Ayo asked.

"Maroons are those escaped former African slaves or their descendants in the Americas. They formed independent communities. Those free Black Maroon villages were in the swamps and bayous of Louisiana, Florida, Mississippi, and South Carolina. Maroon villages still exist in Brazil and Jamaica."

Jacques sipped his wine and called the waiter over for another bottle. "'Mrs. Griot' (a name I've given her because I can't recall her actual name, she was our family's chronicler). She described these Maroon villages of Black people, fighting to free themselves — *by any means necessary.*' Then, she talked about Mame, an African woman who helped slaves all along the Congo River in their fight for freedom in the 1890s."

Jacques stared at Ayo and said, "I have a vivid memory of her explanation. In the language of the Mongo people, 'Mame' means *fearless*. Mame fought King Leopold II for twenty years, from 1884-1903, and she helped hundreds of people escape from his brutality.'"

"Zuri and I used to talk about Mame," Ayo said softly,

29

surprising Jacques.

Closing his eyes, Jacques intoned, changing his voice to that of Mrs. Griot. "When we say the name of Mame and of the other warrior women who fought for our people, we invoke their spirits and bring them among us. If we are willing to listen, they will protect us and offer us their wisdom. They encourage us to stay strong. They command us to fight for our freedom together." Jacques sighed deeply and opened his eyes to continue the narrative.

"Suddenly, the drums that had been sounding all day became quieter, softer but still beating. The adults who had been talking and laughing with each other most of the afternoon stopped what they were doing. Both the adults and the children became highly attentive.

"The solemnity of the day changed. Then, the elders and the youngsters recited the names of past leaders. As each name was called, the crowd repeated, '*A-Shay*, so be it, we remember,' and an elder poured purple-colored water on the gray cobblestones.

'Yaa Asantewaa, Queen of the Ashanti.'

'*A-Shay*, we remember,' the crowd said.

'Dahomey Amazons, women warriors of the Fon.'

'*A-Shay*, we remember.'

'Amanirena, Queen of the Kush.'

'*A-Shay*, we remember.'

'Carlota Luhumbi, Queen warrior of Yoruba.'

30

'*A-Shay*, we remember.'

Each *A-Shay* became louder with every pour of the purple water. The liquid entered into the crevices in the earth between the cobblestones as if the spirits were becoming part of the earth.

"Then, when the elder evoked 'Mame, warrior queen of the Mongos,' I felt a tingle from head to foot, as if the spirit of Mame were entering into me." Jacques emitted a heartfelt sigh.

As Jacques finishes his story, he became very still and inward-focused, certainly not at Mimi's with Ayo. To bring him out of his reverie, Ayo says, a little too loudly and slowly, "Your descriptions are exquisite. I felt like I'd been there in Congo Square. I could see the kids playing tag in the heat and the adults catching up on family gossip. I could taste the gumbo, po-boys, steamed shrimp, and that ice-cold Abita beer."

Jacques, leaning back in his chair, his eyes closed as if in a trance, says, "When we called up Mame, I had vivid images of a large, tall, dark woman waging war against her oppressors. She looked like my mother. I feel very close to my mother, and Zuri does, too." Then, he opened his eyes and smiled. Jacques is back.

Jacques asks, "Am I talking too much?

Ayo says, "No, this is what we are supposed to do on a first date."

Jacques smiles with relief. He knows he talks too much like

31

he's lecturing.

Ayo continues, "But Zuri told me you like to lecture people and that you are full of information that you want everyone to know. I like it. I'll tell you when you talk too much." Jacques lowers his eyes and smiles, slightly nodding his head.

Ayo returns his smile and waits a minute before saying anything. Finally, she says, "It's getting late. The staff is cleaning up around us. We should probably be heading out."

Jacques asks for their bill, pays it, and he and Ayo step out into the New York night.

Chapter 3

Greenwich Village, Drumming in Washington Square Park

Jacques and Ayo walk into the crisp New York evening, and Ayo takes Jacques's arm. "Your sister also said that your mother had the spirit of Mame."

Jacques nods. "When Mom was younger, she worked with the NAACP. When I was in school, if any teacher dared to treat me unjustly, she fought them. Once I wasn't permitted in an advanced class, and she strode into school and sat in the principal's office until they put me on the roster for the class. By the time Zuri came along, the school knew better than to mess with the Henri kids."

"My mother was also a warrior. She was active in the integration of our Boston schools. She and my dad separated when I was young, and he didn't play any kind of significant role in my life. Maybe Mame's spirit has visited us, too. I come from a long line of military leaders. My cousin Betsy Young was one of just a few Black nurses to serve in the Civil War officially. She even received a pension after the war. Betsy could read and write and set up a school for Black children and soldiers during the war.

After the war, she established a school for freed slaves and fought for benefits for the Black Civil War troops.

"And in more recent times, another of my relatives, Leigh Ann Hester, a sergeant, won the Silver Star for repelling at least thirty al-Qaeda fighters who tried to ambush her convoy in Iraq."

As they walk along the street, Ayo warms to her subject. "I admire those women fighters, but we need warriors who use legal briefs along with those who use machetes. Frederick Douglass said that to win our rights, 'Black people need the ballot box, the jury box, and the bullet box.' He also said, 'Let no woman be kept from the ballot box because of her sex.' I think all the fighters, including the lawyers, teachers, and politicians, need to be infused with the spirit of Mame."

"I agree," Jacques said, smiling at her with one of his melt-your-heart looks.

Ayo slowed down and turned to look at Jacques. "I'm a relative of Shirley Chisholm, the first Black woman elected to Congress and the first Black woman to run for U.S. President. My grandmother told me that Shirley would regale the family with tales of her time in Congress. Shirley really loved my grandmother, who was born in the Caribbean. She often said Grandma influenced her greatly. I think they both had Mame's spirit in them."

The two stop and sit side-by-side on a townhouse stoop. "I hope that whoever gets the 2020 Democratic nomination for vice president also has Mame's spirit in her," Jacques added.

"Yes, we can hope and work toward that," Ayo said. "I've been active in helping register people to vote." She looks at him, looking at her, his strong features highlighted in the glow of the streetlights. "Now, what else can I tell you? I went to a private school in Boston. I've always loved French, studied it all through school, and became fluent while attending boarding school in Geneva."

Ayo stops talking. She's suddenly self-conscious, worried about going on about herself. She's scared off potential boyfriends before; her usual self-confidence is threatening to many men. Then again, she doesn't want to be with a man if she has to act all googly-eyed and demure to keep him. She wants someone secure enough in himself to be secure enough to be with her.

Jacques is encouraged by Ayo's opening up. He smiles with approval, "You speak French, and you became a cop because the military is in your blood. I like that."

"I'm proud of my ancestors," Ayo says. "See, I said 'ancestors,' not just 'relatives.' I picked that up from you. But my family is into public service—being in the military is just part of it. I became a cop to help reform the police, to try to stop the shootings of unarmed Black people."

Jacques snorts, "Yeah, police have been shooting us down for over 300 years. It's only now that everyone has an iPhone that we're catching those bastards in the act."

"Amen," Ayo says. "Let's hope that the more cops who are caught, the more other cops will do the right thing. Maybe they'll learn how to change the discriminatory attitudes they grew up with. Anyway, I'm doing my bit to help. I like my work. I solve crimes and help people. I help bring closure to someone's tragedy. I do as much counseling as I do police work."

Ayo jumps up from the stoop and leads Jacques toward a park bench half a block away. Jacques drifts away again. He looks at Ayo but is back in the Congo. "For centuries, the Mongo people spread along the Congo River, using the river as their source of food and trade. They resisted invasions. But many of their tribal leaders helped Arab slave traders, and King Leopold II built his rubber empire by enslaving the free Congolese. I hope that their descendants feel the guilt for what they did and agree to pay reparations today to the people they enslaved and maimed."

Ayo scoots closer to him, and he puts his arm around her before continuing. "Mame was a proud Mongo, a fierce warrior leader, the queen of Maroon compounds along the Congo River. She was always on the run, always fighting for freedom. The spirits of her ancestors possessed her and protected her from King Leopold's army."

The noise of an ambulance breaks their conversation. Once it passes, Ayo says, "I heard stories about Mame from Zuri. Mame was a superhero, a Wonder Woman of Africa."

"Yes. One of Mame's superpowers was catching the

36

bullets fired at her, then throwing them back at soldiers, killing them instantly."

They get up from the bench and take a meandering walk, circling through Greenwich Village. Walking hand-in-hand, they take in the busy streets of McDougal and Bleecker, checking out the shops and looking at other people. They stop in front of Murray's Cheese Shop. Ayo pulls Jacques in to sample cheeses, and they each buy some fresh Stilton and Blues from England and France.

Jacques takes Ayo by the hand to cross Jones Street and shows her his favorite meat market, Ottomanelli's. Jacques is eager to point out his favorite cuts. While inside, Ayo shows Jacques her favorites.

Jacques beams. "I'm so glad you're not a vegetarian." Ayo laughs in response.

Jacques says, "I love the small, intimate streets of the Village; let's walk them." They walk down narrow Barrow Street to Bedford then to Downing back toward Bleecker. Jacques stops in front of the Churchill Square pocket park, showing Ayo where he sits Sunday mornings reading the Times.

Ayo says, "I'm surprised we've never run into each other. This is my favorite park in the Village."

"Serendipity," Jacques declares. "More proof our ancestors want us to be together."

Ayo locks her arm into Jacques's elbow, and they continue

walking Bleecker full of others just like them, in wonder of each other. They talk non-stop.

"I feel a kinship with Mame," Jacques says out of the blue, oblivious to what Ayo just said. "She's part of my blood. Her exploits empower me. I often talk to Black high school groups about her. The firm I work for has an aggressive mentoring program for public school students. I like to tell young Black students about Africa and Mame and how she represents the disenfranchised. Her spirit enables students to have a voice — to get back at those who injure them, which might include those who do not pay a living wage to their parents or the landlords who allow lead-based paint to stay in their apartments."

On a roll, Jacques continues. "Mame exerts her spirit against those who underfund schools that Black children attend. I tell these high school students that slaves in the Congo strongly believed Jesus would save them, but it didn't happen. Mame's spirit gave enslaved people the emotional impetus to rebel against injustice. That fighting spirit resonates strongly with high school kids. Of course, I've been banned from some schools."

Jacques continues talking and walking faster. Amused, Ayo hurries to catch up. "Hey, Jacques, where are you? Did you forget I'm here? Slow down for a minute."

Jacques is startled. He looks around, a bit discombobulated by Ayo not being by his side. He looks back and sees her. "Ayo, I'm sorry. I get so absorbed in what I'm saying I sometimes lose track of everything."

Jacques and Ayo wind up at Abingdon Square Park at the end of Bleecker Street. Across the street at the corner of Bleecker, Hudson and Bank is the Mediterranean café, Meme. "It's not named Mame, but it's close enough, and I like its North and West African cuisine."

As they sit on a bench in the park surrounded by greenery and purple, lavender, and white impatiens, Jacques asks: "Tell me more about Ayo James."

He brushes a pesky fly from her face. She gives him an appreciative smile and starts again. "I graduated from NYU with a bachelor's degree in sociology, a minor in criminal justice, and took as many French lit courses as I could squeeze in. I planned to go to law school after getting a master's in public administration. My mom was disappointed I didn't. But as a cop, I'm earning my street cred."

Ayo shows Jacques her gold detective badge. "I've been on the force for eight years. Of course, as a woman, I've had to fight my battles. It's probably harder being a woman than being Black.

"I was a beat officer in Brooklyn and Harlem and quickly moved up to detective lieutenant. The NYPD paid for my graduate studies because I promised to devote at least five years to the police force, and I've worked as a cop for eight. When I decide I'm ready for law school, the NYPD will pay for half if I stay with the force for three years after I get my degree. I enjoy my work, even the intense uncertainty of investigations. I know I'm an anomaly in the NYPD, but

I'm good at what I do—solving tough crimes, including homicides. And my colleagues like my attitude—I speak up, even to the boss."

"You have a wonderful spirit," Jacques sighs, "so positive. Me, I'm moody and obsessive."

"Nah," says Ayo. "You're focused on what you believe in. I admire that."

They feel the night breeze and hold hands, naturally, comfortably. They walk close together, and Ayo keeps up with him despite his longer legs and her heels. Jacques slows his pace. They reach her apartment building. They draw each other in, feel the warmth of each other despite their coats, and kiss deeply. Neither wants to go. "I have to prepare a speech for tomorrow," Jacques says, "otherwise, I'd drop pretty obvious hints about wanting to come up."

Ayo gives him a look that says, "any time."

****

Their second date is a week later. Jacques and Ayo share a warm familiarity and an eagerness to probe each other's minds as foreplay to what each hope will be a night of probing one another's bodies. Ayo selects a two-piece orange sweater set and Le High Skinny Slit Jeans with rivets and Versace Jeans Couture pointed-toe pumps. Ayo's research inspires her choice of orange as the color that offers new ideas and releases the body of spiritual limitations. She mischievously thinks perhaps other limitations include the limitations of clothing. At the same time, she believes that the orange color encourages self-respect and respect for others.

When Jacques arrives, he looks stunningly handsome in his slim-fit Givenchy jeans and casual black jacket with a buttoned-up black polo shirt. Glancing down at his shoes, Ayo notices that he is wearing Christian Louboutin loafers with their distinctive red soles. She is delighted that he takes care of himself and even dresses with a French touch.

They walk east on Bleecker to MacDougal in the heart of the Village. MacDougal is throbbing as usual with NYU students and visitors from around the world. Crossing 4th Street, they hear drumming coming from Washington Square Park near the chess tables just a block from Jacques's destination. Drumming in the park reminds both of them of their days as students bopping to drumming circles in the park.

Jacques takes Ayo to a small Italian grotto-like garden cafe, La Vitorra, on MacDougal, a favorite hangout of NYU students, bringing back memories of undergraduate days. They each have an unusual dark beer, Liefmans Goudenband. "I had this beer in Belgium," Jacques says, a bit too professor-like. "It's the aging and fermentation that makes it so special. Smell it."

After a beer and some Kalamata olives and blue cheese, Jacques leads Ayo downstairs into an atrium cafe with a three-person jazz ensemble playing smooth and low in the corner. Very romantic. Ayo and Jacques settle in, taking

41

menus from a waiter in an NYU purple sweatshirt.

"Tell me more about your work, Ayo."

"During my eight years on the force, I've handled a variety of issues. Some of the most difficult involve cases where fathers lose their jobs and take their anger out on their families. One man slashed his wife to death in front of his three kids after a violent argument. It made me think of what Joseph Conrad wrote in his novel about the Congo, and I think it aptly applies to some parts of New York City, too—'the horror, the horror.'" She talks about other cases for a while before lightening the mood. She wants to see Jacques's beautiful smile.

Ayo insists on paying and suggests they have dessert at MarieBelle's Chocolate Café on Broome Street. Jacques is touched; she remembers him saying he always craves chocolate.

They sit under the gorgeous chandelier at one of the small, round marble tables. While drinking unforgettably decadent hot chocolate, Jacques once again begins to drift off, but this time he wants to take Ayo with him.

"You're the first person I've ever told this to, and I'm worried it might scare you off, but somehow I need you to know what happened to me while I was working on a project in Belgium."

Chapter 4

2009—Antwerp, Belgium—Chocolate Hands

"I think I mentioned," Jacques said, "that at NYU, I had a double major in international affairs and African history. I spent my junior year studying in Brussels. Each month, my class traveled to seminars in African countries colonized by France and Belgium — Mali, Senegal, Cote d'Ivoire, and the Congo. One month, we went to Timbuktu, in what is now Mali."

He launches into the professorial mode and explains, "Mali was the site of the great African learning center in the 1500s, the seat of African high culture: music, dance, literature, spirituality, and Islamic thought. The French colonized it in the late eighteenth century and reduced it to just another profit center, trading in diamonds, gold, silver, and Black slaves."

"You're a walking encyclopedia," she quips.

"Yes, and this African heritage stuff is very important to me. I spent ten-to-fourteen hours a day studying. I was a little obsessed, you might say. I had this unquenchable thirst to know more. I rarely went to parties, and I had little social life. I guess that's not healthy.

"I'd say," Ayo affirms.

"Instead, I lost myself in research. The other students poked fun at me because I was so aloof and turned down their invitations. Even now, I don't have many friends because I get so wrapped up in my work. Of course, I try to get to the gym to work out and can have some interesting conversations in the sauna." Before he continues, he takes a deep draft of the now lukewarm hot chocolate. He looks at Ayo and asks, "Should I continue?"

"Of course," Ayo says, permitting him.

"Well, one day, when studying in Brussels, a friend said I needed a break. So, I took a weekend visit to Antwerp. It was just forty-five minutes by train from my apartment. While strolling through an upscale shopping district, I saw a chocolate shop. Chocolate was one of the few luxuries I allowed myself. Here I was at a shop that sold the best chocolates in the world. I couldn't resist."

"Wait a minute," retorted Ayo. "Chocolate? From Belgium? The Belgium Congo, where chocolate is produced? I think I see a pattern emerging here."

"You got it," replies Jacques. You are now figuring out my thinking trends."

"So, anyway, while in the chocolate shop, I eyed tray after tray of temptations under glass. Then, I noticed two blonde, blue-eyed children, seemingly a brother and sister, about seven or eight years old. They were playing in the aisles while their mother shopped. Both kids looked at the brown chocolate hands displayed on the counter under glass and giggled. The boy pretended his arm was a machete, and with chopping motions pretended to cut off his sister's left hand. Their mother asked them if they wanted to eat one. They both squealed, saying, 'Oui!'

"At that moment, nausea hit my gut like a bullet. Pain encapsulated my entire body. It was hard for me to breathe. I rushed out of the shop into an alley alongside the building. I leaned against a wall, slid down to the ground next to a trash dumpster, put my head between my knees, and threw up. After a few minutes, I regained my composure and walked across the street to Antwerp's urban public park.

"I sat on a bench and took deep breaths. Then I looked around, panicked, and became angry. Here I was, a Black man surrounded by Whites. This was the first time in my life I've ever had such a violent reaction to the color of people's skin. I rarely noticed skin color. It never meant much to me. Growing up in New Orleans and living in the Village, color lines were blurred — most of my friends were mixed, or I didn't categorize them as Black, White, Brown, or anything else.

"Often, I'd been the only Black person in a sea of Whites. Never before did I have the visceral reaction like I had in Antwerp. No matter who I was with, I generally felt secure that I was the smartest — and often the best-looking — guy in the room," he adds with a self-deprecating laugh.

"I knew my reaction was irrational. I looked around. It was a lovely day. Families were lounging on blankets with picnic baskets full of cheeses, bread loaves, and sparkling drinks—much like at my family reunion in Tremé. Everywhere I looked, people were enjoying the tree-lined boulevard and the park's manicured flower garden. Children were running and laughing. Nobody seemed to care that I was Black—nobody was paying any attention to me.

"But seeing those chocolate hands brought back what seemed to be a memory that despite the beauty of the park and Antwerp itself, both were built on the slaughter of 10 million Congolese people by King Leopold II. King Leopold ordered his Force Publique soldiers to maim or kill natives who didn't meet his quota for gathering rubber."

Shuddering a bit, Jacques looks at Ayo and continues. "To prove the kill, the Force Publique cut a hand off each corpse. The King was worried that the soldiers would use the bullets for hunting. So, to prove they used the bullets for killing people, he required them to chop off each corpse's hands and bring the hands back to their White officers to count. Then, King Leopold went a step further and punished whole villages for not adding enough to his fortune by cutting the hands and feet off of children.

"These White people lounging in the park were the inheritors of the wealthy nation of Belgium built by Leopold's massacres and pillaging. I felt my body sway as I sat. I looked out over the park, and a haze enveloped me. I blacked out for a minute, maybe longer. When I came to, my head was throbbing in pain. I was frightened by what was happening to me.

"I closed my eyes, leaned my head back, and forced myself to sit upright on the park bench. I clasped my hands behind my neck. I took slow, deep breaths, holding in the air for five seconds—something I learned from yoga. Probably ten minutes later, I slowly stood up. My knees were still wobbly, but I found a café and settled in for a hot black tea while I tried to pull myself together."

Staring at Ayo, he continues his narrative. "I tried to figure out what happened when I saw the two White kids and their mom contemplating eating those chocolate hands. It was as though something excruciating had entered my body. I felt possessed. In Antwerp, Belgium, in the chocolate shop, whatever had gotten into me brought with it blind anger and panic. White blonde, blue-eyed Belgian children were eating chocolate hands that mirrored my ancestors' severed hands—our ancestors. It was revolting. I couldn't sleep that night thinking of how the Belgium elite actually eat chocolate designed in the hands of my ancestors! I'm still bothered by the spontaneous episode."

Ayo stares anxiously at Jacques telling his story. She feels his agony. She's silenced in the horror of his story.

47

Chapter 5

Greenwich Village, "Show me your drums!"

Jacques realizes he's talked for over half an hour about what happened to him in the Antwerp chocolate shop. He senses that Ayo is patiently waiting for him to finish his story and that the server in MarieBelle's is not-so-patiently waiting for him to finish his hot chocolate and vacate the table.

He doesn't tell Ayo about feeling possessed by Mame. Still, he says, "I recently watched a public TV report on Post-Traumatic Stress Disorder, PTSD, and how it can be triggered in soldiers by the slightest thing, reminding them of the violence they had faced or the danger they had been in."

"Believe me, in my line of work, I know lots about it," Ayo said with a deep sigh.

"I began to think about another emotional stress disorder that I've observed across Africa and among African-Americans, called Post Traumatic Slavery Syndrome — PTSS.

"Maybe that's what I experienced in Antwerp, a disorder brought on by an acute awareness of the ravages of colonialism and slavery inflicted on our ancestors. I wonder, do others suffer from this? How do Black people in the United States handle the graphic portrayal of slavery that surrounds us in movies, books, and television everywhere? Maybe African-Americans lash out every day without even knowing why. Maybe we self-medicate and act out through antisocial behavior. Clearly, we are sleeping with anger, as the Charles Burnett film suggests. Maybe we unconsciously hate ourselves for being victims of the terrors of slavery, rape, mutilation, and the horror of 500 years of colonial rule and White supremacy. I think it's the cumulative effect of trauma that is so debilitating to our people. Centuries of trauma have been passed down from generation to generation and are encoded into our DNA. Where is the endpoint? What will it take to break the cycle?"

Jacques is exhausted just talking about it. His voice drops to a hush. His eyes peer into Ayo's for answers, knowing none are available at this moment of his soliloquy.

Jacques drains his cup of hot chocolate. "Maybe we can't handle our history. Maybe I can't handle it, either. But let's go so the waiter can get another tip from the next couple to sit here." Ayo nods and leaves a substantial tip, and they once more enter the brisk evening air.

Jacques and Ayo head into the New York spring night and down the Avenue of the Americas, turning west on 4th Street, and take the promenade along the Hudson River. With Jacques leading, Ayo joins him in singing "Deep

River" and other Negro spirituals about water that enslaved people sang on their way to freedom.

"I looked over Jordan, and what did I see? Coming forth to carry me home...A band of angels coming after me, coming forth to carry me home." Then, they launch into "Swing low, sweet chariot, coming forth to carry me home. Swing low, sweet chariot, coming forth to carry me home."

Neither feels it odd that they began singing together. After singing several songs, Ayo notes, "There are so many songs about slaves using water to escape from slavery."

"Water," Jacques professorially intones, "has always been a metaphor for liberation. Remember, Moses was found floating in a basket in the Nile. John baptized Jesus in a river. When you escape from slavery, you head straight to water because in water, the dogs coming after you lose your scent. Harriet Tubman and many others used water for their escapes. The Ohio River was the freedom river; once over it, runaways were free. Harriet used the Choptank River in Maryland."

Then, Jacques loses the lightness of the moment and says, "Our African ancestors' first experience of water was terrifying. Most had never seen the ocean. They were captured in the interior and force-marched to pens on the coast to wait for slave ships. While imprisoned, they heard waves crashing against the rocks. Then, at the bottom of a slave ship, they heard waves crashing against the vessel. They had no idea where they were or where they were going. The sound of the crashing sea must have been

50

horrifying."

A young Black man approaches them. "Hey man, aren't you, Mr. Mame?" he asks. Jacques smiles. "You really torched the school that day," the kid says. Normally, Jacques wouldn't be able to resist basking in the student's admiration. But not now. He's eager to take Ayo to his apartment. He blows the kid off with a brusque "thanks" that cuts off all additional discussion.

Jacques becomes silent. He walks slowly, his hand in Ayo's. Then, he says, "Let's go to my place."

Without another word, their pace becomes quicker and purposeful through the Village. They enter Jacques's apartment. The first thing Ayo sees is a huge map of Africa hanging on his living room wall, alongside modern African art and ancient-looking African masks. Lining the walls are a variety of drums. "Show me your drums," Ayo says to Jacques.

"These two short drums are Djembes," Jacques explains. He shows Ayo how to hold it between her feet while sitting on one of his overstuffed chairs. Then, he shows Ayo two other drums, Conga drums, about four feet high. "You play these standing up. Your knees hold them in place. They have a deep and sexy sound." He demonstrates, boom, boom, boom, boom.

Jacques then moves to another drum. "This is the Sengba, a bass drum. See, it's shaped like a perfect cylinder, about three feet tall. You play it with one or two drumsticks." He gives Ayo a demonstration and then tells her to try. When she hits the drum, she's amazed at its loud sound. Jacques shows her the intricate carvings on the drums' sides, explaining, "these are more than just musical instruments. They're prized possessions that expert carvers and musicians created. Families keep them for generations."

He pounds on the drum, sending out a rhythmic message. "It's the intensity of the sound that allows drums to link people emotionally."

Ayo chuckles and says, "Other men I've dated talk about batting averages and stock market fluctuations. You're the first to tell me about drums."

They move from the living room into the room Jacques uses as his office. Ayo notes a huge collection of books about the Congo. His bookshelves hold pictures of his family, with skin tones ranging from African dark to European pale white. His mother has a dark complexion, a large forehead, high cheekbones, a strong, straight nose, and thin lips. His father more light.

Ayo examines his bookcase. She reads the spine of many books on the Congo and French-speaking West Africa. There are ceremonial masks, Kente cloths, photos of people, animal wood carvings, and stones marked with villages' names. She observes a section that resembles an altar with a voodoo-like collection of stones and feathers and what appear to be chicken feet, sticks, and a drinking gourd. A large-scented candle centers the altar.

Jacques lights the candle, illuminating the altar enclave in a yellow hue, accentuating the African masks. As the candle flickers, the masks seem to come alive. It's both spooky and sensuous at the same time, Ayo thinks.

As Ayo scans the bookcase altar, Jacques puts on some jazz—vocals by Ella Fitzgerald and Nina Simone, instrumentals by Thelonious Monk and John Coltrane. Jacques brings out a bottle of pinot noir; he holds it up, "Santa Barbara," he intones in his deep voice.

Ayo laughs. Two tall, full-bodied crystal wine glasses magically turn a deep purple-red color. Ayo lifts her glass and says, "To the African drum." They smile warmly at each other, sensually sipping some of Jacques's finest pinot. As a man of experience and grace, he doesn't cut corners on good wine. They alternately sip and kiss.

The music becomes sultrier as the evening goes on, and they dance. Jacques moves comfortably, rhythmically. Ayo takes off her shoes, "I hope you don't mind," she says.

"Being comfortable in your body is important," Jacques says. "Take off anything else you'd like." He takes off his jacket. His tight-fitting polo shirt accentuates his muscular frame.

As they dance, Ayo sees that the dark brown of her skin perfectly complements Jacques's caramel tones. With the lights down, Jacques's skin takes on a deep rosy golden tint. He's not dark gold, nor light gold but a golden color

53

like well-aged pine paneling. Ayo lightly runs her fingers over his face and touches his lips.

Ayo thinks, "Here I am with a light-skinned man after being with dark-skinned guys all my life." Her mother always told her, "The blacker the berry, the sweeter the juice." Most of her family is dark-skinned, and until now, she always thought she would fall in love with a dark-skinned man.

She is intrigued, not just by the beauty of Jacques's Creole caramel color but also by the realization that, in a way, he's Blacker than she is. She has chosen to become part of the police—the police who traditionally work for the oppressors of Black folk. Jacques has chosen to identify with African warriors fighting for liberation against Whites. She remembers her grandmother telling her that light-skinned Blacks feel the sting of racism deeper because, along with not being accepted by Whites, they have to prove their Blackness to Blacks. Her dark fingers stand out on Jacques's caramel face as she gently embraces the contours of his cheeks, nose, forehead, and neck.

Nina Simone is getting to them both.

The more Ayo thinks about color, the more her sexual feelings take over. She has never made love with a light-skinned man.

"It's warm in here," Jacques says. "Why don't you relax and take off that lovely orange sweater?"

Ayo sheds her cardigan, sliding it slowly down her

54

shoulders, eyes never leaving Jacques's.

"Now, may I help you with the next one?" he inquires.

Ayo grins at him and nods. He gently lifts the sweater off her head and seeks her approval to remove her bra. He unhooks it, and before he touches her, he looks at her and smiles appreciatively. "The color of the sweater is pretty, but the color underneath is rich."

She kisses him deeply, rubbing her breasts against his shirt. "This has to go," she says, helping him out of his shirt and undershirt, placing them in a pile along with her clothes.

As Ayo's fingers caress his face, Jacques captures one finger in his mouth. He covers it with his tongue and lips. Jacques takes another of her fingers into the warmth of his mouth, then another. He moans each time he licks and sucks her fingers. She is entering him, not the other way around. She has never experienced anything like this. She presses her body tightly against his, trying to enter him completely. She helps him unzip her jeans, and he puts his hand between her legs, feeling her growing dampness. They are moaning together.

He removes his slacks and his silk briefs and stands erect before her. She quickly follows suit, removing everything else she is wearing and then stands in front of him. He takes her hand and leads her to the bedroom.

In bed, Jacques touches her perfect breasts. He gently holds one then the other in both hands. Her nipples instantly respond to his touch, becoming gloriously firm, asking to be sucked. He realizes he's intrigued — and even more turned on — by her dark skin. Until now, he never thought about the skin color of his women — their intellect, their ideas, yes, their shape, definitely. But he's made love to — and has been a partner for varying lengths of time with — White, Asian, Latino, and African-American women of all shades. He never thought about their color. Maybe sharing his drums with Ayo has brought his sense of Negritude to the front of his mind. Or maybe his fascination with Ayo's skin is part of his fascination with her and desperately wanting to meld with her. He stops thinking and yields to his desire.

For her part, Ayo can now answer the question she asked herself about Jacques in the coffee shop: is it his alluring smile that captures her soul? His athletic muscles are strong and beautiful but do not make her feel small or weak. His penis is perfectly shaped but not bullying; it doesn't want to conquer her but share itself with her — to fit into her body and complete her.

When Jacques enters Ayo, he's giving, not taking.

Afterward, they lay on their sides, facing each other, holding each other, their legs intertwined. Jacques reaches down and covers Ayo with the black comforter and black silken sheets. Jacques suddenly understands why it feels so right to make love with a dark-skinned woman: Ayo drawing him into herself is like all of Africa accepting him, despite his light skin. Blending his color with hers and filling the dark room with their heat and heavy breathing is bringing African love into the heart of Greenwich Village.

Light skin, dark skin, black sheets, golden candlelight, and John Coltrane's Love Supreme bring both Ayo and Jacques closer to their roots than they've ever been; closer to feeling they've not only entered each other but have come home to a world that welcomes and protects them not because of anything they have done but simply because they exist. Their sleep is deep and full of enchanting dreams.

When Ayo wakes, Jacques is admiring her. She wordlessly returns his look and meets his lips. He runs his hands over her back, her breasts, her triangle and enters her with his fingers. She draws his erection into her mouth, tasting her own juices and his mixed together from the night before. She puts him inside her, and he stays there a long time before they climax together. "Yes," is the only word they whisper to each other as they fall asleep again.

The next time Ayo awakes, Jacques isn't there. He's sitting in his office, answering emails. She walks in naked and kisses the top of his head, and he pulls her onto his lap. They're helpless. There's nothing they can do but head back to bed and spend the next hour actively exploring each other's bodies.

Later that day, Ayo is very, very late getting to the station. Still, her captain says nothing because she walks through the office with self-confidence, signifying her obvious state of wholeness and blissfulness. He's never seen her like this before. She smiles at her captain with kind, penetrating eyes as if she were in charge, not him. But her supervisor, McSorley, doesn't care what she does. Ayo is great at her job. She makes him look good. Plus, she's rarely ever late. McSorley just smiles at her and says, "Good morning Queen James." He always says she is descended from African royalty.

Chapter 6

Love and Hate in Greenwich Village

A yo suggested to Zuri that they double date. Zuri was dating a copywriter, working for a pharmaceutical advertising agency. He was tall and elegant and had the complexion of Malcolm X with a hint of reddish hair. He and Zuri met through a friend and had gone out a few times before.

The two couples agreed to meet one Saturday afternoon in September when the weather was perfect. Ayo said she heard about a quirky place — the Lexington Candy Shop, and they decided to try it out. They drove there and miraculously found parking. The four of them — Jacques, Ayo, Zuri, and Edwin — sat in a high-backed, dark-wood booth. The soda fountain ran the length of the restaurant, and simply looking at the many delectable selections encouraged patrons to try some special ice cream flavor. The four shared a gargantuan sundae in a huge bowl laden with hot fudge, whipped cream, and nuts, topped with a maraschino cherry. Long spoons allowed them to dig into this divine dish with its combination of four flavors of ice cream — vanilla, chocolate, chocolate chip, and caramel.

"I'll need to swim extra laps," Zuri said as she inserted her spoon.

"I'll run an extra mile," Ayo pledged, inhaling with delight. Jacques and Edwin followed their lead and dipped their spoons into the sundae.

Edwin, feeling his way in this crowd, began innocuously. "Hey, did any of you see the new Xanax ad on TV?"

"I try to tune out all ads whenever possible," Jacques responded. "Why do you ask?"

"I was part of the team that wrote it," Edwin explained.

"What's it like writing as part of a team?" Ayo asked.

Edwin became animated. "It's great. One person says something, and the others piggyback on it. We have a chance to provide immediate feedback to one another. My team has a fantastic dynamic; we're all on the same wavelength, and it's an incredibly creative, collaborative environment."

Jacques responded, "I've worked with many groups, but never quite that way. Usually, I write a draft, and that written version is passed around with each person on the team, inserting his or her suggestions in a memo. After getting their input, I decide which comments to consider and then implement them."

Edwin noted, "My group is pretty freewheeling. We're intense but uninhibited. After we nail a campaign, we often go out for drinks. Things can get pretty wild. I'm very close to them."

Their conversation and the ice cream eventually came to

an end. Jacques made his excuses, "I'm sorry I have to end our get-together, but I have some pressing work. I'll take Ayo home with me."

They paid the bill, said their goodbyes, and went their separate ways.

Back in the car, Jacques commented to Ayo, "I love my sister, but I couldn't wait to get away from her latest loser boyfriend. There's something shifty about him."

Ayo suggested, "Perhaps it starts with the product he's writing about. Xanax is now on the radar as a potential carcinogen."

Jacques harrumphed and shook his head. "What would you like to do now?" he asked. "We've never walked across the Brooklyn Bridge, and today is such an extraordinary one; we should take advantage of it."

Ayo agreed. They walked across the bridge, holding hands, enjoying the sensation of being above the traffic, looking down, and seeing the water below them. When they finally reached the other end, they kissed, looked at each other and began the trek back across the bridge, going the other way to reclaim their car. They went back to Ayo's and relaxed.

That evening, Zuri phoned Ayo and asked, "So, what did you think of Edwin?"

Ayo, hedging, said, "He seems okay. How do you feel about him?"

Zuri unleashed her assessment. "As you know, I've dated enough so that I have a set of standards that I've developed. First, is he fun to be around? Do I enjoy my time with him? Does he have a strong sense of humor? So, the second general standard concerns his intelligence. Not just Ph.D.-level intelligence, but some natural intelligence about life. One Ph.D. I dated, couldn't figure out how to transfer his driver's license from Massachusetts to New York and had other issues with basic day-to-day living.

"Now, the third standard is self-confidence. I don't want to be propping up his ego constantly. He shouldn't be an egomaniac but needs to have enough confidence to know when he's done a good job and when he hasn't."

Without any hesitation, Zuri continued, "Of course, he's got to be financially stable. I dated an Adonis, but he was dirt poor. He was supporting his ex-wife and three kids and had no real free and clear assets. When we went out, we split the tab, which I didn't mind, but I knew sharing a bottle of good wine would create problems for him. I liked him, but I didn't want to go back to ground zero."

Ayo listened and asked, "Well, what about feeling a zing for each other?"

Zuri said, "Of course, that's important, but you have to get through all the other hurdles."

"So, how does Edwin fare on your scale?" Ayo inquired.

"Well, he comes off okay, but there's another criterion, a bit difficult to explain. For me, he's got to be sexually unambiguous. I have gay friends and some trans acquaintances, and they're great, but for me, I want a man who's 100 percent heterosexual. I want to feel like I'm a juicy steak, and he's a ravenous caveman. That's important to me. With Edwin, I'm not so sure. He talks about members of his workgroup, and I think there's more than a platonic relationship among them. Sometimes I wonder just how crazy those ad-team nights get."

"Woman, you're a tough cookie," Ayo says. "So, the quest continues?"

"Yes," Zuri said, "yes, it does. And how are you and my dear, darling brother doing?"

Ayo laughed. "Things are great. I'm grateful that I met him and that we're together," Ayo explains, "and I have you to thank for that. I appreciate your introducing us."

"I'm glad," Zuri says. "You both deserve to be happy, and if it's with each other — so much the better."

"Count me in on doubling with you on your next date. I want to see another example of your rating scale in action."

"Deal," Zuri promises. "I'll talk to you soon. After all that ice cream, I've got to get to the gym. Immediately."

****

Ayo and Jacques are in love. It's not a first for either. People get over and done with falling in love for the first time before moving to Greenwich Village, which is for people who know from experience how to be in love: You exchange apartment keys because it's not fair for one partner always to have to go to the others. With keys, you can decide "your place or mine" without a lot of rigamarole. You choose two favorite restaurants, one near each partner's workplace, so that you can meet about whoever has to work late that night without complicated discussions. You do not change the routines you have with friends because lovers come and go, but friends provide the continuity of life. You try to include your lover in these routines.

As he told Ayo, Jacques is so involved in his projects that he has few friends but many acquaintances. Ayo is more social. She enjoys the occasional girl's night out and often calls her friends. Without fail, she talks to her mom weekly. Jacques joins Ayo and her police squad every Thursday at 8 PM to get together for drinks at a bar near the 6th precinct at 233 W 10th. Ayo joins Jacques and his colleagues every Friday for an end-the-workweek-happy-hour at a restaurant near his office, close to the U.N.

They often get together with Jacques's sister, Zuri, who introduced them. One Sunday morning, when the three were having brunch in Zuri's studio apartment in the East Village, she reminds Jacques that he never finished explaining the importance of reparations, a topic she wrote about, quoting Professor M'Zuri, who was speaking at the meeting on Congolese women entrepreneurs.

"First off, Dr. M'Zuri comes from a high-ranking family in the East Congo, an area super-rich in natural resources," he explains. "She has significant inherited wealth if one is to believe the press. She has all the money she needs for her own enterprises and to support African women's projects. She's a real force. By day she's a professor of history, but really, she's an activist.

Don't underestimate her."

Jacques then launches into another one of his stories about an event that changed his life. "This gets a bit complicated, so grab your drinks and a bagel, and I'll give you the background on Critical Race Theory, which is necessary to understand reparations and racial issues in our culture," Jacques said. "I learned about Critical Race Theory during my first year at Columbia. White supremacy and Black oppression are so deeply embedded in the American social system that Black and Brown people in America today still suffer from its effects. They don't start life on an equal footing with Whites. But you know that."

Jacques took a sip from his mimosa and then continued, "Inequality makes the 14th Amendment's equal protection under-the-law mandate meaningless. Black Americans have endured more than 246 years of slavery and 103 more years of Jim Crow. For over 349 years, our legal system denied Black people our rights and prevented us from having the same opportunities that are available to White people."

Jacques looked up, smiling at the two women in the living room listening to him, which obviously makes him happy. "We've had only forty-five years of legal equality — not real equality. And, as you know, America is not a level playing field for everyone."

Knowing that asking Jacques any philosophical question meant a long and involved answer, Zuri and Ayo settle comfortably in their chairs and sip their mimosas. Jacques is ensconced in a big, black leather chair with a large orange, black, yellow, and red Kente wall-hanging behind him.

Jacques continued, "All U.S. laws have been and are still being written by White people, working to perpetuate White supremacy, though most lawmakers today probably aren't consciously perpetuating this supremacy. Nevertheless, there's hope. Laws that once oppressed can be transformed to liberate. The Supreme Court's decision in *Brown v. Board of Education* in 1954 is a perfect example."

Jacques senses the lagging attention span of his audience. Looking at them to reinvigorate their interest, he says, "I'm coming to the issue of reparations that you asked me about last week," he explains. "Thus, under Critical Race Theory, if lawmakers want to fulfill the intent of the 14th Amendment—equal justice for all—then reparations for Black Americans is a viable legal solution."

Ayo stares at the man she recently bedded, who seems transformed into some distant, bookish professor—not the sexy guy who made her insides feel like fire. She is paying enough attention to ask, "Are reparations only theoretical? Has the U.S. ever made any reparations' payments?"

"Yes," Zuri explains. "The United States paid reparations to Japanese-Americans interned during World War II. More recently, survivors of police abuses in Chicago[1] received reparations."

Almost competitively with his sister, Jacques adds, "Reparations were paid to victims of forced sterilization, and Black residents of a Florida town burned by a murderous White mob."

Ayo was eager to join the intellectual Henri team of Jacques and Zuri and adds, "I know the Jewish people in Israel received billions in compensation from Germany, but what other reparations were made in our country, and how could we apply reparations to more contemporary issues?"

Slathering cream cheese on his bagel and taking a sip of his mimosa, Jacques explains, "Native Americans received land from the U.S. government on which they now operate profitable casinos, and the federal government apologized for the many instances of violence, maltreatment, and neglect inflicted on Native peoples by U.S. citizens in 2009[1]. Something similar happened with the natives of Hawaii, whose land was taken from them."

Zuri sighs with some disgust in her voice and adds, "In the few cases of national reparations, the amount given for the injustice was small, but the fact that the injustice was acknowledged is a beginning. Tragically, compensation to Japanese Americans didn't come close to making up for the losses they suffered. No amount of money can wipe

67

out the horror of genocide or inhumane treatment, whether it's the Holocaust or endless land stealing. For Native Americans, the U.S. government stole their valuable and sacred lands. Indian children were forced into inhumane White boarding schools and forbidden from speaking their native languages. No money can compensate for the forced detachment of children from their parents or the loss of important spiritual sites."

Turning to Jacques, Zuri asks, "Doesn't the taking of valuable lands with oil and minerals remind you of what the colonial powers did in the Congo?"

"Until you put it that way, I never realized that North American colonization required subjugating Indigenous peoples to the political power of Christian European kings, and later to the White government who stole their lands or traded them for some trinkets," Ayo says.

"Same playbook," Jacques says. "But we were talking about reparations. My constitutional law professor argued, 'Why not give reparations to Black Americans for an estimated 7.9 trillion dollars stolen from them during slavery?' I've thought about this issue for a while," Jacques explained.

Ayo and Zuri could see that Jacques was getting wound up and was ready to lecture to them. "Before you begin, who would like water?" Ayo asks. She gets up, stretches, pours herself a glass of water, then re-fills the other water glasses. "Stay hydrated, y'all, while we drink these mimosas."

Like a batter ready to hit a game-winning home run, Jacques stands up, straightens his legs, and begins. "Take, for example, the horrors of lynching in America. Over 4,400 Black people were lynched from 1877 — the end of Reconstruction — until the 1960s to keep Black people in the South from voting, thereby keeping them in a system of peonage, a system of slavery by another name. That is, over 4,400 documented and yet another 3,000 plus who are known to have disappeared. They were without recourse to the laws of justice or fairness. Black people were not permitted to be police officers, elected officials, or serve on juries. If they were sent to jail, as they often unfairly were, they became slaves again under the convict-lease system, which forced predominantly Black prisoners — men, women, and children — to work for free on farms or other industries.

"You're aware of Emmett Till, who was killed for allegedly whistling at a white woman. Well, Southern Blacks were imprisoned for all sorts of trumped-up charges like that," Jacques says.

"Great pun, 'Trumped-up charges,'" Ayo says, trying to lighten the atmosphere.

Looking at his sister and Ayo, he says, "The Emmett Till lynching was used to strike fear into the Black community — to teach them not to expect justice from the Southern way of life, which is all part of White supremacy. Now, tell me, what compensation is owed those victims of lynching and illegal imprisonment?"

Before Ayo or Zuri could answer his question, Jacques continues, "In my class, the professor threw the question back at us. 'Should the government just write a $10,000 check to each African-American? Who should receive reparations? Should wealthy Black people like Oprah and Bob Johnson get reparations? Our class had a heated debate that quickly became bitterly divided."

"Sounds like what's happening today with all racial issues," Ayo says.

"We almost had brawls in the class because people were so rigid in their positions. Many students said 'reparation is an unworkable concept' — although we've just discussed how it has precedents. Most Black students tried to develop workable solutions, such as free college education for Black families who earn low incomes.

"One white student said that her family has been living in poverty since the steel mills shut down in her Ohio hometown and asked, 'shouldn't I get reparations, too?'

"After class, as I walked back to my apartment, the words of Malcolm X resonated through my head. Malcolm said that if the government continued to prevent African-Americans from attaining full equality, it might be necessary for them to take it 'by any means necessary.'"

The discussion continues for some time, and despite several mimosas, each of them enjoyed, Ayo senses that their discussion has a strong drag on Jacques, as if an inner spirit is pulling at him. Ayo begins to clear some dishes into the kitchenette, leaving Zuri and Jacques to their thoughts.

Jacques' thoughts eventually turned to Mame, as they always did. His early upbringing in family reunions in Congo Square in New Orleans placed King Leopold II's enslaved and slaughtered Congolese people in the context of Critical Race Theory and the 14th Amendment. He thinks Mame would settle the score.

"But, Jacques," Zuri says, attempting to bring him back to their conversation, "you got sidetracked."

Jacques begins pacing across the living room, and his voice becomes stronger with each step. "Critical Race Theory examines history from the viewpoint of the oppressed, not the oppressor. The people of the Congo are still suffering from the poverty and oppression caused by colonialism. For close to 100 years, Belgium grew wealthy from the crimes it committed against the Congolese people while stealing their valuable resources. At the same time, the Congolese grew poorer and poorer. Belgium didn't leave the Congo until 1960, leaving it bereft of infrastructure or the governance needed to ensure that the people benefited from their natural resources. It's disgusting! I don't like the word 'hate,' but I truly hate colonialism," he says as he finally settles on the couch.

Zuri says to Ayo, "I need another mimosa after that dissertation. I see he still pontificates. And maybe that's why we love him." They raise their glasses, smiling and say, "A sante a professeur Jacques." (Here's to good health

71

to Professor Jacques). Clinking their glasses, Ayo walks over to Jacques and kisses his forehead. Zuri cleans up. Jacques is pleased.

Chapter 7

Greenwich Village, Where's Jacques? Call Mom!

Not long after breaking up with Edwin, Zuri calls her mother.

"Hi, Mom. It's been too long since we talked. Things are going well with me, but I still haven't met anyone who sparks my heart. I was seeing someone, an ad guy, but he didn't measure up. Things are good professionally; I feel like I'm being taken seriously as a journalist. I know the struggles that Black people and especially Black women, have had in this realm, and I'm constantly grateful for my good fortune in having the work I do. But..."

"Honey, it's not good luck. It's hard work, and the Black warrior spirit that rages against injustice doesn't settle for a back seat. Your spirit has made you who you are."

"Thanks, Mom. I've never asked you, but who are your heroes?"

"One of my 'sheroes' was Wilma Randolph, a Black woman runner. She won three gold medals in the 1960 Olympics. The press called her 'the Black Gazelle.' I admire her because life wasn't easy, but she didn't give up. Against incredible odds, she succeeded gloriously."

"Tell me more about her."

"When I was growing up, we had few Black heroes to look up to, and we rarely heard about any Blacks during school—even in our segregated school. So, when I saw a picture of Wilma, I got excited. She was born prematurely. When she was a child, she had polio, scarlet fever, and pneumonia, which left her unable to walk. However, this woman had great determination, and not only did she learn to walk again, but at sixteen, she competed in the Olympics and won a bronze medal with her relay team. Then, as I mentioned, at the 1960 Olympics in Rome, she won gold medals and set world records in the 100, 200, and 4 x 100-meter relay.

"When the mayor of her Tennessee town wanted to honor her in a segregated ceremony in the Black community, she told him that she only wanted to be honored by the whole community, in an integrated ceremony—something rare in the South at that time. The mayor agreed. When she died of cancer at age fifty-four, I cried."

"That's quite a story, Mom. I've heard of Wilma Rudolph but did not know details about her life story. I don't think it's one of the stories you told me when I was little. I remember you used to tell Jacques and me bedtime stories about Black warriors, especially Black women warriors.

"Jacques used to draw them in his notebook. I liked the stories, but they didn't engage me as viscerally as they did him. I knew the difference between reality and myth, even back then. Maybe that's what's lacking in my life now; I

74

don't have enough fantasy to dream the big dream that will propel me to the next level and help me to send out those pheromones to meet a strong Black man who's not afraid of this strong Black woman."

"Honey, just as I told Jacques, have a little patience and believe, and you, too, will meet someone. I never expected to meet someone like your father. You may meet someone who doesn't meet all your criteria, but he'll make up for it in his love for you. You're lovable and will attract the right person. Trust your mother on this."

"Thanks, Mom. Talking with you always makes me feel better. I love you."

"Love you, too, honey-girl."

****

Ayo and Jacques do things New Yorkers never do except when visitors come from out-of-town. They visit the Statue of Liberty; they go to the top of the Empire State Building; they visit the Metropolitan Museum of Art and the Natural History Museum. They even see the Rockettes.

Jacques gets used to Ayo carrying a badge and gun. Ayo gets used to Jacques drifting off when they're together and to his frequent habit of lecturing instead of talking.

They often go to the Churchill Square pocket park and sit side-by-side, quietly reading different sections of the *New York Times*. They annoy each other by insisting on reading aloud something they just must share. They demonstrate their commitment by giving up one of their subscriptions.

Jacques surprises Ayo with a bouquet of purple bachelor's buttons and amaranth flowers. "The florist told me that they symbolize immortal love."

Ayo inhales their scent and draws him close, giving him a deep kiss.

He was about to launch into how they were used medicinally in Africa when Ayo looks at him and puts her finger on his lips, urging him to allow the moment to proceed without a lecture.

When their schedules don't allow them to sleep together, they call each other at night, telling each other fantasies about what they would like to do with the other in bed, on the floor, on a table, in public, wherever. But when they're together, they do none of these things. They have no interest in anything kinky; they simply want to get closer and develop a more soulful relationship.

Jacques has to attend a conference in Brussels about projects in Senegal. Ayo expects him to return to New York in about a week, but he stays away for a month, then two months, and more.

Ayo has intermittent, irregular contact with him during this time. Ayo calls her friend Aisha and complains. "Hey girl, what's up?"

Aisha details the latest IRB review on her thesis and how she's about ready to give up if she doesn't get the go-ahead. "What's going on with you and that dreamboat man of yours?" she asks.

"I haven't seen him for months," Ayo says, her voice rising. "I thought we had something special, but I'm not special to him — I'm the convenient girl here and not nearly as important as his work. It seems he can't be bothered to remember me. I know communication in some African areas is difficult, but there has to be some way he could call or text."

"I'm sorry, honey," Aisha says. "I thought you had a rare relationship."

"I did too," Ayo concludes with a heavy sigh. "Zuri says she hasn't heard from him either."

"Well, if Zuri hasn't heard from him, then it's not you. Maybe something happened to him. Didn't he go to Africa? Things happen there. I don't want you to panic, but anything can happen over there."

"No, his office says he's deep in the forests, examining projects. They told me he's safe. But I have not heard from him directly. I'm worried!"

Chapter 8

Tswambe, His Ancestors and Colonialism's Horrors

Thanks to the ancestral spirits of the Earth, shortly after the soldiers hacked off his hand, Tswambe passed out. His face was still buried in the dung; his life force was eager to join the spirits of his ancestors and flowed out with the blood coming from the wound where his hand used to be. Cow dung clogged his handless arm, stopping the bleeding, saving his life. The Earth as a healing source, he thought.

From dirt and water, we came, and to dirt and water, we go, and back again. It's the cycle of life, thought Tswambe, an idea his father taught him during a coming-of-age ceremony when he was thirteen years old. He remembered his father pouring libations into the cleanly swept soil in front of his home, recalling the spirit of the ancestors. Over and over with each pour, family members responded with, "Ashay, so be it, we remember."

The thick mist coming from the Congo River at the edge of his village surrounded Tswambe. Moisture rose and then fell through the air. The sun gave its heat but little of its light. The green growth was so thick; it was already dark at noon. The only light came from a bend in the middle of the river, where the leafy canopy opened slightly. The air muffled the sounds of the soldiers grunting, burping, and farting while they drunkenly went about the work of hacking hands from corpses with their machetes. Black Colobus and Sun-tailed monkeys playfully jumped across hefty rubber tree branches, not caring about the scenes of horror happening beneath them.

Tswambe felt himself being lifted by his armpits. As he came to, he saw that two women with rifles strapped across their chests and machetes attached to their waists were lifting him. They were as gentle with him as possible. They tied a thick vine around the stump of his arm to staunch the bleeding.

It took him a while to figure out that this woman, Mame, and a band of twenty women warriors had descended from nowhere and attacked the soldiers who had killed most of his village.

Hidden by the thick jungle, the women shot the three White Force Publique officers armed with U.S.-made Remington Repeater Rifles—one bullet downed each of them. The women warriors then jumped out of the foliage and cut off the officers' heads with razor-sharp machetes, creating explosions of blood spurting from their collapsed torsos. Then, the warriors dispatched the fifteen Black troops, who were so stunned they just put up a token fight, a hopeless fight, drunkenly swinging their machetes around. They were more afraid of what their White officers would do to them for wasting bullets than they were of these women. The women overwhelmed the slovenly, drunken band of Force Publique misfits. Killed them all.

The villagers who survived the soldiers' attack stumbled out from their hiding places under huts and the bodies of dead cattle. In addition to Tswambe, two others — a man and a woman — had played dead and lost their hands. Six children, including his daughter, came out of their huts. The soldiers had cut off their right hands before they shot their parents. Because the soldiers were drunk, their bullet had missed Tswambe, but he fell anyway and feigned death. Out of the corner of his eye, he witnessed soldiers raping a naked teenage girl strapped to a tree with the butt-end of their rifles as she screamed for death rather than torture.

Tswambe's daughter walked zombie-like out of their hut. The soldiers had not only taken her hand; they had taken her soul as well. She did not speak for the next two years.

None of Mame's warriors was injured, and she tended to each of the wounded villagers herself as her comrades gave aid. Aside from being frightened to their core, Tswambe and the other villagers were half-starved, near naked, and exhausted from the constant strain of twelve-hour workdays.

Rubber in the Congo came from wild vines in the jungle,

unlike the rubber from Brazil, which was tapped from trees. To extract the rubber, instead of tapping the vines, the Congolese workers had to slash the vines and lather their bodies with the rubber latex. When the latex hardened, they would scrape it off their skin in a painful manner, as it took the workers' hair with it.

Mame consoled them and explained that they should follow her and her warriors up the river into a Maroon haven with food, natural medicines, and protection from the terror they had lived through for years. As Mame led the villagers and her warriors through the jungle cover, she walked with the handless children, including Tswambe's daughter. Mame took her time talking, smiling, placing her arm around each of their shoulders. She learned their names and reassured them. They learned her name and never forgot it. Mame.

Chapter 9

Brussels, Belgium—"We are all Africans"

Jacques ate breakfast in his hotel café, dressed impeccably in business attire—a dark suit with a light blue tie adorned with discrete gold fleur-de-lis in a thin red border. He wore an off-white Ermenegildo Zegna silk and cotton shirt. Jacques placed a euro on the table as he left the hotel, even though the bill included the tip. The taxi waiting for him was a black Mercedes with lightly tinted windows.

After a ten-minute ride through busy streets streaming with buses, cars, and bicycles, his taxi pulled up to a well-appointed office complex. He saw the word UNESCO emboldened in a golden brass plaque across the entrance. As he rode the glass-enclosed outside elevator to the seventh floor, he observed solar panels angled toward the sun embedded in glass windows. "What a great idea," thought Jacques. "Why don't we do this in New York City?"

He entered a meeting with his UNESCO colleagues from the United States and Belgium on the top floor. In French, they discussed the millions of dollars in grants earmarked for clean water and new housing projects in Senegal. During the discussion, not thinking of Ayo, not even thinking of himself, Jacques volunteered to stay as long as necessary to supervise the grant money distribution.

At the end of the meeting, Jacques reminded his colleagues of the increased violence from radical Muslims and poor people of color worldwide. "The rise of terrorisms adds additional urgency to this project," Jacques said. "To fight terrorism, we need to help people obtain decent housing, health care, and education for their children. When people have necessities, the pull of radical ideas is lessened." Jacques circled the oval meeting table shaking hands with his colleagues, who all nodded in agreement with what he had said. For such a young man, they thought he was advanced beyond his age.

When he approached the representative from Senegal, Dr. Barbara Joof-Dior, he firmly grasped her extended hand with both of his and told her that his professors at NYU had spoken about the leadership of the Joof and Dior families in Senegal, starting centuries ago in the kingdoms of the Senegambia nation.

Dr. Joof-Dior thanked him for his courtesy. "We have always believed in ourselves and the concept of one-world and one-people. We want to work with American and European leaders who appreciate our vision of oneness. We are all Africans."[1]

Jacques smiled at her comment, nodded, and said, "I agree, we are all Africans."

"You seem to believe that we are all Africans, c'est vrai? (is

83

that right?)," Dr. Joof-Dior asked.

"Yes, indeed. I frequently tell people, 'We are all Africans,' which puzzles some people."

"Go on, tell me more," Dr. Joof-Dior said.

Jacques continued, pleased that he found a receptive audience in the important Senegalese representative. "We, Black Americans, call Africa 'Mother Africa' because all humans come from Africa — Europeans and Americans, too. After all, the human species started in Africa in the Great East African Rift Valley, from southern Lebanon to Mozambique. We were the only humanoid species to survive.

"About 300,000 years ago, the Out-of-Africa movement began due to climate change[1]. Waters dried up, and animals and humans migrated north up the Nile Valley. The Africans followed the animals for food. Eventually, we Africans occupied all four corners of the world. In Africa, people needed a lot of melanin in their skin to protect them from the harsh sun. Still, after thousands of years in colder climates with fewer sunlight hours, our chemistry evolved because we needed less melanin. Human body colors lightened and evolved over thousands of years, but everything began in Africa."

Dr. Joof-Dior was visibly surprised and pleased that this American seemed to know so much about her people and Africa.

Jacques delighted her even more by saying, "I think I've

read every poem by your President, Scholar Leopold Senghor. He introduced us, Black Americans, to the Negritude Movement in the 1930s, long before our own Black Power Movement. Senghor was a brilliant thinker and a gentleman. He always spoke of a one-world vision. He loved his Blackness and made our color so beautiful, so revolutionary with his words and deeds."

"Merci beaucoup, Monsieur Jacques," Madame Joof-Dior said, bowing her head. "We will prevail. We have no choice. Our history commands it. The theory behind Senghor's Negritude philosophy was to teach the rest of the world that we are all Africans. We all come from the same source, Africa, so we should not separate ourselves. Where did you learn so much about President Senghor?"

"I double-majored in African studies and international affairs. Africa has always fascinated me. The anti-colonial leaders of the '40s and '50s inspired our modern civil rights movement, too."

"It's a shame most people don't appreciate our history and our enormous contributions to the modern world," Dr. Joof-Dior said, "I look forward to working with you in Dakar and our countryside."

"A bientôt a Dakar (see you soon in Dakar)."

They embraced, giving each other three slight, quick kisses on alternative cheeks in the French African tradition.

85

Chapter 10

Dakar, Le Ile de Madeleine, and Nasty King Buzzards

Jacques flew to Dakar, Senegal's capital, for a round of meetings before beginning his real work. He stepped out of an air-conditioned taxi from the airport.

Jacques reached back to close the taxi's door but quickly pulled his hand off the blisteringly hot chrome handle. He headed straight for the hotel's revolving front door to escape the heat. Without seeming even to notice how hot the day was, his driver sauntered to the taxi's trunk, hauled out Jacques' suitcase, and brought it into the hotel lobby. The hotel was on the Dakar waterfront on Boulevard Martin Luther King, Jr. The Terrou-Bi was a pleasant, five-star hotel, inexpensive by European standards.

After settling in, Jacques went downstairs to the bar, where he and Senghor Yade, a diplomat, fell into talking with each other. Yade turned out to be the first cousin of Rama Yade, France's Senegalese-born delegate to UNESCO.

"I love Africa," Jacques said. "I love Senegal, but it's so damn hot."

Senghor shot him a strange look—in diplomatic circles,

you did not curse. Then, he smiled. "Yes, temperatures can reach more than 50 degrees Celsius. Some days are even hotter, but you get used to it. The rainy season in August brings unexpected downpours and more muggy weather."

"Aren't the rains supposed to cool the temperature?" Jacques asked wryly.

"Ah yes," Senghor replied, "but that never happens here. It stays hot in Dakar."

"I know heat. New Orleans has hot, muggy heat," Jacques replied, "but not like Dakar. When I arrived earlier today, it was almost 45 degrees Celsius, what we Americans know as 112 degrees Fahrenheit. It was like walking into a furnace. New Orleans is hot, but Dakar is seriously hot."

They finish their drinks and go together into the restaurant. Jacques orders Caldou, fish cooked in palm oil with vegetables and rice and a lime and peanut sauce. Senghor has bassi salte, couscous with lamb meatballs, and a variety of potatoes—sweet potatoes and white potatoes—white beans, carrots, cabbage, cowpeas, and sweet dates and raisins in a tomato sauce.

Senghor said, "We each are ordering separate dishes. In Senegal, we traditionally all share from one plate. Funny how European customs are invading Senegal. Have you been here before? Do you know about Le Ile de Madeleine, which you can see from your hotel room?"

"Yes," says Jacques. "It's one of the most beautiful islands in Africa. I hear the island is on the list—a potential UNESCO World Heritage site."

They order coffee. The waiter brings each of them a bowl filled with green mangoes and pineapple topped with peanuts for dessert.

"Bird-watchers flock to Le Ile de Madeleine to glimpse rare African birds," Senghor explains. "They're only allowed there on weekends. No camping, no cooking, no eating, nothing is allowed—just birdwatching. The island is uninhabited."

"What about the legend that the island isn't uninhabited?"

Senghor gives Jacques a look of uncertainty about continuing, but he does. "West Africans up and down the coast believe King Buzzards inhabit the island, birds that used to be humans but were transformed into ugly, weak, wretched buzzards that smell worse than rotting human corpses. They come out after midnight searching for refuge from their smell, their pain, their misery. They can't wipe off the rotting slime that covers their bodies. They search for solace but find none. They roam all night long, moaning in misery. They are forever doomed in the living hell of the island, unable to get off lest they be swallowed by the sharks circling the island, drawn there by the smell of rotting flesh. They can never rest. In the dark hours, they scream and moan in endless pain. If you've been on a boat just off the island, you have heard them."

Jacques replies, "Scientists claim the moans and screams are the waves rushing into lagoons and caves along the island's rocky coast, forcing air out to cause that moaning sound, but I believe the folklore. It's not the rushing waves. It's the buzzards crying in misery."

Later, sitting at a desk in his room, Jacques wrote his thoughts about the buzzards:

Long before Christianity or Islam, West Africans followed the concept of animism, a religious philosophy proclaiming all living things sacred: plants, birds, insects, trees, animals, rivers, winds, and the rising and setting sun and moon. Each category of life is imbued with divinity by the god or spirit who looks after it.

When living things stop living, they do not die but join their ancestral community. When a tree dies, it is not dead; it joins its tree ancestors by decomposing, blending with the soil of the jungle floor, and nourishing the earth to produce another tree. When the sun sets, it does not die. It comes back twenty-four hours later as a sunrise. When an animal dies in the jungle, it is not dead. It decomposes into the earth and eventually comes back as a flower, a tree, or a shrub.

When humans die, their spirits reunite with their ancestors, extending back hundreds and thousands of years. Nothing is more joyful to a believing West African than the promise of reuniting with our ancestors when we join the spiritual community in the state Westerners call "death." But the African doesn't die, he enters his spirit community. Enter Le Ile de Madeleine.

89

The ancestors of enslaved people have a special place reserved for African rulers and leader mercenaries who helped the European slave traders. That place is Le Ile de Madeleine. The souls of those who helped enslave their own people are condemned to live on the island. They can never enter the spirit community of their ancestors. They are condemned to wander forever, covered by the stinking slime and rotting flesh of the people they sold into slavery. They are the King Buzzards – never allowed back into the ancestral population of family, community, and love.

Jacques closes his eyes and imagines himself to be one of the Africans who had been captured and enslaved. He paces restlessly around his room before returning to his writing.

More than fifteen million of us West Africans were kidnapped from our villages, sometimes more than 400 miles into the interior. Our rulers sold us to Europeans for guns, rum, salt, and silk.

Ten percent of people captured did not survive the march to the coast and the waiting slave ships. Those who did were shackled into a one-foot by five-foot by eighteen-inch space in the pit of those hulking slave ships and forced to lie for eight to twenty weeks in their excrement in 115 degrees of stifling heat. Thirty percent died before reaching the Caribbean. The sharks could smell a slave ship from miles away and quickly learned to follow slave ships to eat the African bodies thrown overboard. Slave ship captains referred to the route from Africa to the Caribbean as "Shark Alley."

Slavers ripped out virtually all of West Africa's strongest, smartest, and healthiest inhabitants for more than 400 years. The slave masters became extremely wealthy. The Africans were enslaved for four centuries. Le Ile de Madeleine is the hell reserved for the Africans who sold us into slavery. They wander in misery every night for eternity, never to be reunited with their family. It is a fate worse than death. It is the fate they deserve. Never, ever to be rejoined with their ancestors.

Jacques grows both weary and angry. He feels the spirit of Mame, urging him to take revenge. Emotionally exhausted from writing, from remembering his ancestral histories and staring at the beautiful Ile de Madeleine from his hotel window, Jacques falls asleep. All night in his nightmares, he tosses back and forth, chained at the bottom of a slave ship, unable to sleep due to the rolling ship and the crashing waves and the moans and screams of men and women, indeed children too, locked in fetid heat and excrement in complete darkness lying beside him.

In his nightmare, he hears a man, just inches from his face, gasping his last breath and dying. The contorted and sweating man had salt stains around his mouth and eyes.

He feels his shackled hands and feet, and his mind races in horror: Where are we going? Why are we captives? Why do these strange, smelly, drunken red-faced men want to chain us in this hell? Are we going to be stripped of our skin, dangled over hot coals, and eaten? The horror of being at the bottom of a ship chained to rough-hewn wooden planks that launch splinters into his skin at every toss of the ship's pounding wave was unbearable. Night after night, day after day, for weeks on end, he hears the echoes of pounding waves on the ship's bow. Jacques's nightmares only end with the rising sun across the bay with a view of Le Ile de Madeleine from his five-star hotel room with 400 thread-count sheets.

The next day and the day after, he meets with his UNESCO and Senegalese colleagues about their ambitious project of erecting more than 1,000 new homes with clean running water in villages across the countryside.

Jacques goes to the hotel gym for some much-needed exercise. He knows he has neglected his physical activity, which is bad for both his body and mind. Perhaps his spirit, too, is agitated for lack of exercise. A good sweat eases emotions.

He travels about twenty-five miles outside of Dakar to meet with the local elders in the village of Gorom in the Mosquée de Gorom. Everyone speaks French. As a show of their support for the project, the village elders fête Jacques that evening. They thank him for his work, his commitment to the local people, and his dedication to improving the quality of life in Senegal. The feast includes Thieboudienne, the national dish of Senegal composed of fish, rice, and tomato sauce with onions, carrots, cabbage, cassava, and peanut oil. For dessert, they serve the type of beignets Jacques grew up with in New Orleans. He thought Café du Monde's beignets in New Orleans were better, more moist, soft, and tasty, but he dares not say that to his hosts. He has some fleeting thoughts of Ayo, but they became lost in the meetings he holds.

Jacques and his entourage visit villages within a 250-mile radius of Dakar, where clean water and housing projects would be undertaken. This work, he thinks to himself, is why I'm here on Earth. He knows he is making a difference in the lives of people. The spirits of his ancestors, especially Mame, inspire him. He is determined that they would never, ever consider turning his soul into a King Buzzard. He losses himself in his mission and spends the rest of the summer going from village to village, unfortunately neglecting Ayo in the process.

In September, he returns to Brussels for a week to report to various UNESCO-connected groups before returning to the United States. Brussels treats Jacques very well. His expense account is very generous, having amassed two months' per diem cash while in Senegal without paying a dime. He can spend virtually without care. And he does. He enjoys the best food, wines, cheeses, and single-malt scotches Brussels has to offer. He takes several day trips to the Belgian countryside. He goes to a gym and works out and notices how much tone he has lost.

Jacques decides to call his mother, who he has neglected, along with Ayo and Zuri.

His mother is thrilled to hear from him but yells at him for neglecting her. She warns him that his girlfriend, whom she had heard about from Zuri, has every right not to be patient and could be looking around for someone else who values her. Jacques has always been close to his mother. Now, especially since his father died a few years ago, he pictures her roaming around their large Tremé house, alone but tending her garden. His mom's words worry him.

Chapter 11

Brussels, Belgium

On his last night before flying home, Jacques calls Ayo. After thinking about his mother's warning, he is fearful of calling her. So, all week, he ducks making the call. When they talk, she is distant. She has very little to say. He reassures her that he loves her, but she tells him, "Someone who loves someone calls, writes, and stays in contact." He apologizes and hopes that she might forgive him. Over dinner at his hotel, Jacques reads the first New York Times he has seen in months. The headline was shocking: Belgian Princess Elizabeth Attacked by Machete. The article read:

Laeken, Belgium—Last night, Princess Elizabeth, heir to the Belgian throne, was attacked near the royal palace just outside of Brussels by a masked assailant. The assailant severed her hand at the wrist with a machete. As she lay in near shock, the princess said the attacker put a tourniquet around her arm to stop the bleeding. The princess said she watched in horror as the assailant picked up her bloodied hand and walked down the dark alley with it. Authorities are now combing the area looking for the severed hand.

The attack occurred outside an exclusive shopping area just after sunset. The assailant pulled Princess Elizabeth into a darkened alley, pushed her to the ground, extended her arm, and hacked her hand off at the wrist. Authorities found the blood-streaked machete at the scene. The Princess is resting in the Laeken hospital under armed guard, but her hand is missing.

After Jacques reads the Times article, he goes online to The Belgium INS, an online news service based in Brussels. Commentators across Europe speculate that the crime was a terrorist attack staged by Muslim extremists.

The Brussels Times reports that the Belgian Islamic Council's spokesperson (BIC), Dr. Amin El-Bahraanani, said, "The BIC condemns in our most emphatic terms the senseless and counter-productive violent attack by a madman against the royal family. All citizens of Belgium, including Muslims, offer our sincere condolences to the Leopold family. Bring this criminal to justice!"

The former American ambassador to Belgium, Denise Rosalyn Barnyard, who still lives in Brussels, said, "I have known Princess Elizabeth for over five years. We are dinner and tennis partners. She is a lovely lady, bright, full of life, and very generous with her wealth and time. I cannot believe anyone would ever want to harm this beautiful person. I am devastated."

Jacques wonders about the details of the attack: a severed hand, a machete, a royal family member, a darkened alley near an open venue. What could this mean? He almost picks up the phone to ask his colleagues at the Africa-Europe Parity Group (AEPG) back in New York but decides to wait. He would see them in a few days.

Chapter 12

Back in the USA and Heading into Her Heat

J acques rushes to his office at AEPG, near the United
Nations, immediately after passing through customs at
JFK airport. As soon as he hits his desk, he begins long
days of eating on the run and sleeping at the office. He
dives into writing reports and meeting with his colleagues
and supervisors about his work in Senegal. The heads of
the organization rarely say it, but they constantly need
evidence to show donors that their money is well spent.
However, this is hardly necessary in Jacques' case. His
name on a report is sufficient to satisfy anyone that a
project is important and well-handled. Everybody knows
Jacques is the hardest working, most dedicated person at
AEPG. Everybody also worries he will burn himself out or
have a breakdown.

****

A week after returning to New York, Jacques can finally
unpack, settle into his apartment, and crash. For three
days, he does nothing but sleep and eat Chinese food and
has pizza delivered to his door. He loves watching old
movies late into the night and spends his days in a partial

sleep watching re-runs.

On the fourth day, he gets out of bed at nine in the morning, shaves, showers, and scrambles some fresh eggs he ordered from a delivery service along with other groceries. After eating, he shuffles to the hall table, where the doorman always drops his Times. Nothing is there. He then remembers; he stopped his subscription because he counted on having Ayo's to read.

He sinks dejectedly into one of his black leather wing-backed chairs. Now that he has no work in which to hide, he has no recourse but to allow his very human thoughts and emotions to surface: he feels lonely. Specifically, Jacques feels lonely for Ayo and feels guilty because he knows he must have hurt her — over and over all the time he was in Senegal.

AEPG staffers told him she was trying to reach him, but he did nothing because he did not want to be distracted from his work. Big mistake, he thinks to himself. Was it that he was too afraid to be committed? And he feels afraid that by now Ayo has taken another lover, as his mother warned him. Why wouldn't she? That's what you do in Greenwich Village.

Seeing Ayo was harder for him than facing the dangers of the deep jungle teeming with malaria-infected mosquitoes, but Jacques musters up his courage and calls her. Much to his relief, she doesn't answer, and he talks into her voice mail without fear of response.

She calls back within an hour. Her voice is tight as if she were holding back, saying something. She is brusque, limiting herself to "yeses" and "nos" and "I don't care." Jacques's speech is uncharacteristically halting, and he stumbles over his words, but he manages to ask to see her. She agrees, but only if they met in a neutral place. They agree to get together at noon at Birch's coffee shop, where they were first introduced. Neither says so, but each hope that the noise and the crowd would help them keep a lid on their emotions and lessen the possibility of drama.

It works. At least, Jacques and Ayo are spared the need to talk to each other when they first arrive because they must stand in line to get their coffee and concentrate on not spilling their cups while wedged into the crowd waiting for a table to empty.

When they finally sit down, Jacques speaks fast, as if he is afraid that he would not be able to say anything at all. "Ayo, I know I've blown being with you. I'm sorry I didn't keep in touch, but please believe that I just couldn't. It wasn't just you that I didn't contact. I didn't keep in touch with anybody, not even my mom or Zuri. My project was so overwhelming; it took everything I had. There were conflicts with builders, government agencies, and the United Nations' staffers. UNESCO was worse than the Africans."

He takes a breath and pauses before rushing ahead. "I had to constantly reassure village elders we weren't doing anything to diminish their power or hurt their people. It wasn't that I didn't like the work — I loved it. I so wanted the project to happen — to provide a decent standard of living for thousands of people, to change the course of their lives, so they have clean water, quality education for their children, and a real home of their own.

"I lost myself in work. I hope your new boyfriend doesn't treat you the way I did. I'm so very sorry for hurting you."

Ayo almost laughs and growls at the same time. "What boyfriend, asshole?" Her voice is loud enough to carry a few tables over while Jacques sheepishly looks around to see who is listening. "After what we had together, I certainly won't be ready for anyone else for a long time. At first, I was worried, then angry. Then I tried to focus on remembering you're a pompous, withdrawn, weird, self-centered bastard who I was better off without. But that didn't work; the look of your smile and whatever that thing is you do with your eyes kept messing with my head. I felt more hurt than angry, and I missed you more than I remembered your obnoxious parts.

"And I felt used. You were helping humanity but forgot all about me. I'm human, too! I admire the work you're doing; I really do. And I love your dedication. But when I'm in a relationship, I just can't be put in second place to anything. I've never been able to play second fiddle. I've dumped guys who didn't get that. Of course, I've put my work first many times, and I need a guy to understand that. Maybe neither one of us is cut out for being part of a couple. Especially not this couple."

101

****

Hope washes over Jacques, and it shows on his face. She doesn't have a new boyfriend! But the fear that Ayo was right, that neither one of them was cut out for a lasting relationship, also rings true. Paradoxically, her anger is reassuring.

"You're right. I'm a bastard in many ways. Look, here's the thing: I love you. Shit, that just bubbled out of me. I can work on the pompousness and moodiness, but I can't say that I won't get lost in my work. I wish I could turn it off, but I don't know how."

"Maybe think of it this way," Ayo said thoughtfully, "If you let me in when you're immersed in a project, maybe I can help you with my support, and if you talk about things with me, rather than lecturing me, maybe I can even give you some insights that will help you. And maybe you can do the same for me."

For reasons he did not understand, Jacques starts to cry. "I truly want to try," he says softly.

Ayo was smart enough not to comfort him, not yet. He had some work to do first. "You can't turn your emotions off for months and then expect to start right back where we magically were," she says. "But we can work together. We can both try."

She suggests they start by having dinner together that weekend. "Give me a few days to think. Let's talk Friday. Maybe dinner, I don't know, maybe."

Chapter 13

Detroit 1967: Police Brutality and the "Voice of the Unheard"

To rekindle their relationship, Ayo and Jacques meet at Mimi's, where they had their first date. This time, Ayo orders pinot noir from Santa Barbara. Jacques is moved that she remembers what they talked about their first time here, and his guilt about his treatment of Ayo burns tears in his eyes.

Their food seems to taste especially delicious, and they are soon engrossed in talking. Ayo and Jacques split an appetizer, a Pâté de Porc, composed of Armagnac-soaked prunes, hazelnuts, Dijon mustard, cornichons, and sourdough toast. They each order a seafood entrée and share one another's entrées—each wondering whether they will share more intimately later.

Their conversation is wide-ranging—United States-European-African history. Jacques, for once, does not pontificate but asks Ayo for her opinions and thoughtfully listens to her answers. The mood is warm and comfortable, much as when they were together before he left for Brussels and Senegal.

Ayo tells him about a special movie discussion that might

interest him. After dinner, they see the movie *Detroit*, about the uprising in Detroit's Black community in the summer of 1967 after incidents of police brutality. She quotes Dr. King, "Riots are the voice of people unheard." They remain in the theater for the discussion with the director.

The film evokes strong feelings in Ayo. She says she understands the men and women on the Detroit police force and the pressures they faced, but in 1967, Detroit's population was 70 percent Black while the police force was 80 percent White. Most officers didn't even live in the city, and too many were racists. She is not surprised at the uprising.

"Better pre-service and in-service training are part of the keys to a resolution. But the police force in Detroit and other areas needs to reflect their communities and get better training in mental health and other non-traditional police activities," Ayo tells the group in the theater. "By working with people who are different from you, you learn a lot—including tolerance for diversity, and that people who look different from you face the same problems you do: they have trouble with their kids, with their spouses, or other relationships, with making ends meet, with medical issues.

"And" she says, "some people are just jerks and don't belong on the police force. They should be rooted out during training, but if their attitudes aren't noticed and come out later, their supervisors should put them under watch and kick them out before they hurt someone. The union shouldn't protect them. They're a danger, and they make the good police look bad." The crowd claps.

They walk to Jacques' place, chatting pleasantly but not touching.

Jacques says, "You were dynamite, Ayo. You got everybody thinking."

"I just repeated what police departments around the country are saying. Many now require their officers to take diversity-sensitivity training as part of their pre-service and then attend annual required training, and if they don't do well, out they go."

Chapter 14

Jacques's Apartment – Good Wine, Candlelight, and Fear

At Jacques's apartment, they uncork the second bottle of wine, another Santa Barbara pinot noir. They put on some jazz CDs, turn out the lights, and light some candles. They continue to chat nonstop. They still do not touch.

"Do you think things can get better?" Jacques asks.

"Are you talking about America or us?" she asks tartly.

For the first time, Jacques sputters. "Both."

Ayo looks at him, and he sees the depth of the hurt in her eyes.

He reaches over to kiss her, but she backs away.

"It'll take time to rebuild our relationship," she says.

"I want to try," he reassures her.

She nods gravely.

"And what about in America?" she inquires, allowing him to finish his thought.

"Well, after sixty years of the modern civil rights

movement, police brutality is still rampant. Black Lives Matter is being treated like the Black Panther Party used to be. What's improved, really?"

"Of course, there's been progress," Ayo insists. "Segregation is no longer the law. You can sue if you're discriminated against, and more Black youth are in school than in prison—for the first time in history."

"But we are going backward," Jacques counters. "White wealth is ten times greater than Black wealth. More of us are in poverty today than in 1970. And the police! I know you say they're improving, but Black people are more afraid than ever to just walk down the street or drive their cars. Police shoot four times as many Black men as Whites. Where's the progress?" The intense Jacques is back, intoning his words, not talking to Ayo.

"Calm down, calm down," she says. "Let's enjoy our wine. No, on second thought, maybe you've had too much."

Things turn playful. Jacques grabs his wine glass and drains it, comically contorting his face into an exaggerated imitation of a little boy doing something naughty. They laugh together. It feels good.

Ayo lifts her glass, too. "Here's to us," she says.

"Here's to us," Jacques repeats, with hope and promise in his voice. "And to progress—in the United States and Africa." This time, Jacques sounds uncertain and a little sad.

He makes sure Ayo sees him admiring the way the candlelight dances over her beautiful skin, creating shimmering, changing reds, yellows, and rich browns. He quietly thanks her for her patience with him.

They kiss each other on the lips but lightly. Jacques asks Ayo to stay over, but she's not ready yet. Jacques calls a taxi to take her back to her apartment.

Chapter 15

Greenwich Village: Screaming, Red Blood, Handless Wrist

Jacques would have called first the next day, but Ayo beats him to it. "Damn, I've missed you." After another week, they spend the night together, first at her place, the next night at his.

As Ayo explains to her friend, Aisha, "I should have kept my distance — but I couldn't wait to have him inside me, to feel his body against mine. I missed him so badly. He fulfills something in me that I've never felt before."

Aisha surprises Ayo by giving her some good news. "I've passed the IRB review; now I can finish writing my thesis and get my Ph.D., and I've met someone." They chat excitedly as two old friends. Having Black girlfriends offers Ayo a special perspective — not available through friends at work or even from Jacques. They're her emotional barometer — helping her keep an even emotional temperature during difficult times.

Jacques and Ayo fall back into their comfortable routines,

phoning each other with sexy talk if they can't sleep together, joining each other's group of co-workers at their weekly get-togethers, and sharing brunches with Zuri, who is thrilled they are back together. Zuri is also glad that Jacques has finally surfaced from his latest work obsession. Ayo and Jacques often sit quietly side-by-side in Churchill Square's pocket park, reading the *New York Times.*

Jacques does not renew his subscription.

****

Sitting in the park one warmish late October afternoon, Ayo passes Jacques the front section of the *Times.* The headline screams, *"Another Belgian Royal Attacked."*

A member of the Belgian royal family was attacked last night in Greenwich Village. Someone severed Lady Clairece Elizabeth Alice Von Struben-Haagen's hand from her wrist with a razor-sharp machete. The victim, 24, is a New York University student. She is in stable condition at New York University Medical Center in Lower Manhattan. She told police that after the attack, her assailant wrapped her arm in a bandage to stop the bleeding. However, she was unable to identify the assailant.

The police did not recover the severed hand but found a bloody machete at the scene.

"We have launched a full-scale investigation to establish a motive and find the perpetrator," Police Commissioner

James O'Neil said. The attack is the second violent attack against Belgium's royal family this year.

Jacques's stomach muscles tighten, and he feels dizzy. He hides his reaction from Ayo and says nothing. He's afraid to. He almost lost her once; he doesn't want to push her away again.

He pretends to hear Ayo's comments on the article and responds with a nod, but nothing more. He says to her, "The world's gone mad."

****

Back in his apartment that evening, Jacques feels relief that Ayo couldn't spend the night. The news of the attack on the Belgian princess within blocks of where he lived took over his thoughts, and dark, sharp twinges coursed around inside him. He had a lot to deal with.

He watched the news while he brewed coffee. Maybe it was elitist, but Jacques enjoyed his Peaberry coffee from Tanzania, thinking that it tasted better because it was from Africa, and he liked watching the old-fashioned percolator bubble on top of the stove—reminding him of his childhood. He clicked on CNN. The headline scrolling at the bottom of the screen said Breaking News—Royal Machete Maiming in New York City.

Jacques undressed, went into his bathroom, and stood in the shower. Hot water beat on the back of his neck and head. He thought about the machete attack, but that got mixed in his head with black and white moving pictures shot by French cameramen in the 1900s showing Black children with their hands cut off by King Leopold II's Force Publique soldiers. Their parents had not gathered their quota in pounds of rubber.

In his mind, Jacques saw the blades of machetes falling in slow motion on the thin arms of children. Their hands seemed to drop in front of him onto his shower floor. The black and white images now changed to full color with red blood flowing and swirling in an endless clockwise rush down the shower drain, like the scene from Hitchcock's Psycho, and he heard the screams of children and the pleas of mothers.

The shower water seemed louder and louder and turned into the screams of a young African girl holding her handless arm outstretched, running to her father after Leopold's army severed her hand. Blood spewed out of her arm, dotting the sandy-colored dirt dark red. As the hot shower water enveloped him now colored red, the screams seemed to get louder as the blood swirled faster down the drain.

He saw images of King Leopold II and his royal family living in luxury sipping teas and eating chocolates in the Royal Palace in Laeken juxtaposed against the miserable squalor of the huts in which most enslaved Congolese lived. He saw the chocolate hands-on display in chocolate shops in Antwerp. The screams became louder still; the blood flowed redder, faster. Repeatedly, he heard a CNN reporter say breaking news, breaking news, breaking news — the horror, the horror. His mind screamed – The Horror!

After several minutes in the shower, Jacques's breathing became deeper and slower. He felt calmer and turned off the shower, but he felt a heavy weight in his body and mind. He was unable to move. Slowly, he opened the shower door. Steam seemed to rush away the pain and anguish he felt as the cool air hit him. He stepped out of the shower, grabbed a towel, and began to dry off. Slowly, he began to feel normal, but not before more images flashed through his mind of the violence inflicted on his ancestors.

What's going on, he asked himself? He realized he felt the same as he had in the Antwerp chocolate shop years ago. Maybe the spirit of Mame, with her angry vengeance, was back.

Chapter 16

NYPD Sixth Precinct—A Happy Place

Ayo's boss, Captain Coleman McSorley, called Ayo into his office, She was wearing her purple NYU sweatshirt. "James, you went to NYU, right?"

Ayo rolled her eyes at him. "You know your way around there. Want to investigate the machete attack against the Belgian princess, or whatever she is?"

McSorley had spent thirty-three years on the force and was now a violent crime investigations supervisor. If Ayo was an anomaly on the force, so was McSorley. Neither of them ever knew if somebody Downtown had put them together for a reason or if it were just a coincidence. Since meeting Jacques, Ayo toyed with the idea that the spirits of her ancestors had something to do with it, but she didn't tell anyone, not even Jacques. She and McSorley loved each other in the way mentors and mentees do. McSorley was like a loveable grandfather to Ayo.

McSorley grew up in the Bronx, the perfect Irish-Catholic kid: an altar boy, a star baseball player, a straight-A student in Catholic school. He attended a Jesuit College on a full scholarship. McSorley was tops in golf, philosophy, sociology, and Catholic studies. He could have become a

114

golf pro but instead went into the priesthood. For five years, he took a vow of poverty and devoted himself to serving the less fortunate.

McSorley was an intense and voracious reader of moral philosophy and stumbled upon Catholic liberation theology. He soon grew to believe that God was calling on him to help the "meek inherit the earth." He became convinced that the Gospel was a roadmap for making the "first last and the last first" and that the most important thing he could do is to help "feed the hungry, offer drink to the thirsty, and heal the sick." He volunteered at the Dorothy Day Catholic Worker centers in the Bronx and Brooklyn and wrote for the Catholic Worker. He often got into deep trouble with his abbot and bishop, arguing with them about God's existence and His mercy. Eventually, weary of McSorley's insatiable questioning of their faith, his superiors forced him to choose between the monastic life and newfound beliefs.

Working at the Dorothy Day Center with troubled youth, he met Catholic police officers who suggested he join the police force and put his body where his mouth and pen were, and that's exactly what he did. He became a cop for the same reason Ayo did—he wanted to work with and help protect the poor.

He became a cop's cop. Sometimes pedantic or standoffish, he was beloved by the officers he supervised. He always gave them articles about peace, non-violence, and moral philosophy. His cops put up with him because he offered them respect and encouraged them to explore their intellectual capacities while working with the community. He recognized a kindred spirit in Ayo James.

When he asked her if she would like to work the machete attack at NYU, Ayo lit up. "Is the Pope Catholic?" she asked with a wide smile. "What do we have so far?"

"Nothing. Except the victim is a member of the Belgian royal family going to NYU. And since you went to NYU, you're perfect. Talk to Jason; he's got the files. Get back with me on what you think. But listen, James, the Mayor is on this one! He's watching us. The State Department is on the mayor, and the United Nations is on the State Department. No one wants this to turn into an international incident. Get back to me by the end of the week."

Ayo wondered to herself why the Belgian royals after the second attack didn't all hire security. Perhaps they each thought it'll never happen to me. If the royals did have security, then the maimer was devious enough to evade the security and accomplish the goal.

Ayo knew McSorley didn't pick her just because she had gone to NYU. He picked her because she was his best detective. McSorley knew she knew. That's one of the things he liked about her — she was confident. He also got a kick out of her wiseass mouth. "Is the Pope Catholic?" Indeed, he is!

Chapter 17

Greenwich Village: "Jacayo" Rambling down Bleecker Street

Their friends call Jacques and Ayo "Jacayo" because they fit together perfectly. They're both highly intelligent and witty when they want to be. And they will talk—and talk, and talk—about everything from wines to international politics. They get angry together— really and truly angry—when they see or read about something they consider unjust. They both seem to believe that what they call "the spirits of their ancestors" are somehow helping to guide their lives.

They each consider their work to be their calling, not just a job, and they support each other because they each believe in what the other is doing. Sometimes they give each other ideas and helpful suggestions, but mostly they support each other through reassurance that when work comes first, they understand.

If Ayo doesn't show up for dinner because there's been a murder on Hudson Avenue and forgets to call Jacques, he understands, even though he's spent four hours preparing the most delicious coq au vin ever. When Jacques forgets to show up or even call Ayo because he got immersed in a project to ensure that a village in the Congo gets clean water, Ayo tells him she admires what he's doing; even though she bought two expensive tickets to a Broadway show to share with him, and when he couldn't go, she invites her girlfriend Breyona.

Afterward, Ayo and Breyona go out for drinks and have an opportunity to catch up. Ayo has known Breyona since elementary school, and now that she was in New York, Ayo is delighted to renew their friendship. Breyona asks about Ayo's mother, who she remembered fondly from when Ayo's mom led their Girl Scout troop. "I remember your mom as a strong woman," Breyona says. Ayo agrees.

Most often, Ayo chooses to spend her free time with Jacques—even when he drops out at the last minute. Fortunately, despite both of their difficult schedules, they love each other, and their friends say that's lucky because anybody else would have a hard time putting up with either of them.

Jacques soon receives an assignment to once again go to Brussels and Africa on a project, and once again, he doesn't know when he'll return.

Ayo warns him that she won't be around if he neglects her again.

Jacques believes her and promises to phone, text, or email every day he can. Jacques realizes how important Ayo is to his life. He knows he can do great things abroad, but when Jacques comes home, he wants someone to talk with and with whom to share his thoughts and love. Not just anyone, though. He wants Ayo.

Ayo wants to be stern but tells him she's proud of him, even though she knows she'll be lonely while he's away. She phones Aisha, and they plan an all-woman fun get-together, including Zuri. Ayo prepares herself for another extended period without Jacques but realizes that despite her love for him, she has other outlets in her life, and they are important, too.

Chapter 18

A History of the Congo—Not a Pretty Picture

As part of the fundraising for Jacques' projects, his company books Jacques to lecture about King Leopold at the event venue of 583 Park Avenue. This place, originally the Third Church of Christ Scientist, was restored in 2006. Jacques' company hopes that when the wealthy donors look up at the original 2,500-pound chandelier, they will be enlightened and lighten their wallets — and if the ambiance doesn't inspire them, that the open bar will. The opulence is in keeping with the big donors' expectations, and the free-flowing open bar should ease their restraints.

After his introduction, Jacques looks over the crowd of more than 200 people and strides onto the stage. The screen behind him show scenes from the project.

Pointing to the housing units being constructed, Jacques explains, "The scenes behind me show the reality now. Tonight, I want to tell you why such housing is needed and how the people of the Congo have been raped and cheated, and why you can now do something to remedy this. I want to tell you the story of King Leopold II. Those who have visited Belgium have probably seen his magnificent buildings. Indeed, he is called 'The Builder King.' But what is the true cost of those buildings? How many people were killed in the name of his empire?"

His company knew that Jacques was an expert in the Congo and thought that with his sensitivity and scholarship, the truth about what King Leopold had done would unleash the pocketbooks of many of the lecture's attendees, allowing them to build more infrastructure to improve lives in the Congo.

Jacques, in a cream-colored suit and red tie, looked out at the audience, hoping they will be generous. "In Antwerp today, you see beautiful buildings and magnificent cultivated gardens courtesy of King Leopold II, but there was another part to this man — this king — a shameful part.

"Let me set this in the proper historical context. And it's important to note that the highest levels of the United States government played a role. Let me suggest that our sins, the sins of our government, allowed the shameless events. Each of you can now demonstrate your better angels by helping the Congo rebuild and forge a new identity. Some have called for reparations.

"Your contributions tonight will help go toward the swing toward democracy. As you listen to this story, understand what our ancestors did, and help to repair the harm with a donation to a new Congo."

Jacques looks across at his audience and continues, "In March of 1885, Leopold Louis Philippe Marie Victor — Leopold II, King of the Belgians — was eating lunch in his palace with his wife, Marie Henriette of Austria. He told her he was relieved that representatives of twelve European nations, the Ottoman Empire, and the United States, had concluded their meeting in Berlin after seventy-two days—November 15, 1884, to February 26, 1885—and had agreed to put much of central Africa under the control of his 'philanthropic,' non-competitive International Association for the Exploration and Civilization of the Congo.

"Thanks to the German Chancellor, Otto von Bismarck, the representatives peacefully sat down with a map of Africa and drew lines around areas to be allocated to each country." Jacques glanced out at his audience and exclaimed, "What audacity!"

"Instead of fighting among themselves, European nations could now use their resources to bribe or fight the rulers of the 'savages.' Yes, these leaders referred to the people of Africa as savages. Their goal was to extract the African continent's riches: gold, diamonds, rubber, ivory, oil, copper, cadmium, cobalt, iron, and the labor of Africans themselves. When the conference began in 1884, European countries controlled only 10 percent of Africa, but with the agreements reached, by 1915, they occupied and colonized 90 percent of the continent. What audacity! The only two countries not occupied were Liberia and Ethiopia.

"This period was later called 'the Scramble for Africa,' and Leopold wanted to become part of it. Belgium was a latecomer to the club of colonial empires, but its members were not eager to expand their numbers. For many years, Leopold tried to acquire a colony for Belgium in Africa or Asia. He even tried to buy the Philippines from Spain but to no avail. Getting the agreement out of the Berlin conference took years of lobbying, promising each European nation favored status in the Congo, then assuring them that all countries would be treated equally."

After taking a drink of water, Jacques continued, "Leopold desperately needed to expand Belgium's power. The aristocracy wanted it, and the general public demanded it. The king understood that unless he remained popular, the power of the monarchy, already diminished, would be thoroughly destroyed. And the only way to remain popular was to give the people what they wanted. As things stood, the Labor Party was growing. Labor unions would soon become legal, universal male suffrage was about to become the law of the land, child labor had been outlawed, and a public school system had been established. What's worse, Leopold had lost the right to have a final veto over legislation despite his best efforts.

"But Leopold still presided over the Council of Ministers, and he wanted to hold back the tidal wave of democracy as long as possible. He had to deliver. Now that Belgian workers had won the right to share in the nation's prosperity, the unions demanded that they do more to gain overseas colonies that would bring in more wealth. They were against slavery within the mother country because it created unfair competition with free labor, but that didn't apply to overseas colonies.

"Leopold decided that if he couldn't walk in the front door of the club of empire nations, he'd sneak in through the back. He came up with the supposedly philanthropic International Association for the Exploration and Civilization of the Congo (IAECC) and encouraged other nations to join it.

"Leopold's plenipotentiaries to the Berlin conference, Gabriel van der Straten-Ponthoz and François Auguste, Baron Lambermont, convinced the delegates that the IAECC wouldn't compete with other nations economically. Far from it. IAECC's main goal was to bring Christianity and civilization to the natives. The area under Leopold's control would be a free trade zone, open to exploitation by corporations worldwide. Leopold was going to call it the Congo Free State (CFS). It would be located between land controlled by France and territory controlled by Portugal. Situating the area there would allow these nations to make peace with each other and share the benefits of Leopold's land.

"At the Berlin conference, the diplomats agreed that France would get land bordering the Congo Free State on the northwest, called 'the Republic of the Congo.' Portugal would control the territory on its southern border, to be called 'Angola.'

"Here's where it gets especially interesting," he tells his audience almost conspiratorially. "Sir Henry Morton Stanley, the Englishman who attended the conference as the representative of U.S. President Chester A. Arthur, was

Leopold's most enthusiastic supporter—naturally because Leopold paid him. Stanley had explored the Congo for Leopold a few months before the conference began.

"American President Chester A. Arthur was the first world leader to recognize Leopold's sovereignty over central Africa. He said, 'The Government of the United States announces its sympathy with and approval of the humane and benevolent purposes of the International Association of the Congo.'"

Jacques's tone rose and rouses the audience to acknowledge the deep irony and perversity of the statement because the Association was anything but humane and benevolent.

"The area thus became Leopold's personal property, not a colony of Belgium, but his and his alone.

"Initially, Leopold lived up to his pledge that the area would be a free trade zone. Corporations from everywhere came to the Congo. There were no limits on, for instance, the slaughtering of elephants for ivory or forcing natives to dig mines for cobalt, plant seeds for cocoa, or collect the sap of rubber vines. However, Leopold soon bought out the other nations, which were members of the IAECC, with money borrowed from the Belgian treasury. He set up the Congo Exploration Society, which was free to engage in economic activity.

"King Leopold was, quite frankly, audacious. He wasn't content with simply ruling Belgium. Oh no. He wanted

125

colonies. Colonies could provide him with unlimited access to their wealth. Leopold began to violate the free trade provisions of the Berlin Treaty directly. He created a monopoly in rubber production by imposing sky-high export duties and driving out many non-Belgian companies.

"What's more, Leopold issued three decrees: 1. Henceforth, farmers and small business people were not allowed to sell their goods to any entity except the state, which offered prices so low that the farmers had to let their fields fallow; 2. All land not being used for farming or other production would subsequently be owned by Leopold; 3. The Congolese were required to pay high taxes in the form of their labor in collecting rubber and had to meet quotas set by White people in Belgium and other countries. Leopold, who had earned worldwide praise for freeing the Congolese from Arab slave traders, had reduced the Congolese to slaves of the state. That state, of course, was Leopold himself."

Hitting his stride, Jacques tells the audience, "Leopold was rapacious, first in seeking ivory and then in getting rubber out of the Congo. He wasn't content to hire people to work for him. He enslaved the natives and gave orders for his military composed of other men of the Congo to enforce a quota system for rubber.

"In the final decade of the 19th century, a Scottish veterinarian and inventor, John Boyd Dunlop, invented an inflatable rubber bicycle tube. Others soon saw the need for similar tubes for automobile tires. The growing popularity of bicycles and automobiles caused the global demand for rubber to go through the roof.

"Now, here's a little-known fact for you: rubber comes from a type of sap that flows from rubber trees. The sap, called latex, is a sticky, milky colloid drawn off by making incisions in the bark. Natives lathered themselves with the latex to gather the rubber and then peeled it off their bodies to be transported for refinement into the rubber that was ready for commercial processing."

Jacques dramatically takes out a whip and cracks it against the podium. "The overseers used the chicote—a whip of raw, sun-dried hippopotamus hide cut into long sharp-edged strips, which quickly could remove the skin from a man's back. The overseers employed painful lashes to motivate the men to gather ever-more rubber. You don't have to imagine how much the threat of these painful lashes motivated men to gather ever-more rubber." As he spoke, Jacques clicks through images of his story on a screen behind him, unsettling images of Congolese being brutalized.

"Monetary incentives and greed motivated the chain of command—from the top, good old King Leopold, and down through the company agents who were paid large concessions on top of their salaries based on the profits they generated. This payment system gave them personal incentives to force native people to work harder for little to no pay.

127

"The only way to achieve the almost impossible quotas was using terror. The terror came from the Free State's army, the Force Publique. This army, composed of White officers, came mostly from Belgium but also from other European nations. Black African soldiers were forced into the King's army, though some of these soldiers were recruits. At no time were there more than about 900 officers. Under them were some 19,000 soldiers recruited or conscripted native Africans. At first, they came from colonies owned by other European nations, but they were almost all Congolese as time went on. Others were slaves or orphans brought up to serve the colonial army. The army cultivated its brutal game plan of destroying villages, taking hostages, raping, torturing, and extorting the people.

"Men who didn't fulfill their quota of gathering enough rubber were killed or mutilated. Women and children were often taken hostage until men fulfilled a quota, during which time the women were raped repeatedly. The Force Publique sometimes eradicated entire villages that failed to meet the quotas as a warning to others." Jacques paused before adding, "Some of the soldiers were cannibals and ate some of their victims." A ripple of collective horror circled the room. The Force Publique took graphic pictures.

Based on what the screen displayed, the audience's eyes dropped at the sights, and they slowly shook heads side to side, sadly.

"Leopold never sent more than 3,000 White people to administer the Congo Free State, an impossible job for such a small number, but why spend money on administration when the whole purpose of colonization is to reap huge profits?" Jacques rhetorically asks the audience.

"Leopold became the richest king in Europe, and an enormous amount of money flowed through him into Belgium. He used much of his wealth to build public works such as schools, libraries, parks, theaters, and museums benefiting Belgians. He also built a second palace in Brussels, where monarchs and their staff would work. The king would no longer have to run the government from Laeken, the site of his residential palace. While he was at it, Leopold also built himself a grand palace in the south of France, in Evian.

"Leopold's Congo Free State lasted from 1885 to 1908. After years of reports that Leopold and his Force Publique committed atrocities against the Congolese people and that half the population of the Congo, about ten million people—though some say the figure is higher - had died, the Belgian government paid off the steep debts created by Leopold, gave him a fortune for the area, and re-named the country 'the Belgian Congo.'

Hearing a gasp of recognition from the audience, Jacques continued. "Joseph Conrad, in his 1899 novel, Heart of Darkness, popularized the artfully suppressed reports of the horrors. The book's cover is now portrayed on the screen. Over the years, Leopold used his many contacts at the highest levels of power in Europe to discredit or repress any reports about atrocities in the Congo. He denied ordering his troops to cut a hand off natives who did not meet their rubber collection quotas. 'Cut off hands — that's idiotic,' he told the press. Today, some people would undoubtedly call it 'fake news.' Leopold said, 'I'd cut off all the rest of them, but not hands. That's the one thing I need in the Congo.'

"Finally, Leopold was forced to appoint a Commission of Inquiry with hand-picked members (excuse the pun) ready to conduct a sham investigation. However, the commission came back detailing the same atrocities observed by all the other investigators.

"Leopold died in 1909, less than a year after he ceded his lands to his nation. Although some of the crowd lining the streets during his funeral booed, Leopold was loved and admired by the Belgian people by and large.

"The shame, the shame," Jacques concluded. "This is the stuff they don't teach you about in school."

His audience fully embraced his talk. The donations flowed like the fine wines. Ayo was in the crowd listening. She was moved by his presentation and came to appreciate his work even more. That night was a special night to them both.

Chapter 19

Brussels, Belgium—Gateway to the Congo

Jacques's speech was a major success and earned enough money to support the next step in developing the Congo project. UNESCO matched the funds Jacques raised. Jacques flew from New York to Belgium and met with European Union officials about healthcare clinics in the Congo. They discussed the construction of at least sixteen clinics about 100 miles apart along the 1,865 miles from Boma at the Congo River's mouth to Kisangani at its midpoint.

Over the next two months, Jacques was to meet with local officials at each potential clinic site. He called Ayo and discussed the timeline and the finances of the project but reminded her that she had his heart, no matter what. He explained that the project would be completed in about three years and cost about 50 million euros, but he would be coming home periodically because he needed to be with her. The United Nations, the World Bank, UNESCO, the United States, France, and Germany would fund the work. Belgium's contribution was the smallest, a mere 2.5 million euros.

With Ayo's blessing, he promised to communicate with her weekly, albeit with a warning that the Congo's isolated and thick jungles may not cooperate with his technology. After this agreement, he felt relieved that his love would be waiting for him upon his return.

This agreement would allow him to devote his attention and energy to his life's mission—honoring his ancestors, conjuring their spirits, and giving them his thanks. He would do this not in the safe, elite Congo Square of Tremé but the very heart of darkness, the jungles of the Congo. In the Congo River basin, he imagined that he would not only be home, but he would also be free from the ravages of American racism and White supremacy and re-united with his ancestral soul. And who better to re-unite with than the mother of resistance and the warrior of freedom, Mame.

After that, he called his mother again and updated her about his plans. She was not happy with his being gone for so long, but he mollified her by promising to return periodically. He promised his mother that he would be in touch with her more often than on his prior trip. He knew conversations with Ayo and his mother fortified him, and their forthright, loving spirits inspired him.

Chapter 20

The Democratic Republic of the Congo, So Rich Yet So Poor

Jacques took his old and tattered copy of *King Leopold's Ghost: A Story of Greed, Terror, and Heroism in Colonial Africa* (1998) by Adam Hochschild with him to refresh his memory of the grisly history of the Congo. He wanted to be fluent in its history while meeting with local Congolese officials. Jacques hoped to visit villages and sites mentioned in the book and imagine the terrors that his people had faced due to King Leopold II's reign. He wanted to pay his respects to his ancestors and re-dedicate himself to bringing economic development to the French-speaking African countries that the colonists had robbed.

Sometimes Jacques had nightmares about the Congo as he slept in his five-star hotel bed. He dreamed he was a Congolese villager a hundred years ago. He woke up in a panic, sweating, and tossing his body across the bed, trying to avoid the slash of a machete wielded by Force Publique soldiers directed at his wrist and even at his penis.

In his dreams, he saw handless children and women spread across the ground naked and face down, their hands and feet tied by ropes to stakes as they were quartered. The slave enforcers whipped other women for not gathering their quota of rubber. Jacques could not control his nightmares. He woke up almost every night to escape from them.

But despite this, every day, Jacques pushed on into the Congo River Basin, starting in Boma and working his way north and east. For the next two months, he visited more than twenty potential sites to develop health clinics. After eight weeks of grueling travel up the Congo River, Jacques needed some R&R before returning to New York, some quiet time alone to shake the depression and anxiety caused by his work and to revel in the exhilaration of accomplishment.

Chapter 21

Antwerp, Belgium — It's Official, a Statue to Cut off Hands

Jacques went to Antwerp for a holiday before flying back to New York. He spent five days eating some of the best food in Europe, visiting museums, reading the New York Times and the International Herald Tribune every morning, finishing some novels and history books he had been trying to get through, and walking the city's perfect gardens and parks. And calling Ayo and mom.

He avoided all chocolate shops.

One Sunday morning, Jacques was jogging along the Scheldt River near his hotel and saw the twenty-foot-tall statue of Silvius Brabo in front of Antwerp's City Hall. He stopped abruptly and stared. Brabo held the severed hand of the monster Antigoon, which spewed water, symbolizing arterial blood spurts. Brabo looked like he was about to hurl the hand into the river.

The legend is that a thousand years ago, Antigoon, a very large, monster-like figure, blocked the bridge over the river. He would not let anyone cross unless they paid him a toll. If they did not, Antigoon cut off one of their hands and threw it into the river as a lesson to all those who might try to use the bridge for free.

One day a young man, Silvius Brabo, tried to cross the river, and Antigoon confronted him. Brabo, being strong and right-minded, wrested Antigoon's machete away from him and cut off Antigoon's hand instead of having his own hand severed. Brabo then tossed the hand into the river. Antigoon lumbered off, holding his handless arm dripping blood along the road. No one ever had to pay another toll. People across Europe have interpreted the story as a call to action opposing unjust laws and oppressive rulers.

Despite the late hour, the restaurant in Jacques' hotel was crowded, and he had to share a table with a local young woman. They talked about the Brabo statute and the legend behind it. She said, "the myth had such strong appeal that the city's name, 'Antwerp,' is actually a Dutch word that means 'to throw a hand.'" Jacques nearly spilled his drink. He thanked the woman for the cultural history lesson and excused himself, heading upstairs to his room.

He sat on his bed and thought about whether King Leopold got the idea of punishing people by chopping off a hand from the Antigoon-Brabo story. He suddenly realized that the severed hand symbolized Antwerp and realized that the severed chocolate hands could symbolize freedom. However, Jacques still shuddered at the memory of seeing them and realized that they, too, could easily be the hands of his ancestors. Now he understood the courageous story of Brabo that King Leopold expropriated for his own sinister and wicked purposes.

The next morning, Jacques jogged for a long time to bring himself back from being lost in the past. Afterward, he went to a café to meet Stefan, a student from a wealthy Belgian family who Jacques had tutored in the past. Jacques brought him Things Fall Apart, a book by Chinua Achebe, describing how European colonization had destroyed the indigenous societies of West Africa and created a situation in which otherwise stable nations disintegrated into chaotic tribalism and violence.

"In fact," Jacques told Stefan, "After King Leopold II's rule ended, Belgium occupied the Congo for fifty more years, exploiting its people and natural resources until 1960 when the movement led by Patrice Lumumba won Congolese independence," Stefan said he had learned some of this history, but not much, which surprised Jacques.

Jacques continued, "Lumumba's election didn't curb corporate greed. Foreign corporations continued to exploit the Congo's labor and gobble up its natural resources. Lumumba demanded the corporations invest in the social and economic improvement of the Congo and pay their workers fair wages. They refused. The American CIA engineered a coup d'état led by Mobutu Sese Seko, a general in the Congolese Army, with the support of corporate Belgium. In September of 1960, Mobutu's thugs dragged Lumumba out of the Presidential Palace, beat and shackled him. They threw him naked in the back of a stifling hot, filthy army truck swarming with insects, drove him miles outside of Lubumbashi, the capital of Katanga, and shot him dead.

"Using Mobutu as their puppet, the Belgian government took back control of the country and its rubber, ivory, and diamonds."

Stefan interrupted, "I didn't know anything about this. I went to the best schools in Belgium, but they taught us very little about our history. All I ever learned is that we sent hundreds of Catholic nuns and priests into the Congo to bring healthcare and education to the Africans." His face showed he felt ashamed. He did not know his history.

Jacques said, "Read Things Fall Apart. Then, read King Leopold's Ghost by Adam Hochschild. They both provide a detailed, historically accurate account of Belgium's role in the murder of at least ten million Congolese. But watch out, if you read these books, if you learn the truth about your country's history, you may ask yourself, 'what will I do about it?'"

Stefan said, "Black Belgian students and Congolese kids recently demonstrated on campus for Belgium to pay reparations to the Congo. I didn't pay much attention to them at the time. Is this what you're talking about?"

"Exactly," said Jacques. "Those students were demanding

138

fairness from Belgium toward the Congo. They knew their history. The people of Belgium don't know the history of what their country did in the Congo. Do you think that's an oversight or a deliberate omission?"

"I guess you could argue that it's a deliberate omission!"

"Yes," said Jacques, "Deliberate. Trust me, and we get too much of that in the U.S."

Despite Jacques's lecture, he and Stefan enjoy a pleasant meal. They drink a few cold, sweet mimosas and splurge on a typically robust Belgian brunch, including mussels el frites marinated in a white wine sauce with clams and shrimp; gray shrimp croquettes; rabbit and prunes, and waffles with fresh cream and strawberries.

Stefan and Jacques talk for two hours and drink too many mimosas. They laugh loudly, but so do the other patrons in the cafe.

After his brunch with Stefan, it is early afternoon. Jacques walks alone along the river toward his hotel. Although somewhat fatigued from too much food and too many mimosas, Jacques feels awake enough to do more jogging and walking into the night.

Later that evening, near midnight, Jacques sits in his hotel room, reading and enjoying a lovely view of the city having just come in from a jog. He hears sirens scream through the streets of Antwerp below him. Antwerp is normally a calm city with virtually no crime. It's rare to see police cars and police officers in the city, let alone hear sirens. Jacques walks to the window and looks out into the night. More sirens and more police cars rush by. Red and blue lights interrupt the serene dark of a peaceful Antwerp evening.

As the red and blue lights faded out of sight, Jacques returned to reading and dozed off with his novel lying across his chest and his feet propped up on the end of his couch.

The next day Jacques reads the French-language paper, Le Soir, in his hotel café. The headline, "Another Royal Maimed."

Jacques read the article.

ANTWERP—An assailant maimed a seventeen-year-old member of the Royal family by a machete attack last night in a sporting park in the city center. The victim, Henrietta Josephine Van Housen, is the first cousin to the prince of Düsseldorf, Germany, and is a member of the Belgian royal family. She is the third member of the Belgian royal family, attacked by a person wielding a machete. The victim's left hand was cut off her arm.

Police found the bloody machete at the scene. They did not find the hand. European officials, police say, are investigating these attacks.

Jacques reads several different news accounts. He asks himself, who would maim Belgian royalty? In the next nano-second, he thinks, "They deserve it." At the same time, he realizes that this thought was not at all appropriate.

Or is it? He feels conflicted.

He calls his mother, and they talk until he feels somewhat comforted. He rehashes the maiming in his mind. No innocent persons deserve to have their hand severed, but he thinks to himself, are members of the Belgian royal family innocent? How innocent is Princess Henrietta? What did she do to deserve to live a life of luxury simply for being born into a royal family in the twentieth century? But then again, why does a teenage girl have her hand severed from her arm simply for being born in the Congo in the nineteenth century?

Jacques continues to ruminate. What is history, and who controls the knowledge of history? Then he thinks, who interprets history? Who has the power to withhold this history from the Belgian people? Why is the history of the Congo and King Leopold II's reign of terror not taught to Belgian youth? Why do Americans know little about their own history of violence against Black people, Native Americans, Mexican and Chinese people? Does keeping people ignorant of their history benefit them or those who want to keep them unaware? Why were enslaved Black people not permitted to learn how to read and write? Is there a pattern here, muses Jacques?

Is history about past events? Or is it the present informing us of the future. Could history really be the future - the future of reparations? Or as Brenda Jones, author of Queens of Resistance said, history is the future "that all of us will one day have to confront if we ever want to heal and transform the legacy of hate, human bondage and their pivotal role in the wealth-building of the Western world."

How do we alert everyday people and political leaders to the future if they refuse to know who they are in the past?

These maiming of royalty are shaking Jacques to his core. They conjure his ancestry. He's getting depressed reading about them.

Chapter 22

Greenwich Village: Hand Goes Missing on Upper East Side

Jacques calls Ayo as soon as he arrives back in New York. They enjoy a very satisfying reunion in her apartment and pick up right where they left off. Over the next week, they go to a Broadway show, intake jazz at the Village Vanguard, and art-house movies at the IFC Theater on 6th Avenue just around the corner from Ayo's apartment, and, of course, they take walks in Washington Square Park. Jacques plays in a couple of chess matches, but Jacques, as good as he is, gets crushed by the homeless dudes in the park. Jacques tries to show off his basketball skills to Ayo by playing pick-up in the West 4th Street courts, but the local dudes crush him in hoops, too.

He tries telling Ayo, "Listen, I'm much better than what you saw. These cats play street ball, and I play real basketball."

Ayo rolls her eyes at his excuses saying, "Sorry, dude, those guys are just better, admit it. Street ball is practice for the NBA. Maybe you need to spend more time in the gym."

Jacques grimaces then shrugs his shoulders and says, "Thanks for the vote of confidence. Just don't tell our friends." They kiss. They smile. They love the Village and each other and keep walking.

After being home for three weeks, Jacques is alone in his apartment, reading a novel and half-watching CNN. He isn't paying much attention until a talking head interrupts her commentary, saying, "Breaking News: This just in. There's been another attack on a member of the Belgian royal family." She continues.

"The Duchess of Wingate, England, Lady Elizabeth Riley Alistaire Cornwallis, sixty-one years old, an English royal who married into the Belgian royal family, was attacked just hours ago on the Upper East Side of Manhattan on East 82nd Street between Park and Lexington Avenues. She was walking her poodle when an assailant grabbed her, knocked her to the ground, and cut off her right hand with a large machete-like knife. The attacker tightly wrapped Lady Elizabeth's arm in a black towel to stem the bleeding and walked calmly away with her dripping hand. The blood-streaked machete was left behind.

The attacker called 911 with the Duchess' cell phone and reported her exact location; a police dispatcher told investigators.

The attacker spoke in a slow, deep, and muffled voice, saying, 'I have severed the hand of a Duchess. She needs immediate help at 112 East 82nd Street. Send help now. She is bleeding profusely.'"

Chapter 23

NYPD Sixth Precinct—Her War Room, Her Questions, Her Answers

Ayo sat in her precinct office, her desk covered in files, photos, stats, and news clippings about the attacks on the Belgian royal family. While absorbed in thought, she gets up and paces around her small but comfortable office. Her office is adorned with family photos, green plants, and colorful Kente fabrics hang on her wall.   A NYU pennant tacked to her ceiling dangling down.

Ayo turned to arrange more crime scene photos, newspaper headlines, and photos of the royal family going back to the 1860s on her walls and bulletin board, creating a war room to help her find the perpetrator of these dastardly crimes.

She re-reads for the third time reports from police officers in Belgium and New York. She reads first-hand reports in French about the attacks. The only thing the attacks had in common was that whoever used the machetes wore gloves, leaving no fingerprints. The forensics experts found rubber resin on the handle of each retrieved machete. One of the experts speculated that the rubber was from the Congo. They were attempting to trace the rubber resin to its origins. The irony, she thought bitterly.

Captain McSorley knocks on her door. "Come in."

"Whattaya got, James?"

"It's strange, Captain. It's just…weird. This guy's a nut. A smart nut. And he doesn't want to get caught. At least, the person who called the police dispatcher sounded like a 'he,' but it could be a woman. In any case, the voice was filled with compassion. It was soft and even kind. Educated. Sophisticated. Confident. And there's a trace of an accent. Want to hear it?"

Ayo plays the 911 call the attacker made after the Upper East Side maiming. McSorley listens carefully. "Sounds like a man, but not an American man."

Ayo says, "I'm running the call through the Voice Data Tracking System. I'll get the results tomorrow. I'm really not sure that it's a man's voice."

"Keep me informed, James. Do you need any help?"

"No, Jason is doing a great job. He's giving me every scrap of a lead I can ask for. Thanks." By this time, Ayo was not even looking at McSorley. She was staring at the photos of the royal family. When McSorley leaves her office, Ayo is standing and staring at the photos she just tacked up.

Ayo goes over to her computer and once again looks for everything she could find about King Leopold II and his royal family. There were hundreds of data points, articles, and books about the family. She sees accounts of King

Leopold II's violence against the Congolese people and the Force Publique chopping off hands. Her face contorts when she looks over photos of children with severed hands. She feels convinced the person or persons maiming the Belgian royal family is taking revenge through these horrendous crimes.

Ayo types in many words and phrases that she hopes could offer her clues:

- *King Leopold's detractors in the twenty-first century*
- *Who hates King Leopold II?*
- *Today's Congolese enemies of Belgium*
- *Congolese enemies of Belgium's royal family*
- *The Congo today and the Belgian royal family*
- *The Congo, Belgium, and twenty-first-century relations*
- *Repairing Belgian and Congo relations today*

With this last entry, an article details the construction of new health care clinics along the Congo River. It mentions that the project's manager considered it to be a type of reparation due to Congolese people for the atrocities committed by King Leopold II in the nineteenth century. The article stated:

Jacques Joseph Henri, the project manager, said, "These clinics cannot repay all the harm done by the early colonialists in the Congo, but they are a start. We are pleased that the United Nations, UNESCO, the World Bank, France, and the U.S. government have committed significant resources for health care along the Congo River,

148

the infamous river of the oppressive rubber and ivory trade in the nineteenth century."

Ayo has not discussed the maiming's with Jacques at any length. The subject seemed to upset him too much and drive him either far into his shell or on a tirade of a lecture. Anyway, she always practiced separating her personal life from her job. But the story jars her into wondering whether Jacques' insights might help catch the culprit (or culprits) responsible for the mutilations and put a stop to them. Solving crimes and protecting people were the top priorities of her life, so over dinner in an East Village café, she asked Jacques for his help.

One sentence in the news article attributed to Jacques piqued her curiosity, "These clinics can't repay all the harm that's been done...." What or how could one repay the Congolese people for the horrific terror, she wonders? How would Jacques answer that question?

Chapter 24

Greenwich Village: Awa-Ava Painting in the Park for Africa

Ayo and Jacques meet at the North Square Restaurant in Washington Square Park on McDougal Street and Waverly Place. They are the only people there at 4 PM on that warm and breezy Friday. For a while, they gaze out the window at the people who flock to Washington Square every Friday afternoon: NYU students, innovative street performers, cutting-edge musicians, rising comedians who try out new material, sidewalk chalk artists, world chess champions, all breeds of weirdos, weed sellers, scam artists, acrobats, filmmakers, and bocce ballplayers.

For the next hour, Ayo and Jacques speak in French about the violent attacks on the royal family and discuss the history of the Congo and African colonialism. Jacques answers all of Ayo's questions thoroughly and thoughtfully. In the process, he gives her detailed descriptions of his work.

Ayo, the professional NYPD detective that she is, probes Jacques' mind for his ideas on what type of person would want to maim royal family members and asks for advice on the next steps of her investigation. Jacques says he understands the revenge motive of the perpetrator. "After all, I can trace my lineage to the Congo. I closely identify with my ancestral roots."

Jacques describes, once again, his family's pride in their African heritage and his feelings about the horror inflicted on the Congolese people. He speaks with an encyclopedic knowledge about how the European nations divided up the continent at the Scramble for Africa conference and the crimes against humanity committed by King Leopold II and all the European powers that colonized Africa for over a century. He gives Ayo citations to reference books detailing the atrocities.

Ayo tries to absorb the voluminous information Jacques offers, taking thorough notes in her investigation journal. After an hour or so, she looks outside and suggests that because it's such a beautiful day, she and Jacques should walk through the park. They leave the café for the park. They stop for a while to watch men playing chess, and because he was defeated so soundly the last time he played, Jacques declines to play them again.

Walking along, they listen to a jazz combo and applaud an acrobatic team of very athletic Black youth who leap over themselves while cracking jokes. Jacques and Ayo throw a few dollars into the bucket that the acrobats pass around after the performance. They laugh when members of the troupe explain, "You can give now, or you can give more later tonight—if we have to rob you." Everyone assembled around them laughs uneasily.

They saunter toward the grand circular water fountain in the center of the park, with its spray sprouting thirty feet in the air. They stop in front of a young Black girl painting a picture of the fountain on a canvas. Ayo asks her name and how old she is.

"My name is Awa-Ava. I'm thirteen."

"Why are you painting the fountain?" Ayo asks.

"I like the fountain, it's pretty. The silver water sparkles up through the air, and it reminds me of Paris. It's hard to paint sparkling silver water."

"I sure couldn't do it," Ayo says. "Are you from France?"

"My family lives in Paris, but we're from Senegal," Awa-Ava answers as she turns back to her canvas.

"Senegal!" exclaims Ayo in French. "OMG, I studied in Dakar, Senegal." She exchanges pleasantries with Awa-Ava in French. Next to the young artist is her mum. Awa-Ava says, smiling brightly with very white teeth, "This is my mum." Her mum, reaches out her hand and says, Bonjour, je m'appelle Oumou-Mariama." They exchange pleasant words in French, and then Ayo gets back to her painting.

While walking away, Ayo looks back and says to Jacques, "Imagine those handless children in the Congo speaking French at the height of French Impressionism! How many of those children could've become painters if they'd a chance to study in France? Someone needs to pay for what happened to handless children who look just like Awa-Ava!"

Jacques nods and listens but says nothing.

They walk further, pointing out places that meant a lot to each of them when they were students at NYU. They continue, heading up 5th Avenue. After walking slowly for more than forty blocks, they arrive at Rockefeller Center and enjoy the frenetic scene of tourists gawking at the NBC Tower at 30 Rock, flocking into St. Patrick's Cathedral, and buying authentic New York City hot dogs from vendors. They buy a couple of hot dogs and slather them with spicy brown mustard, crunching down and squirting out juicy fat.

Ayo and Jacques devour the city, enjoying each other, sharing stories, laughing, and talking in French. They taxi back down to the Village and have dinner at a Thai restaurant on West 3rd. They walk along McDougal Street, where the lines at Mamoun's Shawarma Sandwich Shop, the Comedy Cellar, and Cafe Wha!, wrap around the block. They turn on Bleecker Street, heading into the West Village, teeming with thousands of people walking, lounging, laughing, and dipping in and out of cafés and boutiques. The night is magical. They love the city, and the city loves them back. And they love each other.

Then, once again, on the next day, Jacques's work pulls him away from Ayo, but this time for only one week, to attend several UNESCO meetings in Europe.

Chapter 25

Paris, France, Monet Paints with One Hand

Jacques' first meeting was in Paris, a two-day gathering of policy analysts regarding development projects in French-speaking Africa. He attends as the representative of the Africa-Europe Parity Group (AEPG).

He enjoys Paris and loves everything to do with French Impressionism, especially Monet, so after the meeting, he spends two more days visiting Musée D'Orsay, Musée Marmottan Monet, and Monet's house and gardens in Giverny. He also wanders through the 6th arrondissement, the Jardin du Luxembourg, and the Latin Quarter, which remind him of the French Quarter, Tremé, and Greenwich Village. These three American communities have the same verve, panache, and creative energy as Paris—which is why he stays comfortable and alive in them.

That evening he calls both his mother and Ayo, and his mood is buoyant and vibrant, filled with the beauty of Monet. Ayo tells him that she misses him but is crazy busy at work and has kept much of her tension at bay by going to the gym at least five times that week.

On his last night in Paris, French newspapers report an attack on Princess Louisa Maria Elizabeth Leopold, Archduchess of Austria-Este, twenty-two years old. The maiming occurs in the fashionable 16th arrondissement near the Musée Marmottan Monet, where Jacques had been the day before.

Every television station in France interrupts its programs with the news. On one station, the newsreader said: "This just in from Paris: A fifth Belgian royal was attacked.

Someone attacked the twenty-two-year-old Royal Princess of Belgium, Louisa Leopold, as she entered her apartment on Avenue du Marechal Maunoury tonight after she attended a friend's birthday dinner.

The princess told investigators that she was putting her key in her front door lock when an assailant jumped, seemingly out of nowhere, and cut off her hand holding the key. She could not see who it was and did not even realize her hand was severed until she saw her arm spurting blood. She screamed for help. The princess just graduated from the Sorbonne and had started a job as a fashion consultant with François-Henri Pinault of the Kering Group on the Avenue des Champs-Élysées.

The shiny silver steel machete streaked in red used to maim the princess lay on the steps leading into the apartment glistening in soft, peaceful yellow light. Police did not find her hand. This attack is the fifth such attack on a member of the Belgian royal family over the past year."

A newspaper report said that the princess was resting in the Clinique de la Main in Paris and that the Mayor of Paris, Anne Hildago, had already visited her.

Paris was on high alert, but the police, yet, had no information about the perpetrator or the motive. As with the first four attacks, no one claims responsibility. The police uncover no clues except for the bloody machete without fingerprints but with a slight bit of rubber resin on the handle. The police forensics confirm that it was rubber from the Congo.

Jacques is once again shaken to his core. He can hardly think. Congo rubber...severed hands...machetes. Going through his mind over and over was something Malcolm X said when President Kennedy was killed: "The chickens have come home to roost."

Then, he thinks about the pattern at each crime scene— each hand is missing, but a machete is at the scene. Being the movie buff he is, he thinks of the classic line from the scene in The Godfather when the Corleone family murdered a snitch in a car out in the middle of nowhere: "Leave the gun, take the cannoli."

Leave the machete, take the hand.

The next day, Jacques rents a car and drives through the Chunnel to his second meeting in London.

Chapter 26

London, England, "Ironic Justice"

T he multi-national meeting lasts only four hours but seems to take forever. Jacques wants to talk about the solid work his organization is doing and detail the work that isn't being done but should be. He does not get a chance. He is forced to spend all afternoon listening to representatives of European countries bloviate about how much their governments are doing to help the poor, benighted people of Africa. Jacques knew firsthand that most of what they said was BS.

He has no desire to stay in London any longer than necessary and books a flight back to New York for the morning after the meeting. That night he stays at the Best Western Hotel on Shaftesbury Avenue and gets a ticket to the musical Jersey Boys in the West End. On the way back to his hotel, he stops for a few beers in a local pub and then goes to his room for a good sleep.

The next day, while waiting for his plane at Heathrow, Jacques picks up a copy of the London Times. The subject of its front-page story was simultaneously broadcast over the television monitors dotting the airport: "Belgian Royals attacked for the sixth time, the latest attack in London:

In a shocking attack, someone hacked the hand off a sixth member of the Belgian royal family, Prince Joachim Stuart Leopold, with a short, razor-sharp machete blade last night in West London.

The prince, twenty-five years old, is now being treated at the Chelsea and Westminster Hospital, West London. The prince was outside his home in Knightsbridge, near the Underground Station at Hyde Park. The prince was returning home after attending a show on Shaftesbury Avenue.

The attacker walked toward the prince, grabbed his right hand, pulled it forward, and sliced it off at the wrist. He then dropped the blade and ran away with the hand. The prince told police it all happened so fast; he did not get a look at the attacker but saw that the attacker was dressed in black and wore a hat. Police are reviewing CCTV footage of the area."

Newspapers and media reports throughout Europe condemn these attacks as a concerted terrorist plot, possibly seeking revenge on the Belgian royal family for King Leopold II's crimes committed against the Congolese people over a hundred years ago.

The Anti-Balaka, a terrorist group in the Central African Republic (CAR), has issued a statement stating, "We may or may not have carried out the attacks, but we believe the attacks are just punishment for the terror inflicted on the Congolese people for centuries. No Belgium or French official was ever brought before the bar of justice. Terrorism? No. Justice? Yes."

"These attacks," according to the Anti-Balaka, "are justice rendered." The CAR, which borders the Democratic Republic of Congo to the north, was a colony of France until it won independence in 1960. The Anti-Balaka is not an Islamist group. They are militant Christians fighting Muslims in central Africa.

'Anti-balaka' means 'anti-machete.' The group uses automatic weapons to fight whoever they consider anti-Christian in Africa, and the group considers all Muslims to be anti-Christian. The Anti-Balaka fighters carry gris-gris, spiritual charms around their necks to ward off harm.

Police are investigating leads to the Anti-Balaka to determine if they are the group targeting the royal family. Since 2013, the Anti-Balaka had beheaded on videotape numerous Muslim men in the CAR. Analysts believe the 'anti-machete' terrorists used machetes to attack the royal family as a show of 'ironic justice.'"

Chapter 27

Greenwich Village Invoking Franz Fanon and Cafe Bombings

Ayo picks Jacques up at JFK when he lands. They hug and kiss. After travel pleasantries and work updates, she dives right into a discussion of the progress she's making on the maiming cases. She explains that she is working with forensic investigator Jason, who just completed a computer search of all CAR immigrants living in and around New York City. Ayo wants to pick Jacques's brain for insights and knowledge about the Anti-Balaka group.

Jacques is eager to help. They forgo reunion sex and go straight to a restaurant in the Village. Jacques turns on his professorial persona and tells Ayo about his research on the Anti-Balaka. "European authorities have tracked this terrorist group since 2013. They're much like extremist militia groups in the United States who believe they're above the law and are protected by God. The Anti-Balaka formed after the Islamic coup d'état in the CAR led by Michel Djotodia. The coup overthrew Christian Prime Minister François Bozizé."

"So, you're saying they're Africa's version of right-wing, Bible-beating nuts?" Ayo asks.

160

Jacques sidesteps Ayo's questions, sips some wine, nods affirmatively and continues, "Djotodia expelled all the Christian soldiers from the CAR army and replaced them with Muslims. The Christian soldiers took their weapons and fled to the bush and the hills establishing Christian communities and forming Anti-Balaka maroon cells. Since 2013 they've engaged in guerrilla warfare against the Muslim-controlled government. They hide in the jungle along river swamps and sweep into cities, murdering Muslim militia. Because the Anti-Balaka wear dark green, they're virtually impossible to find in the thick jungles. Many villagers harvesting rubber for American rubber corporations feed and protect them."

Ayo interrupts. "I've read that some of the guerrilla cells take the names of African women warriors who fought the colonists."

"Yes. Warrior cell names include Mame, as well as Nzinga, Amazonia, Yaa, and Queen Nanny. Queen Nanny was a runaway slave in British Jamaica who established a successful maroon compound and independent state high in its Blue Mountains. The British never apprehended Queen Nanny. Today, she's one of the national heroes of Jamaica and Haiti. Leaders of the Haitian revolution against the French in the eighteenth century often invoked Nanny's name. In Jamaica, she's known as "Queen Nanny of the Maroons.""

Jacques runs out of answers. "I really don't know much about modern terrorism, but I understand why anti-

161

imperialist fighters do what they do. Remember the movie The Battle of Algiers?" Ayo admits she hasn't seen it. Jacques continues, "We'll have to rent it sometime. It's about the 1962 Algerian struggle for independence from France. In one scene, French police interrogate a revolutionary and ask, 'Why do you people bomb our cafés and kill innocent people? Your actions are acts of cowardice.'

"The revolutionary responded coolly, 'Okay, I tell you what. Give us your guns, your communications equipment, your tanks, your massive arsenal, your helicopters, and your jet fighters, and we'll stop bombing your cafés. We fight with what we have. You have the firepower. We have our will to win.'"

"Like the Vietnamese," says Ayo. Jacques nods yes.

As Jacques speaks, his eyes burn into Ayo's heart. His sincerity is scarily on target. As a Black woman, she understands — you do what you can with what you must to survive.

Jacques conjures up Frantz Fanon: "the poor must use every resource to topple the oppressor even if it means that innocents will die. No one wants to see civilians die in a civil war, but it's unavoidable. Their death is not the fault of the oppressed.'"

Ayo nods in agreement and adds, "Fanon was brilliant. Died so young, at thirty-six, just like Martin, Malcolm, Bobby, and John. I loved reading him in French. So much intellectual passion. The wretched of the earth will rise, eventually. They always do.

Chapter 28

Jacques's Apartment—Again and Again, Even More Surprises

Ayo and Jacques usually stay at Ayo's. Her apartment is close to her work, and she doesn't know from day to day what her hours will be. For the first night of their week-long Christmas break, Jacques cooks Ayo a sumptuous pre-Christmas dinner of rosemary roasted chicken with lots of butter. They talk about how Julia Child said that to be a good chef, one needs to know how to make a roasted chicken at night and an omelet in the morning—both with lots of butter. Both with lovemaking. Child was so right-on!

Ayo listens as Jacques tells tales about Africa. When he's not a professor, barraging her with details, he can be a griot, a storyteller. Jacques weaves African myths into his stories. She listens, enraptured, and almost feels as if Mame has captured his soul as he speaks. His sensual storytelling is improved by great wine and sultry jazz—the power of taste, sex, and spirituality. They make love in the kitchen while the chicken is roasting and sip pinot, then make love after their meal, sipping French cognac by candlelight that accentuates their colors and curves. They make love the next morning making omelets together.

164

The next day, they meander for hours down Bleecker Street, shopping for the holidays. They see the big Christmas tree with its thousands of lights at Rockefeller Center and go ice skating in Bryant Park. Both are superb skaters, no mystery there.

When they return to Jacques's for the first time in weeks, Ayo notices he added a photo to the altar honoring Congolese culture. The photo sits on a bookcase shelf in his study. The gruesome photo shows a Congolese father squatting on the ground, looking dejected and horrified at a hand and a foot of his children lying on a wooden porch. The Force Publique had maimed his kids to punish him for not collecting enough rubber. Leaning against the bookshelf, with the tip of its handle in front of the photo, is an old machete. Ayo feels an icy shiver run up and down her spine. Her mind spinning out of control.

Next to the machete is a small, cobalt blue bottle with a cork top. Ayo dares not open it, fearful of what was inside. Behind the blue bottle, a new item is on the altar — an African mask. Ayo becomes more curious yet worried that more and more African artifacts — especially machetes — are on Jacques's bookshelves. So as not to alert Jacques to her worry, she innocently asks about the mask, "I love African masks. What's the story behind this one?" she asks, pointing at the new addition.

"That's called a Mbuya mask. It represents a woman in sickness. See how her face is contorted in pain? Congolese African masks inspired Picasso. You can see these images in his painting Les Demoiselles d'Avignon. Here, I'll show you." Jacques pulls a book on Picasso from his shelf, showing Ayo the painting.

"That's fascinating! I've always wondered about some of the faces that Picasso created. Looks like he also stole from Africa. Did he ever acknowledge his inspiration was African?"

"Of course not!" Jacques blurts out.

"But why do you keep these horrid things on your mantle, like this photo of cut-off hands and machetes?" she asks in frustration.

Jacques responds in a solemn voice, "I never want to forget. I never want to forgive, either. I'll only forgive when justice is rendered. The photo inspires me to do more for my ancestors. Mame's spirit pushes me to continue my work."

Ayo puts down her water and stares at Jacques. His words confuse her. She was raised in the Christian church of forgiveness and redemption, and her faith encourages her to move beyond the pain and suffering and forgive those who have "trespassed against us." Never forgiving, to her thinking, causes too much weight, too much baggage. Too much pain.

She asks again about the machete. Jacques says, convincingly, "An elder in the Congo gave it to me. It's an essential tool in the bush. He said he used it to clear his land and build his hut. He was proud of its practical purpose and offered it to me as a gift. Of course, I had to accept it. But for me, it's also a symbol of the oppression of colonialism. I display it, so I don't forget the hard work and struggles of my people." Ayo accepts his explanation, although with caution. She then asks, "What's in the blue bottle?"

"Water from off the coast of the Congo, at the mouth of the Congo River. The Congolese call this bottle Minkisi or Kisi for short. It's a spiritual vessel containing the water spirit, a protector of life. It's a lucky charm. Very African. Remember when we wandered through the village singing songs about slaves and water? Besides, blue cobalt bottles have a resonance in West Africa." Ayo doesn't pursue why that is afraid of an endless lecture.

Ayo nods. "Yes. I could feel the spirit of our people." She begins singing, but Jacques is entrenched in his lecture.

Jacques continues. Ayo is his captive audience. "Have you ever read Mark Twain's book, King Leopold's Soliloquy? He wrote it in 1905 after reading accounts of the atrocities committed by the king in the Congo. On certain editions, the book's cover has a dramatic and provocative image of a Christian cross and a machete." He moves along the bookcase, locates his quarry, and hands it to Ayo.

She grimaces at the sight of the cover. "That's not my Christianity. Mine is a gospel of love, not violence. I believe in the power of redemptive suffering, the power of forgiveness through love. We call it 'Restorative Justice.' It's a power that heals, it's not a power of revenge that only invites more revenge," she says sadly, shaking her head. "What did Dr. King say? 'An eye for an eye leaves the world blind.' No, I'd rather go with the Christian power of love."

Ayo shrugs her shoulders and shakes her head slightly, saying, "You are a very interesting man, Jacques Joseph Henri," emphasizing his unique name.

Jacques smiles at her with his warm eyes, giving her a peck on the cheek, then turns to the living room door. As he walks toward the door, he turns back to her, saying, "You're not wrong. And yes, Dr. King is right. Redemptive suffering does lead to redemptive healing. But someone must pay for the harm King Leopold II committed. That's called accountability, every culture believes in accountability. Maybe both are right." Jacques opens the door, leaving Ayo on her own as he heads to the supermarket.

"I'll be right back. Gotta get rosemary."

Alone in his apartment, she reads the titles of the books in Jacques's study. Most of them are about West and Central Africa and the Congo, French-speaking Africa.

Jacques also has photos of his family on his bookshelves. Some look European with blondish hair and bluish eyes; some look like French Creoles; others appear very African. The photo of Jacques's mother shows her dark complexion, large forehead, high cheekbones, and a strong, straight nose. She resembles a woman warrior, Ayo thinks.

Then Ayo notices the group photo of the royal family of Belgium, with yet another machete leaning on the bookcase directly under it. Ayo is stunned to see a machete and a picture of the royal family. Ayo thinks, "This is too bizarre." She takes a closer look and sees that the family has different shades of skin color. Maybe some are well-tanned from sunbathing in the Alps, she surmises. Several of the young men look like Jacques.

Ayo's inner cop takes over. After all, she is a detective, trained to examine in detail every potential clue, no matter how far-fetched, unlikely, or small. She remembers reading Langston Hughes's writings on passing for White. Hughes wrote that children of mixed races often are the most militant opponents of racism. Jacques seems to fit that stereotype. He is part of an elite, well-to-do Black American family, light-skinned, but he has dedicated his heart and soul to building Black racial pride.

Ayo turns in the direction of his desk and sees that tucked into the corner of Jacques's large desk are file folders— each containing detailed information about the members of the Belgian royal family, in alphabetical order. Each file contains their full name, where they live, and what foods they favor. He had compiled the royals' photos, profiles, complete bios, even what car they drove. Ayo feels spooked. Jacques is obsessed. She feels a knot growing in her stomach as a horrifying thought goes through her mind: the attacker took all the hands, which meant he must be keeping them somewhere. The attacker has them on ice, perhaps. Ayo shuddered. What was in Jacques's freezer?

She reluctantly opens the freezer door above the refrigerator. In typical Jacques' style, meats and veggies were well-organized in vacuum-sealed plastic pouches: chicken, shrimp, andouille sausages, and okra for making gumbo. Jacques labeled each pouch in neat, graceful lettering. Far back in the right-hand corner, however, was a plastic container with no label. Ayo pulled it up from among the stacks of frozen wraps. She hesitated to pry off the lid because she knew Jacques would be back shortly. She overcame her dread and quickly opened the container. Inside, neatly arranged, were small packets of frozen soft-shelled crabs.

No severed hands.

Ayo felt immense relief, but her inner police detective could not shake off her suspicions and surprises beyond surprises.

Chapter 29

NYPD Sixth Precinct—Snowstorms and Scary Schizophrenia

Three snowstorms blanketed New York City in January and February. It was bitter cold and impossible to do much outdoors. Many people did not even go to work. Crime was down because it was too cold for the criminals, too.

Jason walks into Ayo's office with a folder filled with reports on serial criminals. They all said essentially the same thing: serial violent criminals and killers suffer from various forms of trauma caused by the violence they experienced when they were young. Evidence shows that 75 percent of serial criminals were people who masked their traumatic experiences by dissociating themselves from their memories. Sometimes, this dissociation resulted in them adopting a different personality from time to time, a personality completely different from their "real" selves. They act out their trauma by detaching themselves from themselves and attacking other people, almost like they are strangers in their own body.

As Jason walked her through his research, Ayo says, "this is very helpful, Jas. It only increases my field of suspects by four million people, just about half of New York City."

Jason laughs at her wit. "I'm working on better stuff for you. Be back later." Jason walks out of the office while she pores over the documents.

Ayo likes Jason. They occasionally go out for coffee to ease the tension they both are under. The mayor wants to apprehend the attacker, if in the States. The UN is talking about it, and its international news. The pressure is on them both. They bond knowing it.

She learns that Jason grew up in a small upstate New York town, Sackets Harbor, about sixty miles north of Syracuse. A very conservative rural area. After graduating with a criminal justice degree from the George Washington University, he went back to New York, seeking a more liberal atmosphere. In New York City, Jason did not have to hide his gayness. For the first time, he could express who he is—and associate with others who also are gay. For a few years, this freedom became wildness. Eventually, he returned to school, earning his master's degree in forensics at John Jay College, one of America's best schools for criminal justice studies. In his thirties, he realized that he wanted to build a serious professional life and have more in a relationship than just a sex partner. He found Andre, a Black man, a few years younger who also had not come out to his parents.

For the last few years, Jason and Andre were a couple, and Jason said he felt elated that at long last, someone understands and cares for him. He said, "I truly love Andre—he's someone very special."

Ayo trusts Jason, and he adores her. She can confide in him—just as he could in her. They have an easy-going, respectful relationship.

Jason is a great researcher. Ayo read and reread the studies Jason gave her and read and reread the police departments' reports from where the maiming attacks took place. She stared at the photos of the royal family, looking at each one intently. They were perfectly dressed, looked perfectly happy, perfectly rich, and perfectly secure in the superiority granted by their royalty. Ayo then turns to look at photos she had found of Congolese children with their hands severed from their arms.

For the third time, she went over one of the studies Jason acquired: Early Childhood Trauma and Dissociative Identity Disorders. It defined dissociative identity disorder (DID) as "a severe condition in which two or more distinct identities, or personality states, are present in—and alternatively—take control of an individual." The report continued, "This condition is commonly known as a split personality or multiple personality disorder. Often, when a second personality gains control of a person's body, their normal personality has no memory of this time. However, the second personality can remember the actions of the original personality." Ayo continues reading. "The second person is completely different from the original person. The disorder is also known as 'acute schizophrenia,' with two or more 'people' occupying one body."

173

Ayo returns to staring at the photos of the royal family. She intensely studies their noses, eyes, smiles, skin color, and hair texture. Ayo again notices that several royal family members and Jacques share the same looks, even body types. She wonders if, instead of suffering trauma from directly experiencing violence as a youth, Jacques suffers from what he called Post Traumatic Slavery Syndrome (PTSS). Because of his PTSS, he carries anger at the past oppressors of his people and self-hate because his people were victims for so long, while he has led a relatively happy life. And suppose, Ayo thought, Jacques also carries inside him the DNA of the worst oppressors, the Belgian royal family. And probably he knows it. If that were the case, he would be both the oppressor and the oppressed – at the same time!

Put all this together, having roots in both the Congo and in the Laeken palace—wouldn't that be enough to put anyone at risk of suffering from a split personality?

Questions beyond questions, Ayo thought, now more confused than ever.

Chapter 30

Garnet Hill Lodge, the Adirondack Mountains— Sweet

Jason suggests that Ayo and Jacques take some time off together for fun.

Over the Presidents' Day weekend, Ayo and Jacques take a getaway to the Garnet Hill Lodge, a romantic (but expensive) ski lodge in the Adirondack Mountains of upstate New York. The brick fireplace is inviting, and the Alpine pine ceilings enhance the rustic charm.

Ayo loves to watch Jacque's skiing, slaloming down the most perilous slopes, agile, sleek, and strong. So beautiful. Jacques loves to look at Ayo, no matter what she's doing. They share the best red wines, the best single-malt scotch and eat the best Stilton cheese on this side of the Atlantic. It is heavenly for both. They feel so right together, it's hard for either of them to remember what it was like before they met.

But Ayo, the cop, has her suspicions, and they continually punch through the cocoon of love for Jacques that comfortably wraps around Ayo, the woman. She knows she must talk to Jacques about what she's been thinking. She's sure that Jacques' answers will satisfy her suspicions and that they will both get a good laugh out of her foolishness.

She must talk to Jacques. But she'll wait until they get back to the city. No point spoiling this lovely interlude. For more than a month, Ayo has been taking some heavy-duty antacid to calm the pain in her stomach—her body's reaction to her rising swells of stress.

Chapter 31

NYPD Sixth Precinct—Finally, We Meet Mame

Ayo could not uncover any hard evidence incriminating Jacques. Still, it was hard to ignore the fact that a lot of circumstantial evidence pointed his way. When each of the six maiming attacks was committed, Jacques was nearby—in Laeken, in Antwerp, in Paris, in London, and twice in New York. Ayo saw that Jacques was collecting additional detailed information about the Belgian royal family members, and she also realized how fixated Jacques was on the crimes Leopold II had perpetrated against the Congolese people.

Currently, Jacques is active in an organization of policy wonks, trying to develop workable proposals for Belgium to give reparations to the Congolese. And then there was Mame. Jacques was convinced he carried the spirit of Mame in his soul and felt her anger. Mame wanted justice for the Congolese people, justice by any means necessary.

Ayo, the cop, wanted to solve the mystery of the maiming. Ayo, the Black woman, understood and sympathized with the motive behind the attacks and wanted to protect her lover. Ayo, the cop's suspicions grew, but the more they did, the less Ayo the woman wanted to confront Jacques. Her stomach ulcers grew worse. Some days it seemed her whole body was in revolt—with fierce headaches and muscular aches—like the flu, but she knew it was no virus or germ. It was the tension ransacking her body and her spirit.

Caught in this internal conflict, Ayo did nothing but work hard on the investigation, digging deep and desperately trying to find leads away from Jacques. She found none.

Winter faded away, and spring returned to the city. She opened her apartment windows and felt the spring breeze and breathed in the aroma of the city—hot dogs, silver linden trees, and saw the beauty of the flowering pear and the crabapple trees along Sheridan Square. Though she was troubled, she still saw the beauty around her.

Ayo had not discussed the case with Jacques since they had their conversations about it when he returned from London. Whenever Jacques asked, she said it was against NYPD rules for her to disclose any information. Jacques never pushed her to say more. He almost seemed relieved that they could not discuss the matter.

By May, Ayo's investigation was at a dead end, and Captain McSorley said either she comes up with something or he would move her to other projects. That's when Ayo, the cop, and Ayo, the lover, had a battle royale. Ayo, the cop, won. She had dedicated her life to solving and stopping crimes—no matter what. Ayo could not bear to see the NYPD halt its efforts to stop this horrible maiming spree. She felt compelled by her code of ethics to talk to her captain.

She told McSorley everything she knew and suspected about Jacques. She then repeated it all to a city prosecutor. McSorley knew Jacques from the many times he had joined the squad at the tavern after work. He liked Jacques and knew that Ayo loved him deeply. McSorley understood immediately how difficult it was for Ayo to come forward and what it cost her to do so. He reassured her repeatedly that she had done the right thing.

He took her off the case and suggested she take a week's vacation, maybe go to Boston and visit her mother. He gave her administrative leave, free money, and time off. McSorley was truly like a work-father to Ayo.

She agreed. She hated to lie to Jacques, but she told him that her mother was ill, and she was going home to Boston to spend time with her.

****

With Ayo out of town, the Sixth Precinct detectives visited Jacques at his AEPG offices. They asked him to come with them to the station for an interview. "You have unique information about the Congo and Europe that could be valuable to our investigation into the maiming of the Belgian royal family. We'll drive you to our offices and bring you back in the late afternoon." It was a pleasant, professional interchange. Jacques agreed to go.

Several detectives interviewed Jacques in the interrogation room of the Sixth Precinct and showed him a gruesome photo of the severed arm of the elderly Belgian-English royal, Duchess Elizabeth. They played him the recording of the voice calling 911. At the moment the voice says, "I have severed the hand of the Duchess," Jacques exploded.

Something triggered Jacques. He rose from his chair in a rage. He waved his arms in the air and mimicked the slashing motions of a machete—just as the young boy had done in the Antwerp chocolate shop years ago. His eyes were fierce, and his voice dropped several octaves. His face turned red. He moved into a corner of the room, placing his chair between him and the detectives.

He lifted the chair and told the detectives that he would cut the hands off all the Belgian royals. "It's right and just," he screamed, "for all the suffering they caused over the centuries." Jacques was like a cornered animal. He talked in a language that was part French, part English, and part Congolese, raising his voice louder and louder. After several minutes, he fell to the floor and cowered behind the chair. Breathing hard, whimpering, "the horror, the horror" over and over again... "the horror, the horror." Finally, he curled up into a fetal position in the corner under the chair and cried. Whimpering, he settled down breathing hard.

The detectives were initially startled, but they were pros. They calmly asked Jacques to calm down and told him, "everything will be alright." Their voices were soothing, but one detective had his hand on his service revolver. Eventually, Jacques calmed down, continuing to whimper quietly under the chair in the corner of a gray, nondescript room. The detectives helped him up from the floor and placed him in a chair at the table, telling him softly that he would be okay.

In his normal voice, Jacques looked up at them and asked, "What were we talking about?" One of the detectives told him that he had blacked out. Jacques looked around him, puzzled.

The officers brought him to a room with a heavy iron door with a window and a cot. He could not understand what was going on but was very compliant and exhausted. After about two hours, uniformed police officers handcuffed him and put him in the back of a closed-in truck with cushioned walls and seats. A police officer watched him from the front seat through a window. Jacques was confused and asked for Ayo repeatedly. The police officers assured him that they had contacted Ayo, and she would contact him.

Chapter 32

Bellevue Hospital Center: Who Really is Mame?

The padded police paddy wagon delivered Jacques to Bellevue Hospital, where he was put in the maximum-security unit. He was confused, terrified. Psychiatrists, internists, and social workers took turns examining him for three days straight. Then, various specialists and technicians tested him and interviewed him for a month. Police detectives interrogated him almost daily. NYPD officers searched his apartment and took anything that might be evidence, such as the two machetes, photos, and his thick pile of dossiers on the Belgian royal family.

Over and over again, he swore he had never hurt anyone in his life, let alone had maimed anybody with a machete. But he could not prove his whereabouts during the six maiming episodes and said that he believed the maimings were justified. He ignored the warnings of his public defense lawyer telling him not to speak to the police. He said he had nothing to hide.

He was officially charged with assault, attempted murder, and possession of deadly weapons.

His mother flew up from New Orleans and hired a top law

firm to defend him. Ayo returned to New York during the first week of Jacques' confinement and had to submit to being interviewed by a forensic psychiatrist. She told him she suspected Jacques was a descendant of both the Mongo people, who were victims of Leopold's brutality, and of those Belgians who had perpetrated that brutality. She was almost sure Jacques knew this about himself, albeit unconsciously, "if that makes sense," and that it was one of the factors causing his schizophrenia.

A DNA test confirmed that Jacques was, in fact, a member of both King Leopold's family and a descendent of the Mongo people—a child both of royalty and enslavement. Likely his great-great-grandmother was raped by a Belgian royal more than 100 years ago. Over the 500-year history of European enslavement of Africans, children born of rape of African women by European slavers were common. Strong evidence shows that Mame was raped as a young girl when the Force Publique first entered the Congo River Valley when she was fifteen. She bore a child and raised her to be a warrior. Her daughter grew up to be her first lieutenant. She was by Mame's side when her band raided rubber camps, freed the slaves, and took them to safe Maroon communities.

It could be that Jacques is descended from Mame herself; maybe that's why he's convinced her spirit permeates his body.

Ayo avoided asking anybody whether Jacques knew that she had turned him in. She couldn't face being told that he knew. Nor could she bring herself to see him at Bellevue. Ayo still felt that as a police officer, she had no choice in doing what she did, but that made matters worse for her—maybe she should have just quit the force and let someone else handle it. Tormented with guilt and virtually paralyzed by inner conflict, she couldn't go back to work. Captain McSorley understood. He told Ayo to take personal leave, as much as she needed, to get her head straight. Her job would be waiting for her when she was ready to come back. If she needed medical leave, he would make sure she got all she needed. She was a very valued member of the force, and more than that, she was the captain's favorite detective, his work-daughter.

Jason called Ayo a few times and told her that he admired her bravery but understood how devastated she felt. His voice calmed her but did not compensate for the physical toll of the weeks of stress and strain. She was now a shell of her former self. On her bleakest days, she thought back to the day she had seen Zuri out of the blue and almost wished that day had never happened.

Chapter 33

NY State Supreme Court, Manhattan: Who's on Trial, Jacques or Mame?

Despite its name, the criminal division of the Supreme Court of New York State is better known as the NY Supreme Felony Court. However, it is not the highest court in the state—the New York State Court of Appeals. The New York State Supreme Court has a court in each borough that hears serious felony cases. The court that heard Jacques's case was in Manhattan.

Jacques's mother, who Ayo had never met, was there, and so was Zuri. The jury was composed of seven women, five men—five Blacks, four Whites, two Hispanics, one Asian—a reflection of the new America, a country where in some areas, the minority is the new majority, especially in New York City.

The judge was John McCarthy. Of all the judges in New York, he was probably the best-suited to hear the case. He was compassionate and bent the rules to permit both the prosecution and the defense to include as much information as possible. He relished banter; he possessed a quick mind and quicker wit. He wanted to ensure that everything could be done to find the truth.

Jacques' lawyers filed a technical, medical plea of Not Guilty By Reason of Insanity (NGBRI). They had three psychiatrists examine him. Each said he suffered from DID, Dissociative Identity Disorder, and each described Jacques's two separate personalities for the jury.

One expert witness, Dr. Joshua Rawls, a Harvard University philosopher considered by his peers to be the father of modern-day moral and political philosophy, said Jacques's alleged crimes were rational and logical actions done in the interest of justice as fairness, a concept he had pioneered.

Professor Rawls discussed his theory as it related to the so-called "spirit of Mame." He testified that "Many children in the Congo today experience the feeling of having a soldier in the King's Force Publique lift his machete and swiftly slice off their hand. They are taught about the crimes committed by the former king. They imagine their arm spouting blood seeping into the hot dirt, screaming loud matching the screams of their mother. The trauma caused by the actions of Leopold's army has been passed on from one generation to the next, starting in the 1880s. The trauma never dies.

"If it's true that Jacques committed the maimings—and I'm not saying it is—then he was trying to put an end to the suffering that burdens today's Congolese. Trauma begets trauma. By severing the hands of the royals, he hoped to end the cycle of ancestral trauma. He hoped that the internalized terror would finally stop because the

Congolese would feel that justice had been done by doing to these royals what was the only just and fair thing to do. I refer to this concept: justice as fairness."

Many other expert witnesses spoke about the horrors committed in Leopold's name and described the recent maimings as reparations to the Congolese people in the form of "justice as fairness". Isn't it fair for a few royals to lose their hands to bring reparations and inner peace to the people of the Congo after King Leopold stole their wealth, labor, and natural resources in such a brutal and violent way? The inhumanity of the past has left the nation of the Democratic Republic of Congo so very poor today. Mame's spirit within Jacques hoped to end the modern-day trauma.

African history and culture experts testified that Jacques had a special gift to feel centuries of pain. This gift allowed the second personality, the spirit of Mame, to emerge and commit well-intentioned but misdirected actions. One African expert said that the Mongo people believed that those who have joined the ancestors, like Mame, intervene in the lives of the living. By saying their name, the spirits are willing to listen. Jacques remembered the lessons he learned as a child in Congo Square, intensely listening as elders explained West African spirituality and called out women warriors' names. "A shay, so be it, I remember."

Sitting at the defense table, Jacques understood what the psychiatrists and the others said, even though he was "not" an expert. He knew they were talking about him as they delved deeply into West African religiosity and the memory of West African spirituality that carried itself across the Atlantic Ocean in the bowels of slave ships.

Jacques recalled what his grandmother in Tremé once told him in the back garden of his house on Esplanade Avenue. "You can take the African out of Africa, but you can never take Africa out of the African. We remain, first and foremost, Africans in America!" Then, they walked through the garden and made homage to the voodoo artifacts.

For those souls to survive the horrid conditions at the bottom of a slave ship, his grandmother would say, "They had to transport their psyche, their spirit, into another world." Only those who could remember their spiritual strength in Africa before being kidnapped, chained, and thrown into a 115-degree hellhole of a slave ship could survive the twelve-week Middle Passage from West Africa to the Caribbean. Jacques knew he had a special power of remembrance. He had a special power to know who he was, and more importantly, who he is. Jacques believed he was descended from Mame. Jacques was "the hope and the dream of the slave," as Maya Angelou would say. He/she was a fierce African warrior, albeit a woman warrior.

"Queen Mongo Mame is not dead," one expert witness said. "She lives in the spirits of those who fight to be free and to bring justice to those harmed in the past. Mame is not just the revenge of 500 years of African slavery. She is the arbiter of justice as fairness. She will not forget nor forgive until justice is served—until her universe is balanced."

Of course, the prosecution objected strenuously to such defense, calling it non-sense. The prosecution was much simpler; Jacques was a maniac, a monster who maimed innocent and good people. Lady Clairece Elizabeth Alice Von Struben-Haagn, the twenty-year-old NYU student who had been maimed, sat in the courtroom. The prosecution called her to the witness stand. She was sporting short blonde hair and no make-up, she was dressed in a white suit, with a light blue blouse and dark blue heels. She approached the witness box, and all eyes were on her handless arm. She walked slowly, slightly swinging her arm. Everyone stared at her every move. Sitting softly in the witness chair, she looked straight at the jury, resting her handless arm on the witness box rail wrapped in a white bandage. Her handless arm was obvious resting neatly across the oak-wood railing as if it were somehow a prop in a drama. Indeed, it was.

The prosecution asked Lady Clairece about her studies at NYU in sociology and medicine. Lady Clairece explained that she served as a volunteer in the Lower East Side for the homeless and devoted most of her Sundays to volunteering at the Dorothy Day Clinic on Houston Street. She wanted to go to medical school and work with the poor in Africa. There could have been no more a compelling witness. Everyone in the courtroom knew she offered powerful testimony for the prosecution. Why would anyone want to maim this young person of good will and good intentions? Everyone looked at Jacques after she spoke and lifted herself out of the witness box with one hand.

"But what responsibility should the Belgian royals of today have for the crimes of the past?" a defense attorney asked the jury. "What payment should they make for the enormous wealth and the privileges they now enjoy? Surely, they owe something. That's just fair. Fair is fair!"

The defense called Jacques to the stand. When Jacques took his seat, Mame emerged startling everyone including the judge who was taken aback at first as two armed Bailiffs stood near ready to act if Mame became violent.

Judge McCarthy allowed "her" to speak, despite the prosecution's objections that he rule "Mame" out of order.

Mame rejected the idea that the ones who were maimed were "innocent." His lawyers tried to restrain Jacques from incriminating himself, but Jacques could not keep Mame from saying whatever she wanted. Judge McCarthy was relishing the banter. He loved the free-flowing exchange of ideas if they did not violate the decorum of his courtroom. The debate raged.

Mame defended Jacques for doing what was right and forcing the world, especially the Belgian government, to compensate and pay reparations to the Congo. Mame put the United States, France, and Belgium governments on trial—condemning them for the murder, rape, and maiming of at least ten million Congolese.

Jacques's lawyers knew they were setting a precedent and were especially prepared. They said Jacques suffered from Post Traumatic Slavery Syndrome (PTSS), a set of behaviors, beliefs, and actions caused by trauma suffered by enslaved Africans and passed down from generation to generation for over 250 years.

The lawyers cited a study in the Yale Journal of Medicine, which showed that Black men in North America suffered disproportionately higher incidences of high blood pressure, obesity, and diabetes, now called "Diabesity." During the trauma suffered in the Middle Passage and during 350 years of slavery and Jim Crow, which the defense defined as "the trauma of domestic terrorism," Black men and women survived, working twelve-to-fifteen hours a day in 95-degree temperatures in the South, picking cotton and cutting sugarcane by holding salt in their bio-systems as a natural defense mechanism against the stifling heat and humidity. The punishing work forced salt to embed into their systems for survival. But today, the salt in their systems causes hypertension, obesity, and early death.

"Diabesity," the lawyers explained, is a new medical concept developed by George Washington University public health professor Walter Dentz. He explained the twin-ailments of diabetes and obesity are predominantly found in African-Americans. "Diabesity" is a result of centuries of poor socio-economic conditions wrought by systematic racism and White supremacy, relegating African Americans to a cycle of poverty, poor health care, and early death. The professor argued convincingly that substandard health care for African Americans for four hundred years caused more deaths than slavery, police violence, lynching, crime, and accidents combined.

The defense disclosed that Professor Dentz was a student civil rights activist in the Student Nonviolent Campaign Committee (SNCC) in Mississippi in the sixties. The defense team said Dentz saw firsthand the abject poverty of African Americans in the Mississippi Delta. In the Delta today, Black people face higher poverty, obesity, diabetes, hypertension, poor housing, inferior health care, and more deaths than in any other section of the country. The jurors' eyes reflected the compelling nature of this testimony.

The defense said only the strong survived the Middle Passage. The jury sat transfixed by these arguments. Even the White jurors were glued to every word from the university experts. The professor convincingly explained, "You had to be mentally, emotionally, and physically superior to withstand the punishing captivity below deck and then to endure the rape and forced dancing at the top of the slave ship when the slave's captors brought them up on deck to wash off the urine and feces after a week of living in stench and absolute darkness."

A psychiatrist specializing in trauma, Dr. Marcus Thompson of the George Washington University Medical School and Sirius XM talk-show host on health and public policy, noted that the trauma Africans experienced shackled in holding pens for up to four months in captivity after the agony of being torn from their families and villages must have caused permanent melancholy, depression, loss of self-esteem, sleeplessness, and suicidal tendencies. The trauma was carried over to their children and grandchildren and led directly to more than 400 years of Black people distrusting White people. "That's PTSS," the defense argued.

The defense explained that W.E.B. DuBois called this phenomenon "double consciousness." Black people in a predominantly White world must understand that they live in two worlds simultaneously, one White and one Black, but the White world is organized against them, which leads to the feeling that they are always traveling on water — like traveling on the Atlantic Ocean from Africa to the New World. Blacks always tread water in a White supremacist society, always conscious of drowning either by macro-aggressions, such as lynching or micro-aggressions of Franz Fanon's "The Gaze", the way Whites always look at Blacks as suspicious people — never to be trusted. They remain forever fearful of drowning in a White-dominated world, always treading water, always feeling like they're about to die. That's PTSS. It's a constant internal and external stress making them so exhausted their immune systems weaken, malfunction, over-salt itself leading to stress.

Jacques' lawyers referred to Post Traumatic Slave Syndrome by Dr. Joy DeGruy, a professor of social work, who stated that PTSS is not a disorder that can be treated and cured clinically. Instead, PTSS requires social change in individuals and institutions that perpetuate inequality and injustice toward the descendants of enslaved Africans. The lawyers also cited a 2014 article in The Atlantic that asked: "If the American medical establishment recognized PTSS as a disorder, will it recognize 350 years of violence in slavery, macro- and micro-aggressions against Black people?"

The prosecutor had a different interpretation. He claimed that Jacques Henri was a mass maimer who deliberately attacked innocent victims at will. The prosecution was relentless, objecting over and over, and sometimes granted a "Sustained."

Unlike most judges, McCarthy allowed, over the prosecution's adamant objections, all the testimony the defense presented. He seemed fascinated by every academic, arcane, and even bizarre thing said in his courtroom.

Ayo tried to attend the court sessions every day and listened intently. She avoided Zuri and nodded at Jacques' mother but dared not speak to her. She still loved Jacques deeply and felt extremely guilty for her part in putting him on trial, locking him away. When Ayo came home each night, she no longer felt like the warrior Mame but like a sellout, a betrayer of both the man she loved and of her people. She lost fifteen pounds from her already lean frame. She could not eat.

Occasionally, Ayo reached out to Aisha and Kayla and welcomed hearing their voices — anything to distract her from the raging guilt tearing her apart. Jason also called her, his cheerful voice halting some of the bile she felt constantly rising from her stomach.

When Ayo phoned her mother, instead of getting sympathy, she learned that her mother, her tower of strength, had cancer and would soon need an operation. The news felt like a machete to her heart.

After three weeks of history lessons, psychological analysis, and testimony given by a "spirit," the jury adjourned.

"Stress is stress," Jacques' lawyers argued in their closing statement. "The stress soldiers experience in combat happens in short episodes but is not any more stressful than a lifetime of stress in a White supremacist society."

The prosecutor objected! "Cutting off the hands of innocent people is also a 'crime against humanity!'" The prosecutor called for severe punishment for Jacques's assault with a dangerous weapon and attempted murder. He said that Jacques should be put away for life, with no chance of parole, and called Jacques a "deranged monster — no better than Hannibal Lecter." Everyone in the courtroom knew the reference to Hannibal — the fictional murderer who ate his victims, not unlike some of the very real Force Publique soldiers. The courtroom sat stunned at the reference. Some nodded their heads in agreement. All arguments pointed to Jacques being convicted of seven violent attacks with the intent to kill.

After five days of deliberation, the jury returned. They took their assigned seats in the jury box. As they entered the courtroom, they looked proud, yet exhausted, of the job they had done as citizens. Emotionally drained, they looked as weary as a punched-out boxer by the ordeal. They sat in their assigned seats, tired, upright and dignified, but with a gleam of "thank God we can go home". After a slow processional seating with a dramatic flair, Judge McCarthy asked the jury's forewoman, Ms. Banita Anderson, if the jury had reached a verdict. She stood and said, "Yes, your honor." Judge McCarthy asked her to give her written verdict to the bailiff. She handed the bailiff a folded paper.

The bailiff handed the paper to Judge McCarthy. The judge slowly unfolded it, read it, looked above his eyeglasses at Jacques, and then at Jacques's prosecutor and back again. He slowly removed his eyeglasses. He then asked Ms. Anderson, "Have you come to this decision on your own as a jury and in accordance with the rules outlined in this court?"

"Yes, your honor."

"Do you and your fellow jurors fully understand the consequences of your decision today?"

"Yes, your honor. We deliberated fully cognizant of the severity of the charges."

The judge re-folded the paper, returned it to the bailiff,

who handed it to the forewoman. He then said, "Madam Forewoman, please read the jury's verdict to the court. Mr. Henri, please rise."

Forewoman Anderson directly faced Jacques, unfolded the paper, and said: "The jury finds the defendant, Jacques Joseph Henri, not guilty by reason of insanity on all seven counts."

The courtroom exploded. Observers cheered or booed, and in New York City fashion, depending on their opinion of the verdict, cursed either the jury, the judge, or the Belgian royal family members who were present. The royals hung their heads, shaking them left and right in protest. Jacques's family rejoiced at the verdict. Some people hugged; others slumped in their seats. The judge pounded his gavel, asking everyone to refrain from demonstrating in his courtroom, warning them that they would be ejected. The press had already bolted out of the courtroom to file their news reports.

After hearing the jury's verdict, Judge McCarthy ordered the bailiff to "escort Mr. Henri to the State of New York's Psychiatric Hospital Division at Bellevue for evaluation. A determination of Mr. Henri's status will be made in this courtroom after I receive the evaluation. This court is adjourned." The judge slammed down his gavel.

Jacques was confined indefinitely to the maximum-security wing of Bellevue Hospital. Editorials across the nation condemned the verdict. They said that Jacques had gotten away almost scot-free after committing a series of horrendous crimes. One tabloid headline read, "Crazy Like a Fox—Machete Slasher Sleeps Well with Three Meals a Day, a Game Room, and Cable TV."

Chapter 34

Greenwich Village with Ayo Alone

Ayo suffered severe depression and anxiety. She woke up several times each night, wondering what happened. How could she fall in love with a maniac, a mentally ill man, a demonic psychopath? What was wrong with her to have misjudged Jacques so badly?

She wondered if she could ever find anyone remotely as charming and sensual as Jacques, someone passionate about his beliefs, who spoke fluent French, could cook like a great chef, and make love even better.

She worried about Jacques — this brilliant, compassionate man who was now confined to a mental hospital. Her hopes were like the packed soft crabs in his freezer — bundled up and frozen.

She prayed that his ancestors would protect him.

What made everything a lot worse was that her superiors praised her detective work. For getting her lover and soulmate locked up in a mental hospital, Ayo received a pay raise and a promotion to Senior Lieutenant Detective. Even the mayor commended her work.

She was no longer able to keep herself away from work.

Being alone was too painful, too terrifying. At home, Ayo was so on edge that she was afraid of her own shadow. She needed to focus her mind on something, anything, other than him. She threw herself back into her job and tried to lose herself in her work.

When her friends called her, she mainly listened. She felt that a part of herself was missing. Nothing was fun anymore. When she forced herself to go to the gym, she mindlessly stood on the treadmill. It seemed a metaphor for her life—running in place but not getting anywhere and still feeling exhausted.

And she asked over and over again, why would the ancestors do this to her and to Jacques? Questions beyond questions.

Chapter 35

Brussels, Belgium: My Dog Ran Off with My Hand!

The arrest and internment of Jacques Joseph Henri brought great relief to the Belgian royal family. They would have preferred if the jury had found him guilty and that he was put away for life—that would send a message to anyone else who might think about "seeking justice with machete"—but with him out of the way, the royals hoped there would be no further maiming attacks. Just to be sure and send a message, they didn't end their expensive security detail, but slowly phased it out without publicity.

Shockingly, two months after the trial, there was another attack. Duchess Ashley Leopold, the great-great-niece of King Leopold II, was walking her black poodle at dusk when, as she later told the police, her hand, still holding the dog's leash, was grabbed from behind. The attacker stretched out her arm and severed it at the wrist with a machete. Feeling the tension from the pull of the leash

201

disappear, the dog joyfully ran off, dragging the leash with the hand still wrapped around it. The hand bounced along the green grass, spotting it red with blood, while blood poured out of the Duchess's arm. The attacker calmly threw a black towel at her, speaking in French with a deep, almost haunting voice, "Here, wrap your arm in this towel. You will be okay."

The perpetrator ran after the dog to retrieve the hand. After a few seconds of the hand bounding across the lawn, the hand dropped from the leash. The attacker picked up the hand, dropped the machete, and fled.

The Duchess wrapped her arm in the towel and ran after her poodle for a few minutes before collapsing on the grass. She managed to pull her cell phone out of her coat pocket with one hand and called the emergency services. Blood spurted out of her arm, covering her face, white clothes and streaking her blonde hair. She wrapped her arm again. She picked herself up off the grass, staggered toward the streetlights at the edge of the park, stood in the middle of the street, and waved down the first car that came along. Fortunately, it was a park service vehicle. She knelt in the middle of the street, holding her arm wrapped in a bloody towel, screaming. The driver helped her into the front seat of the car. He looked in horror at the duchess's blood-soaked towel and quickly sped to the nearest hospital.

The Duchess told the police that the attacker was short, thick, strong looking, dressed in black with a black hat, and able to swiftly leave the scene after picking up the hand.

Newspapers across Europe quickly exploded with headlines. They read: "#7 — Seventh Royal Family Member Maimed" and "#7 Copycat Attack." Commentators throughout the world condemned the attacker as a copycat villain. Talking heads said that the more media exposure a crime receives, the more likely copycats would follow.

But not everyone supported the "copycat" theory. One commentator said, "Maybe there are several serial maimers." The media was abuzz with talk shows on who and why the royals were under attack. And not all commentary was complimentary to the king's descendants. The world seemed to be talking about the sins of King Leopold II.

Chapter 36

NYPD Sixth Precinct: Thai Cuisine and Football?

In her mind, Ayo agreed that the seventh attack was probably a copycat crime but hoped it was not. She was ashamed of herself for thinking this, but she hoped the real maimer was still out there and would strike again. It meant that Jacques might be exonerated, even if he could not leave Bellevue, even if he were still "crazy."

She read every account she could find about the latest attack, studied the transcript of Jacques's trial, and again reviewed all the evidence she had collected. Maybe she could find some flaw in the conviction. Anyway, she said to herself, detectives are supposed to go down every path in an investigation, even if it leads to a dead end. She strode up to Captain McSorley's office, stuck her head in the doorway without knocking, and said in the most nonchalant, disinterested tone she could muster, "Hey Cap, you want me to reopen the case against Henri in light of number seven?"

McSorley responded curtly, not looking up from his reading, "No, that's not for us to decide. Let the prosecutor worry about that. We have too much to do. Besides, James, you're too close to it."

Ayo stood defiantly in the doorway, her hand on her hip. He could feel her eyes staring at him. McSorley looked up from his reading and said in a softer voice, "Hey, look, Ayo, I know you had a personal train wreck with Jacques. It's got to be very hard for you. Stay on your projects but do what you think is best. The commissioner and the mayor are very impressed with your work. And the United Nations, too. But do the right thing, whatever the hell that is." He paused, looked deeply into her eyes as if she were his daughter, and said, "Hey, Jean and I are having some friends over Sunday afternoon for the Jets game. Wanna join us? I'm ordering Thai food for football—ain't that nuts?"

Ayo said, "Yes, and thanks, Cap. What do I bring?"

"Nothing," said McSorley, "But bring a friend if you want to."

Ayo pivoted in the doorway and slunk away. She could bring a female friend; perhaps Aisha would want to go with her. However, more importantly, Ayo had gotten her go-ahead. Tomorrow she would visit Jacques and try to get him to understand the relatively good news.

Chapter 37

Bellevue Hospital Center: Maybe Mame Knows Who Maims

A yo had visited Jacques twice before, but he was sedated on phenothiazines, and he'd been uncommunicative and unaware of her presence.

This time though, Jacques seemed to have at least one foot in the here-and-now. For the first time since his arrest, Ayo and Jacques talked to each other frankly. They discussed the seventh maiming. Jacques always maintained he was innocent, but deep down, he considered the possibility that maybe his second personality—Mame—had, in fact, been the attacker.

And there was this: Jacques was not convinced Mame was merely his "second personality." Maybe he was a direct descendent of Mame, and her spirit had entered his body when he was a child. At times, he could swear he heard Mame gloat that she had committed the maimings to get justice and fairness.

But either way—if Mame were Jacques's other personality or a spirit of his actual ancestor—the authorities would not let him leave Bellevue until they were convinced that he could get rid of her.

Ayo wondered out loud, "Where do we go from here?"

Jacques did not know. Neither did Ayo. But then Ayo said something strange. "Maybe Mame knows. She's apparently very smart and cunning. And courageous. Maybe she will reveal the answer to us."

With that thought, Jacques and Ayo just stared at each other. Ayo began to cry. Jacques perked up, "No, baby, don't cry, please. Let's figure this thing out. I love you."

Chapter 38

Evian, France: Two Lady Dog Walkers Meet

Evian, France, is a beautiful city at the base of the Alps that borders France and Switzerland on Lake Geneva. Evian is also known as Evian-les-Bains because of the rich mineral waters flowing into the lake and spas from the famous mountain range. The world-renowned Evian-branded water comes from here. The town was the favorite vacation place of European royalty for two centuries. Nearly every European royal family has or had a lavish residence or two in Evian at one time. Evian was the idyllic summer home of the rich and the richer.

Ironically, or perhaps paradoxically, this is the town where novelist Mary Shelley located her Frankenstein, whose titular doctor murdered his wife, Elizabeth, on the second night of their honeymoon. Victor Frankenstein had a dual personality: one, a loving husband; the other, a mad, monstrous deviant.

On a warm, soft summer evening at dusk, walking along a quay on Lake Geneva, a short, stocky, well-dressed Black woman wearing a light-yellow blouse, soft, silky black pants, and black Ferragamo shoes walked her white poodle. She sported a large, floppy white sun hat covering her well-appointed short twists adorned with cowrie shells. She wore dark sunglasses. She walked behind a young woman, slowly walking a very cute brown, tan, and black Yorkshire terrier, hesitating here and there to look over the beautiful lake scenery.

The woman in front was Belgian royalty, Laetitia Luisa Leopold. She was the thirty-eight-year-old Duchess of Brabant. As the duchess paused to admire the poetically beautiful spewing *Le Jet d'Eau* fountain in Lake Geneva jetting 30 meters in the air, the Black woman with her poodle passed in front of the duchess. After a few steps ahead, she slowed down, looked back, and said, "I love your Yorkie, male or female?"

The duchess answered, "Thank you. She's female, named Gigi. Your poodle is darling. What's its name?"

"Monga. She's a pure Congolese breed."

"I've never heard of the breed 'Congolese.'" She looked puzzled but said, "Well, she's a very pretty young lady." She bent down to pet Monga.

The Black woman asked the duchess petting her poodle, "You're the Duchess of Brabant, correct?"

A bit startled but still smiling, the duchess said, "Why, yes. And who are you?"

"My name is Mame. And I, too, am pure Congolese."

Even more, puzzled, the duchess struggled to maintain her composure. "That's interesting, I have always wanted to go to the Congo. I was once in Senegal and Nigeria but never the Congo. What a fascinating country you come from."

Mame replied, "Oh yes, it's a fascinating country. You must visit someday."

The duchess smiled, relieved at the warmth in the stranger's voice, but couldn't see her eyes, nor even her very dark face which were partially covered by her over-hanging floppy hat and overly large dark sunglasses.

The Black woman then reached into her large leather light-yellow Gucci purse matching her blouse and pulled out an envelope with the duchess's name on it. "Here's a letter for you, madame. It's an open letter to you, the king, and the Belgian Parliament. You are receiving it at the same time as the others."

The duchess was now startled, puzzled, and scared. She took the envelope staring at it. The Black woman turned and quickly went in the opposite direction, walking upright and proud. Her poodle moved with the same prideful stride. Woman and poodle walked earnestly into an adjacent parking lot where a black sedan with dark windows awaited. The driver opened the back door. She lifted her poodle into the car and took her seat. The car slowly left the lot, turning into a lane of trees and flowering shrubs disappearing. Gone.

The duchess watched, paralyzed with fear. After a few moments, she opened the letter:

"I chose to spare your hand. You are our messenger. We

sent this letter to King Philip-Alexander, Prime Minister Michel De Gaul; President of the Chamber of Representatives, Monsieur Bartholomeu De Woeven; two Belgian newspapers, Le Soir and Le Derniere Heure, and two leading newspapers in the Congo, MediaCongo and 7sur7. Please forward this letter to your immediate family members. We will not sever any more hands of the royal family if:

1. Belgium acknowledges and apologizes for the murder, rape, mayhem, exploitation, and severed hands of 10 million Congolese under the reign of Leopold II;

2. Belgium pays reparations of 1 trillion euros to the Congo over a ten-year period to be used for education, health, environmental and economic development to begin within ninety (90) days;

3. Belgium must commission an independent investigation of the assassination of Patrice Lumumba in 1961 and publish its findings;

4. Belgium must erect three museums examining the history of European slavery and colonization in Africa: one in Boma, one in Katanga, and one in Antwerp.

5. We will continue severing the hands of Belgian royalty unless Belgium acts on the above reparations within ninety (90) days. Only Princess Esparada-Maria Leopold will be spared because

she has tried to make amends for King Leopold's horrors."

— Mame and the 10 million.

Chapter 39

Across the World: Mame Strikes Again!

M ame knew that Belgian officials would dismiss the demands in the note outright or drag their feet. She also knew the two leading newspapers in Brussels and the Congo would make her letter front-page news. They did:

- "Royalty Terrorist Makes Demands"
- "Belgian Parliament to Debate Royalty-Maimer Threat"
- "Belgian Press Questioning King Leopold II's Legacy"
- "What Does Belgium Owe the Congo?"
- "Reparations for Crimes Against the Congo Debated Behind Closed Doors"
- Papers and newscasts also dug up Jacques's case:
- "Wrong Man Convicted of Severing Hands of Belgian Royalty?"
- "Who is the Machete Attacker?"

The New York Post ran a front-page headline: "Henri, the maimer? Were we wrong?"

And so, the debate began. Newspapers across the world ran the open letter. They asked, "Who is Mame?" Never was there a public airing of the atrocities committed by Belgian royalty and its government in the nineteenth and twentieth centuries. Belgian historians, intellectuals, and government officials started speaking out immediately — for and against the threat and demands of Mame.

Newspapers weighed in with editorials. Radio and TV reports covered Mame's letter every night, and talk radio exploded with unending commentary. The Catholic Church condemned the letter's threat but then said in the same sentence, "Belgium must acknowledge their true history in the Congo that was never taught in public schools."

For decades, left-wing organizations and newspapers had advocated that Belgium make amends to the Congo by telling the truth about its history in the central African colony. Universities began teach-ins on campuses. Students demanded disinvestment from all Belgian corporations in the Congo until reparations were granted.

The leading university in Belgium, the University of Leuven, with a student body of 58,000, invited the most respected American public historian on the concept of reparations, Ta-Nehisi Coates, to address their students. Mr. Coates was expected to talk at the university's largest lecture hall, the Auditoria, seating 1,100 students. Student passes to the talk were gone within twenty minutes of going online.

The university moved the lecture to the football stadium, seating 5,500. It was standing room only when Mr. Coates arrived. He delivered a persuasive argument that reparations were due to the Congo — much like reparations given to Israel of nearly 100 billion dollars due to the death of 6 million Jews. Belgium's King Leopold II killed more than 10 million Congolese. University students chanted, "Reparations Congo, Reparations Now!"

Belgium's leading conservative Catholic newspaper and think-tank condemned any government negotiations with Mame or any capitulation with the maimer. The Catholic Archdiocese statement argued that Belgium and the Catholic Church brought civilization to the Congo. Previously, Congolese tribes were at constant war with each other, with the victor performing cannibalism, they argued.

The Catholic Church's official position was that Belgium brought civilization to the Congo by providing infrastructure, schools, health clinics, and sanitary conditions to backward, uncivilized people. The Church never refuted that 10 million Congolese were murdered in the process of "civilizing" the people or exploiting the country's supply of rubber, ivory and labor power.

The issues of reparations received extensive discussion, especially on college campuses. One student reminded them that in 2017, The International Criminal Court awarded symbolic reparations of 230 euros (about $250) each to nearly 300 people who lost relatives, property, or livestock or suffered psychological harm in a deadly attack on a Congolese village in 2003. The judges also awarded symbolic collective reparations, which included "housing, support for income-generating activities, education and psychological support" for victims.

In other words, much chatter and many symbolic actions occurred. Still, nothing was really done, except that every member of the Belgian royal family now had armed police protection twenty-four hours a day. The cost of protecting more than 150 royal family members was estimated at over one million euros per month. The Belgian people were beginning to wonder if it was worth it. All of Europe's police forces were looking for Mame.

Chapter 40

Lubumbashi, the Democratic Republic of the Congo, Again?

Ayo continued to read up on the Congo's history, thinking that the additional background information could help Jacques. The New York Times provided some hefty background information in their Sunday editorial section on reparations—providing high-level arguments on the case for or against reparations.

Until she met Jacques, Ayo was not greatly aware of the richness of the Congo. She learned that Lubumbashi is the capital of the Katanga Province of the Democratic Republic of the Congo. Katanga has enormously profitable mining companies, and its mineral wealth includes cobalt, cadmium, copper, coltan, uranium, diamonds, and gold. The French, Germans, and Belgians have mined Katanga for 150 years.

At the end of the nineteenth century, local chiefs fought against the European colonizers' incursion on their land and pillaged their natural resources. But the chiefs also supplied the Arab slave trade with African slaves captured in East Africa. The most powerful chieftain was Mwinda M'Ziri Tabora. Chief M'Ziri brokered a relationship with German and Belgium mining companies to permit the exploration and mining of his land and his people's employment in exchange for guns and profits from the mines. M'Ziri even forced captives from other defeated tribes in the province into forced labor in the mines — slavery.

Ayo recalled what Jacques had told her and assumed M'Ziri was sentenced to live in the next world on Le Ile de Madeleine as a King Buzzard.

By the late nineteenth century, M'Ziri was one of the richest men in all of Africa. However, in 1891 he was violently deposed from his kingdom in a move organized by European corporate interests using local tribal factions paid large sums of cash. Before his death, he ensured that his ill-gotten riches flowed into his coffers and his family's financial cash hideaways. Even today, profits from the mines totaling millions of dollars per year flow into M'Ziri's twenty-first-century family funds. His descendants are very, very rich.

Ayo read a little about one of those descendants, University of Lubumbashi history professor Kwasie Sharita Bambassi-M'Ziri. Ayo thought back to conversations with Zuri about M'Ziri — a strong, entrepreneurial woman interested in supporting other African women entrepreneurs. Zuri told her that M'Ziri does not need to work and owns homes in Belgium, France, and New York City. She also has a private jet on standby anytime she needs it for travel. She received the best schooling in Africa, Europe, and the United States, earning her Ph.D. in history from Yale. Her father and grandfather both have an endowed chair at Yale after donating millions to the college. Those donations secured a slot for Professor M'Ziri to achieve her Ph.D., although her scholarship was at the top of her class. She now works as a history professor because she loves teaching.

Ayo looked up whatever she could find on M'Ziri online and discovered a Huffington Post article about her. Professor M'Ziri inherited more than wealth from her great-great-grandfather. She also inherited his conviction that his kingdom was divinely directed. Chief M'Ziri did not tolerate anyone who challenged his rule, and his rule was to assure that his people, his tribal nation, would never fall prey to outside colonizers. He took no prisoners.

Professor M'Ziri knew very well the chief's power and privilege. She learned at an early age that she was the continuation of Chief M'Ziri's victory over the White domination of Africa and her people. Each time she stood at her podium; she demonstrated his Africa-First philosophy.

****

One morning, six months after someone delivered the note to the Duchess of Brabant in Evian, Professor M'Ziri moved deliberately through her house on the outskirts of

Lubumbashi. She lived in a very upscale community of large, stately homes with well-manicured lawns and gardens. High iron fencing surrounded her home, and red and purple bougainvillea vines covered the fences. A Mozart concerto played in the background, and two luxury cars sat in her driveway, both high-end 700 Series Mercedes, one black, the other silver. She lived a life of elite luxury.

She sat in her kitchen enjoying Mozart arias, sipping her cup of coffee, a green and gold can of Tanzania's finest Peaberry rested on the kitchen counter. She wore a stunning Tanzania sari made of fine silk. Around her shoulders and neck hung a black silk scarf that seemed to float in the air when she walked. She moved toward the refrigerator, where a mirror hung on the wall. She looked at herself and adjusted the cowrie shells in her short twists and locks. Then, she stretched a few of them and patted her locks into a shapelier style. She stopped for another sip of coffee. Mozart further calmed the already peaceful and lush morning of golden sunshine, floating arias and lazy luxury.

Her first class was at 11:00 AM, and she had some chores to attend to before that.

She arranged seven boxes on the shiny black marble countertop in her kitchen, each measuring 10 x 10 inches square. Each box had red gift-wrapping paper with the words "For You" printed in gold to be tucked inside, extending over the box edges, ready for its contents.

The professor approached her large, glossy black refrigerator with slow steps but deliberate movements. She pulled on a pair of everyday kitchen rubber gloves; then, she opened the left section of her freezer door. She brought out seven vacuum-sealed plastic bags, one at a time. Each bag contained a frozen item. She wrapped each one in cheesecloth, followed by aluminum foil, and then placed each of them into its own plastic Ziploc bag. After zipping them, she put each one in a box and gently folded the red gift wrap over the Ziploc bag. She added a small beige card in a red envelope with typed words on each card—one verse of *Congo*, a poem by Vachel Lindsay published in 1914:

Listen to the yell of Leopold's ghost

Burning in Hell for his hand-maimed host.

Hear how the demons chuckle and yell

Cutting his hands off down in Hell.

She carefully inserted the soft red envelope atop the Ziploc plastic and covered the contents with the red paper, and on each box, she slid the lid into place. She meticulously tied a red velvet ribbon around each one, securely crisscrossing the ribbon over the box on all four sides tied tight.

Once all seven boxes were prepared, she then placed each into a mail-courier pouch necessary for airmail. "AVION" was printed in bold blue lettering on all sides of the mail pouches. Each mail pouch was pre-addressed. She bent over behind the countertop, lifting a small suitcase onto the black granite counter. She placed the seven blue and white mail pouches into the suitcase.

When she was done, she pointed her remote at a console on her kitchen table, turning off the lights and the sounds of Mozart's concerto. Leaving the kitchen by the back door, she carried the suitcase to her silver Mercedes. Then, pointing her car's remote at the back of the car, the trunk popped open, and she placed the suitcase in her trunk.

With her remote, she started her engine, got in her car, and put the car into gear. She slowly approached the gate. When the gate opened, she drove through. She watched from her rear-view mirror as the gate close behind her. She pointed her remote again at her back gate, activating her security system. She then put her silver Mercedes into gear and slowly proceeded with ease.

Professor M'Ziri steered herself to the campus in her Mercedes. She arrived at her lecture hall with her thin crocodile leather briefcase, walked to her classroom, and settled in at the front, preparing her notes for the day's lecture on North African history.

Professor M'Ziri was short yet sturdy. To her students, she was impeccably dressed in her green and red Tanzanian wrap with a black and gold-lined silk scarf around her shoulders. She was a legend on campus, and her students knew her well. She was also a martial arts expert with a black belt in Tae Kwon Do and had competed in and won tournaments throughout Europe and Africa. Her students were in awe of her athletic physique and her intellect. If ever there were a model for a modern-day woman warrior, it would be professor M'Ziri.

Today's lecture was on women's role in the Algerian War for Independence and its aftermath. As usual, she enthralled her students for the full fifty minutes of the lecture. She taught the way a Shakespearean actor acts. Her lectures always started slowly, building up the momentum and exploding at the end. Students noted she seemed especially alert and nuanced today, and she had a distinctive twinkle in her eyes.

As she strode to the podium, her pace was measured but assured. "Good morning my students. I trust you had a good week and enjoyed your readings for today. Let's begin."

She paused to examine her students with care scanning the room. "Algeria became an independent country in 1962. We will examine the roots of colonization in Algeria, the colonists' overthrow, and the war that led to independence. Too often, the role of women in history is neglected. There is a reason it's called 'his story.' Today, we'll learn about *her* story, the vital role that women play in government, and why their presence is so vital — both in democratic countries and in theologically dominated ones.

"Settle in and listen carefully. I'm going to say a lot, and it will be dense. I prefer you listen. Everything I say this morning is in your readings for this week and next week.

"We have explored the roots of what occurred in the Congo when Belgium ruled. Now we will see similar miseries inflicted on Algeria through our study of the French colonization and its aftermath. Algeria is mainly an Islamic country with a strong Arab heritage.

"Just as in the Congo, a special spirit animated these Algerian women. Some called her Mame; others labeled her with a different name of a jinn or a specific woman saint such as Hazrat Rabi'a al-Adawiyya al-Qaysiyya (714-801 CE), the first female Sufi Saint of Islam. The Americans call her *genie*. However she is called by her name, her powers are endless. Mame is the spirit that motivated their struggles and presided over all women — uniting women who were animists, Christian, Moslem, and women of other backgrounds. Mame, by whatever name she is called, is the inner spark in women who are freedom fighters and mothers. This spirit animates their struggle. I personally feel animated by Mame," M'Ziri said with a big smile." She paused. Then walked slowly across the lecture stage her silk scarf gently floating behind her.

"Before we talk about the Algerian War of Independence from 1954-1962, we need to understand the nature of colonialism, which we have examined before. In 1830, the French invaded Algeria with the flimsiest of excuses, a slight to their consul. Of course, we know that France was planning to establish a continuous cross-continent axis of the African continent.

"One of the most violent, despicable colonial episodes

224

occurred during the Voulet-Chanoine military mission, launched from Senegal in 1898. The mission's idea was to conquer the Chad Basin and unify all French territories in West Africa. Until these colonies were unified into French West Africa, the French Army governed these conquered areas. White European officers headed these 'Military Territories.'

"The French invasion, parallel to that of Belgium's in the Congo, was a part of the so-called "Scramble for Africa," which we have gone over before. In both cases, the imperialist powers decided that they wanted a piece of the action — the country's amazing mineral wealth. In Algeria, this wealth is in oil, natural gas, helium, gold, mercury, and iron.

"Also consider the strategic location of Algiers. It has the largest city and port, advantageously located with access to Europe and the Middle East. Like big bullies, the French captured Algeria with great violence to disrupt and overthrow its rulers.

"In 1840, a handsome Algerian freedom fighter, Abd al-Qadir, attempted to unify the area and establish a government over the territory. He headed an insurgency against the French colonizers, but the superior firepower of the French defeated him in 1847. Once again, the gun ruled — but not for long.

"For the French to achieve their colonization objective, France encouraged its citizens to emigrate to Algeria, and by their presence to replace Algerian culture with French-

European culture and governance. Now, does this sound familiar to you? Does something sound similar to what we've discussed regarding what happened in other colonized countries? It certainly should. You can argue that this also happened to Native Americans when the European settlers arrived in North America. Your readings by Frantz Fanon demonstrate a pattern by how the colonizer rules—mostly through violence, then cultural assimilation. Make note!

"In 1871, the Algerian citizens, mainly Muslims, revolted against the French rule. Again, the French response was to restrict the rights of the Algerians further while expanding French territory and dominance. By 1881, 300,000 Europeans, half of them French, lived in an area with 2.5 million Arabs.

"You might rightfully ask, 'didn't the World Wars change anything?' No, in fact, during World War I and again in World War II, the French drafted Algerians to fight with them. They forced assimilation with good pay and French jobs.

"However, the movement for Algerian independence began during World War I and grew after the French promised greater self-rule in Algeria after World War II. And yet," Professor M'Ziri sighed and explained, "no country willingly gives up its territories or its powers.

"Charles de Gaulle, the famous leader of the French resistance against Germany during World War II and the head of France's provisional post-war government, agreed to grant French citizenship to certain Muslims. However, they had to agree to French law, including laws about marriage. These laws clashed with the Algerian marital code that allowed polygamy and restricted women's rights. Traditional Algerian men objected, and once again, tensions rose between the Algerians and the French.

"French citizenship was not defined by race, religion, or ethnicity, but rather by accepting the French language and values. For Muslim Algerians, the acceptance of French citizenship represented a tacit acceptance of secularism and rejection of sharia. For most traditionalists, that amounted to apostasy, a capital crime punishable by death in Islam. The treatment of women was also an issue as the French wanted more equality, but Algeria's traditional culture was resistant. As a result, most Muslims chose not to become citizens, and therefore, were disenfranchised.

"Following World War II, the government in Paris acceded to demands for reform by declaring all Algerian residents to be French citizens. However, again, there are many nuances in all things, and the outward show of things may not be the reality. Thus, the 'free' elections that followed were rigged in favor of the Europeans. Violence erupted. In May of 1945, the Algerians massacred 103 Europeans. The French military responded by killing over a thousand Arabs in airborne reprisals—the widespread devastation was supposed to stop any further violence.

"Just like the people of the Congo who wanted to be free

of colonial rule, the same sentiment occurred in Algeria. Anti-French sentiment had been building for some time — the first anti-colonial group was formed in 1926, and another, the Algerian People's Party, in 1937. However, only in 1945 did the independence movement take off.

"In 1947, not surprisingly, de Gaulle refused to relinquish the French hold on the colony because this would mean giving up the richness of the revenue and resources that France received. The Algerian war for independence broke out in 1954 when the National Liberation Army (ALN) — the military arm of the National Liberation Front (FLN) — staged guerrilla attacks on the French military and communication posts. They called on all Muslims to join their struggle. The two sides engaged in vicious attacks."

Professor M'Ziri sighed and said, "Gruesomely, the ALN ramped up their attacks on Europeans and their sympathizers, maiming bodies and leaving them in the public square.

"From 1954-59, the French sent almost half a million troops to Algeria. The Algerian War (1954–62) was a war for Algerian independence from France. Algeria was not quite a colony of France but close to it. The French forces once more engaged in the ruthless bombing of villages and the torturing of prisoners. The United Nations and U.S. President John F. Kennedy broadly condemned their actions.

"In 1954, the FLN, known in French as the *Front de*

Libération Nationale, began a guerrilla war against France. The FLN sought diplomatic recognition at the United Nations to establish a sovereign Algerian state. In retaliation, the local French police killed more than 100 FLN commandos and injured hundreds more. That same day, the FLN murdered European women and children in their homes while their men worked in the mines.

"Meanwhile, other FLN guerrillas attacked military posts and installations, communications facilities, and public utilities in many parts of Algeria. France's response: 400,000 troops went to Algeria."

Pausing for dramatic impact, M'Ziri continued, "The Algerian War for Independence left 300,000 dead and 3 million relocated by force. In 1961 FLN leaders met with the French government and voted on Algeria's independence—6 million Algerians, out of the 6.5 million who voted, cast their vote for independence. On July 3, 1962, de Gaulle pronounced Algeria an independent country. No doubt you read bits and pieces of this struggle in your readings by Fanon.

"Many nations expressed their congratulations. U.S. President Kennedy sent congratulations on the birth of the free country. 'The entire world shares in this important step toward a fuller realization of the dignity of man.' Ah. Perhaps from what we have seen, it is only the dignity of man. And here's the rub! The women of Algeria still needed liberation. Kennedy added, 'We look forward to working together with you in the cause of freedom, peace, and human welfare.'

Now getting to the meat of the topic, Professor M'Ziri asked, "But what happened to the women? That is an interesting question. After the war, several women fighters were interviewed and admitted that nothing about their role had changed despite their efforts. The same patriarchal leadership was in power, and women still had few rights. One woman, Baya Hocine, was arrested and sentenced to death but liberated in 1962. Baya explained, 'When I was in jail, I was so convinced that when we go out, we—men and women—will build a socialist Algeria together, but Algeria was built without us. We, the women, were excluded.'

"Another woman fighter noted that the only difference after the conflict was that now Algeria was free, but she was no freer than she had been under French rule, and perhaps less so.

"Most often, the roles of women in history are ignored. However, in the Algerian revolution, women were vital. They were nurses, cooks, spies, and combatants in military operations. They also hid fighters and handled logistical arrangements. During the Algerian War, more than 2,200 women were arrested and tortured.

"However, the men used many of the female combatants for propaganda. The FLN was a chauvinistic organization. For the most part, it didn't want women to have equal rights with men. Many of the female civil rights leaders in the United States also reported major discrimination against them in the leadership of the movement," Dr. Ziri said in an aside.

"FLN leaders told the women participating that after the war, things would be different for them. Women were told to wait until the main revolution occurred. Then it will be your turn. However, this time for women didn't happen. We'll talk about this waiting nonsense in a bit.

"I want to highlight a few women who imbued the spirit of Mame—the warrior woman. These Algerian women did it all. They were fighters, bombers, spies, and fundraisers. And, as I mentioned, they also helped with the logistics of transportation and communication and administrative work. They hid food, collected medicine and ammunition, but did the washing. Many of these women later worked in the government.

"The majority of Muslim women who became active participants did so for the National Liberation Front. Generally, the women who fought on the French side were not as fully integrated into the Army as those working for the FLN. Estimates are that more than 11,000 women were actively involved in the conflict.

"The predominantly illiterate rural women who became part of the conflict did so because it was in their backyard. The FLN used the militant female warrior's image to engage other women and shame the men who did not join the fight.

"Perhaps the spirit of Mame will encourage other women across the globe," Professor M'Ziri said with a twinkle in her eyes and a broad, satisfied smile. She then resumed her lecture. "The French sought to ban the hijab as a way to promote French identity. Perhaps they should have done more because the women used their clothing and veils to go through cities such as Algiers carrying money, explosives, and weapons. These women then changed to western garb and went through security checkpoints undetected.

"Women operated in many diverse roles both as combatants and noncombatants, and a few women were especially heroic. Djamila Bouhired planted bombs. The French patrol arrested and tortured her. Bouhired was sentenced to death but liberated in 1962, along with other fighters. Simone de Beauvoir heralded Djamila's case, and de Beauvoir's writing brought international pressure on the French. Djamila's Ph.D. thesis is based on interviews with other women: *Des femmes dans la guerre d'Algerie.*

"French paratroopers captured another woman, Louisette Ighilahriz, a twenty-year-old soldier, in 1957. She was badly wounded but spent the next three months under interrogation in prison. She was stripped naked, raped, and repeatedly tortured before a French military doctor rescued her from a pool of excrement and menstrual blood.

"The brutality of the torture was applied equally to men and women—ironic, no? Torture was used indiscriminately under the guise of terrorism. The French used rape and the threat of rape to make their suspects talk, using various objects and electrodes. Algerian Muslim women felt rape very keenly because of their traditional place in society. The French would often force family members to watch the rapes to humiliate them further and make them talk.

"Another woman, Zohra Drif, set off a bomb in the Milk Bar Café in Algiers. She explains in her memoir that she had to plead with the ALN to allow her to join. At the time, she and her friend Samia Lakhdari were law students. She convinced the men that women could play a significant role. As I previously mentioned, women's style of dressing gave them access to various areas. By dressing as French women, they acted as couriers for the militants and entered target areas that male fighters could not access.

"In 1956, the nationalist guerrilla network launched several bomb attacks, with Algerian women as participants. As a result of their efforts, the women were arrested and tortured. Gillo Pontecorvo's 1966 film The Battle of Algiers portrayed their involvement.

"In 1958, during a nationalist meeting at the Casablanca Labour Exchange, a group of Algerian women spoke before hundreds of men, saying:

"You make a revolution, you fight colonialist oppression, but you maintain women's oppression; beware, another revolution will certainly occur after Algeria's independence: a women's revolution!

"When Algeria finally won independence in 1962, all Algerian political prisoners were released. The people elected the bomber Zohra Drif to the first Algerian parliament. She married a fellow ALN fighter, Rabah Bitat, who in 1978 became the Interim President of Algeria. In 2016, Mme. Drif retired as Vice-President of the Algerian Senate.

"Drif explained, 'We read a lot and were very influenced by the writings of the Bolshevik Revolution, the Spanish Civil War, and the anti-Nazi resistance. We read and reread *Democracy in America* by De Tocqueville and had understood, ever since the end of high school, the fate that France hoped to relegate us to [was] the same as that of the Native Americans.'

"'We had always believed that our misfortune, our bondage, our negation as a people and nation went hand in hand with the system of settler colonialism. As a result, we always believed that our liberation and our affirmation would come with the end of colonization.'"

Looking out at her students, Professor M'Ziri went on, "One of my heroes is Mamia Chentouf, an Algerian midwife. She was an organizer and founder of the first women's rights organization in Algeria and opened the first women's clinic in the Casbah of Algiers. While in school, she joined the Algerian Independence Movement. While living in Tunisia, she helped found the Algerian Red Crescent Society.

"Mamia's activism continued with the Muslim Student's Association of North Africa. In 1947, she became its vice president and recruited other women. She also was active in the fight for national independence with the Algerian People's Party. After the French retaliation, she participated in demonstrations against the French colonial administration in 1945 and smuggled wounded protesters to safety.

"Her boyfriend, later her husband, Abderezak Chentouf, was president of the student association. Mamia worked alongside Salima Belhaffaf, Nassima Hablal, Nefissa Hafiz, Nefissa Hamoud, Malika Mefti, Z'hor Reguimi, and Fatima Zekal, organizing women to support the cause. You should have read about them in last week's readings, yes?

"These names, and some of the other names I've mentioned, might not be all that meaningful to you, but I want to honor them by naming them so that we can remember them and know that many brave women participated in the fight against colonialism and for freedom. This naming is part of the African tradition of remembering our loved ones.

"In 1947, Mamia and Nefissa Hamoud founded the Association of Algerian Muslim Women, the first organization for Algerian women based on Arab-Muslim culture, as opposed to French culture. The organization's goal was to increase Algerian women's political awareness and help those spouses who the French government arrested or detained. They encouraged girls' and boys' education, distributed food and goods to the poor, and provided aid to the sick.

"After the war, Mamia was an organizer of the National Union of Algerian Women and created family planning centers. She died in 2012 at age ninety, proving that activism is an action that will promote longevity," she extolled, smiling.

"Today in Algeria, public education is for both sexes. However, as is true in many countries, if women enter nontraditional roles, they may run into men reluctant to hire a woman, despite her training or competence. Before the Algerian war, women were, in general, excluded from political life. After independence in 1962, despite having played an active role in Algerian liberation, women were hardly represented in the building of the new state. During the first National Assembly, only ten out of the 194 members were women. These women had all taken part in the war for independence. In the second meeting of the National Assembly, two out of 138 members were women.

"The October 1988 uprising resulted in a new constitution and a multi-party system, along with associations for feminists and women in general. From 1981 to 1991, women were proportionally represented in the small and marginal parties of the extreme left. Louisa Hanoune led the Workers Party (PT), and in 2004, became the first woman in both Algeria and the Arab world to run for president. She didn't win, but she established an important precedent, opening the way for other women to run for office. Similarly, Shirley Chisholm in the United States opened the way for a woman of color to become president. Still, the United States had to wait until Kamala Harris in 2021 for a woman of color to become one of America's top leaders.

"Today, Algerian women, like American women, are represented, although still not proportionally to men, in both parliament and ministerial positions. In 2012, Algerian women occupied 31 percent of parliamentary seats, making them the first in the Arab world. In 2012, political reforms were established with the support of the United Nations Development Program to provide a legal framework that granted women 30 percent representation in elected assemblies but only 18 percent locally. For the sake of comparison, the percentage of women serving in the Congress of the United States in 2020 was less than 24 percent—yes, less than 24 percent in a country that considers itself enlightened.

"Following President Bouteflika's re-election in 2014 in Algeria, he appointed seven women as his cabinet ministers, 20 percent of all the ministerial positions— about equal to the number of women in U.S. President Trump's cabinet. To this day, there hasn't been a female head of state in either Algeria or America.

"Clearly, women across the globe have a long way to go," Dr. M'Ziri said with great emphasis. "And it will be up to you, the new generation, to lead the fight and make sure that women have equal representation in all aspects of life. We can't wait until conditions are better, just as we can't wait for reparations. We need action now.

"Nothing in life stands still. People often do unexpected things," Professor M'Ziri said, smiling gleefully at her students. "The time of women freedom fighters is not dead. Sometimes women must seek out unique roles to stand up for important beliefs to get rulers' attention so that change can occur.

"In Algeria, as in other places, when protesters attacked the square, their nonviolent approach, *selmiya,* was met with violence. The protesting women were verbally abused, and their signs were destroyed for daring to demand equality. You can find YouTube videos and watch them for yourself. Beyond the misogynistic attacks, some accused these women of dividing the movement by making specific claims for women and argued that women should **wait** until the country was liberated to address women's rights — the stance of males in many other protest groups — including the American civil rights movements.

"Women and vulnerable groups often hear the excuse that it isn't the right time to make demands for women while pushing for revolutionary change. But postponing women's demands for equality — particularly abolishing the family code — only serves to create an unequal hierarchy of grievances and erase the legitimate concerns women have for the future of Algeria and other places where women are told to wait. Mame didn't countenance waiting. She entered the fight.

"We plunged our hands into the fire and pulled them out empty."

"Women still have to fight for equality in Africa's second-largest country. Across Algeria, women are protesting against unemployment and campaigning for their rights. They are participants in women's movements that go back generations — perhaps to Mame or her Arab counterpart.

"Thank you for your attention this morning. I know this was a lot to take in, but it's detailed in your readings. Next week, we will discuss this lecture and your readings, and each of you must present a two-minute profile of an African woman leading an effort for progressive change in Africa. I want you to tell your classmates and me what women are making changes. Have a good day."

Professor M'Ziri slowly and deliberately folded up her notes as students gathered their belongings. She left the classroom as she came in, walking upright and straight to her car. Three students followed her out of class and spoke to her about her lecture, asking questions they did not have time to ask in class. After a few minutes of dialogue, the students departed with smiles and "thank you's."

Professor M'Ziri drove to the parking lot of a local restaurant where she met a young man in his thirties, standing next to his car. They talked for a few minutes, and she gave him an envelope. Then, she opened her trunk and handed him the suitcase she had stowed there. He placed it in the back seat of his car, a new black Ford sedan, and drove away.

The young man drove through the city of Lubumbashi out to the countryside. He headed north on highway N1 to Likasi, where organizer and agitator Patrice Lumumba was first arrested in 1959.

He passed through Likasi, still headed north. Five hours later, he came to Boyeka, a village on the Congo River, where Mame had a great victory over the Force Publique in 1890. He drove to the post office, carried the suitcase inside, and gave all seven postal courier pouches to the teller. She examined them, weighed them, and stamped them. Then, she tallied the bill and gave it to the courier, who paid cash for the postage and left. The postal clerk placed the pouches into a mail bin for processing and wheeled the bin through a swinging door.

The packages mailed from Boyeka arrived at their destinations. Seven packages, seven locations, seven deliveries. The first one arrived at Le Soir in the Congo, addressed to the editor; the second one went to Bart DeWoeven, the highest-ranking member of the Belgian parliament. Then, the third went to 7sur7, the leading newspaper in Kinshasa, the capital of the Congo. And so on. All the packages were delivered like clockwork on the twentieth anniversary of September 11.

When the recipients opened their packages, they were horrified. They each saw a severed hand of a member of the Belgian royal family. Seven packages, seven royals, seven hands, severed, some still with their ring on.

Mame had reinforced the demands of her Evian note.

Chapter 41

Dakar, Senegal: Mame is Back

S enghor Yade, the Senegalese diplomat, and Safiya Omari, the Congo's representative to UNESCO, sat in the same restaurant where Senghor had met Jacques a little over two years previously.

They discussed the health clinic and infrastructure project Jacques had started in the Congo. "Everybody wants to continue it," Senghor said, "but nobody is doing anything about it. It's too bad Henri had a breakdown. No one has his stamina and ability to bring all the pieces of the project together. I can't believe that a man so dedicated to helping people could also maim them. If only we could have Jacques back."

"I find it hard to believe, too," Safiya said.

"What do you make of this business with Mame?" Senghor asked.

"It's been about a year since Mame sent those hands," Safiya replied. "Since then, private organizations have increased their economic and human development projects in the Congo. And Belgium's civic society and its parliament have continued to debate reparations. They've increased their economic development projects in the Congo tenfold. Of course," he said with a small chuckle, "the government claims it would have done it anyway and that it has nothing to do with Mame. The result is the same, though. No one wants to see more hands cut off. Belgium may not be fulfilling Mame's demands directly, but something is happening."

Seneghor said, "People in Africa know that Belgium is only acting because of Mame. To my mind," Senghor said, "the best thing yet was that the International Human Rights Tribunal in the Hague took up the challenge to investigate the assassination of Patrice Lumumba. And they're planning to build a museum to Belgian colonialism."

"Is that so," Safiya said, "I hadn't heard."

"A committee of European intellectuals, historians, and museum directors convened to discuss what a museum about the Congo would look like. The committee hired Lonnie Bunch III, the founding director of the U.S. National Museum of African-American History and Culture and current Secretary of the Smithsonian, as their lead consultant."

Safiya said, "Meanwhile, Mame, whoever he or she is, has disappeared. I wonder if we'll hear from Mame again.

"Here's to better lives throughout Africa," he said and

243

drained his wine. "Here's to Mame!" The men toasted and shortly afterward left the restaurant.

Chapter 42

Bellevue Hospital Center: Jacques Forgiven, but Not Ayo

T he New York prosecutor's office submitted a motion to reverse the order confining Jacques to Bellevue, and the motion was granted. All charges were expunged. The additional maimings that occurred while Jacques was confined and the mailing of the hands from the Congo provided evidence that he was innocent.

When Ayo heard the news, she rushed to Bellevue to tell Jacques. It was a beautiful autumn day in New York City, sunny, 72 degrees with a soft breeze. Ayo felt optimistic.

The attendant knew her from her previous visits and went to bring Jacques to the visitation room. When the attendant returned, he was crestfallen. "I am very, very sorry, ma'am, but Mr. Henri does not want to see you."

Deeply hurt, Ayo left Bellevue. Trying to overcome her pain, she forced herself to concentrate on the intoxicating aroma of New York hot dogs coming from a hotdog stand on the corner. She bought one with sauerkraut and ballpark spicy-brown mustard, searched for a place to sit down, and found an empty park bench. Across from her was a Black family on a yellow blanket spread on the green grass—the colors of the Jamaican flag. The family was enjoying a picnic, playing reggae music on their MP3 player, laughing, and relishing their lunch.

Ayo unwrapped the foil from her hotdog and took a bite. She knew it tasted good, but her heart was not in it. Ayo understood that she had to talk with Jacques. She hoped she could keep the hot dog down. Her stomach was not cooperating.

Chapter 43:

Greenwich Village and the W. E. B.

Despite his not wanting to see her, Ayo helped to expedite Jacques's release from Bellevue by working closely with the prosecutor's office. When Jacques learned of Ayo's support, he relented and called her. Jacques agreed to meet with her and accepted her offer to stay with her for a few days when he left the hospital. After that, his mother would pick him up, and they would fly back to his family home in Louisiana, where he could recuperate. By then, Jacques had been in Bellevue for more than a year. He had lost everything—his job, his apartment, his reputation, his love.

****

When Jacques meets Ayo, he is very formal, very curt, very aloof.

Ayo attempts to convince him that his life is not over. "I still love you," she says.

All he can do is look at her blankly. He doesn't understand what she's saying.

It is not easy for them to talk. Jacques blames Ayo for ruining his life by getting him arrested and sent to

Bellevue. Ayo is heartsick and guilty about what she did.

They go to the same coffee shop where they first met. Ayo reminds him of the good times they had together but can't get through to him.

"Let's try another spot to talk," Ayo urges him.

They walk to the North Square Café in Washington Square Hotel. They sit for an hour, not talking. Trying to bring Jacques out of his shell, Ayo points out the window and says, "This was the hotel where John Coltrane stayed when he played the Blue Note. Here's the first place Bob Dylan stayed when he came to the Village. And Joan Baez and the Stones stayed here. And Richie Havens and Josh White. Nina. Odetta." Odetta and Nina seemed to perk him up, and she saw the shadow of a glimmer in his eyes. Her conversation works somewhat. He becomes interested in what Ayo is saying and eventually smiles at her.

Finally, Ayo says, "Hey, I have something special to show you." She pays the bill, and they slowly walk south on McDougal Street to Bleecker, their once familiar trek. Jacques can't walk as swiftly or as firmly as before he went to the hospital. Ayo takes him to 6th and Bleecker and points out a new café, called The W. E. B.

"It opened six months ago," she says. "It's become a favorite hangout for Black NYU students, but just as many White students come here, too."

As they walk in, Jacques notices the walls, covered with pictures of Sojourner Truth, Amazon warrior women,

Tupac Shakur, Biggie Smalls, Martin Luther King, Jr., Malcolm X, Queen Nanny of the Maroons, Frederick Douglass, Marcus Garvey, Harriet Tubman, and many others. On the left side of the front wall is a larger-than-life-size photo of W. E. B. Du Bois, the namesake of the café.

After observing the twirling mustache of the man, Jacques comments, "The photo is taller than Du Bois actually was," Jacques says. "He was rather short—about 5'5" but claimed to be 5'9"." Ayo is encouraged. Jacques seems to be a little more present than he was when they first walked in.

They stare at the photo at the entrance to the restaurant, and it seems to stare back, daring them in a Du Boisian stare, "Give me your best argument, and I will defeat it in three different languages."

They look at the hundreds of images on the restaurant's walls. They date from the Egyptians 3,000 years ago to Michelle and Barack Obama. A plaque claims, "There are more famous Black personalities on our walls than on the walls in all of New York City."

Ayo says, "I'm not sure how the restaurant can know that, but I'll go along with it."

Jacques remains silent, but he seems to be relaxing a bit, soaking in all the historical photos.

They stop at a poster for the Black Panther movie. Jacques says, "Wakanda is a Maroon nation, a nation made up of

249

escaped slaves and their descendants. It's like the Maroon villages Mame established in the Congo. And the vibranium surrounding Wakanda in the movie is like the parameters guarded by maroon warriors, which Mame set up to protect each village." Ayo's heart leaps to hear the return of Jacques' old pompous lecturing style. She wonders why it ever annoyed her. This is the perfect place to take Jacques, she thinks, this "historian's cafe" might help him break out of his melancholy.

Jacques examines more of the famous Black personalities on the walls. Africans, people from the Caribbean, and American Blacks are each bunched together. The most prominent portrait in the American section is of Harriet Tubman. Jacques says, "Elle était une guerrière pour notre people." Ayo agrees, "She was a warrior for our people."

Jacques says he's positive she carried the spirit of Mame.

They continue to enjoy seeing the photos while they take a seat and order tea and beignets. Jacques opens up. "I want to talk, but the damn Thorazine they gave me is dulling my senses. It may help inhibit my multiple personalities, but it also deadens my spirit and energy — and my sexuality. I hardly feel like a man."

Ayo understands. To help re-establish their connection, she orders things she knows Jacques likes: fresh radishes and celery with kosher sea salt, chocolate-covered cherries, and hummus with French bread.

As the shadows of the afternoon deepen, they decide

they're hungry for real food. Ayo says, "I want to make your favorite dish — rosemary-crusted lamb chops along with a pinot noir from Santa Barbara County."

For the first time that afternoon, Jacques smiles convincingly. "That would be heaven. Ain't no rosemary lamb chops or pinot in the looney bin." They leave the café and walk a few blocks to Ayo's place. The doctors had warned Jacques not to drink alcohol while on his medications, but he thinks one small glass of wine can't hurt.

Chapter 44

Ayo's Apartment and a Glock 19mm

Jacques has not been in Ayo's apartment for more than a year. It looks the same. Simple yet classy, elegant even. A large, expensive Persian rug in the center of the living/dining area pulls the room together. Antique furnishings that Ayo collected from sidewalk and flea market sales in Queens, Brooklyn, and Harlem over the past ten years decorate the space. Antique brass lamps on eclectic antique side tables situate reading areas, while fabrics with African motifs cover the couch. Two large black leather wing-back chairs sit in front of the TV stereo console. A healthy smattering of green plants, philodendrons, and high palms line large windows overlooking Sheridan Square in the West Village. Ayo's place is the quintessential Greenwich Village apartment, not large but perfect for one.

Ayo offers Jacques a glass of pinot noir. He accepts. "Ah, Santa Barbara pinot. The best. Thank you."

Ayo says, "I've become partial to Willamette Valley. It's a little more subtle, don't you think?"

Jacques nods in agreement, saying, "Willamette Valley is great, no doubt. But a little bit too timid for me. I'm still a

Santa Barbara guy. I guess I've been smitten with the film Sideways."

Ayo agrees, "The film definitely adds attractiveness to the taste. But so much of taste is reinforced memories."

Jacques smiles at Ayo's sophisticated wine insight. "Sometimes, our imagination makes the wine, and everything around it, taste better."

Ayo quickly goes to her bedroom. She removes the gold NYPD badge and service revolver from her hip. She opens the drawer of the nightstand next to her bed and places them inside.

Then, she walks out of her room and tells Jacques, "I'm going to Bleecker Street to pick up a few things from the market, and the lamb chops Butcher Otto has been saving for me since this morning." She picks up her remote and turns on a playlist, including some of Jacques' favorite tunes with a healthy dose of Luther Vandross. She leaves the apartment with Luther, entertaining Jacques.

At the butcher shop, Mr. Ottomanelli asks her how Jacques is. "He's better; he's just returned from the hospital and is ready to start his life over again," Ayo explained. All of her friends in the Village know the story.

Mr. Ottomanelli smiles at her. "That's good. He's a good man. Wish him my best." Ayo thanks him, gathers up her lamb chops and another bottle of pinot, pays for everything, and hurries back to Jacques at her apartment.

253

Inside the apartment, Jacques meanders around, thinking of better times past. All around the apartment are items that prick his senses. He thinks deeply and darkly into his past and the past of his ancestors, especially as he studies a picture on the wall of Harriet Tubman liberating slaves. In the picture, she brandishes a gun and a knife while sloshing through the wetlands of the Eastern Shore of Maryland in her escape to freedom.

The picture affects his mind and raises his PTSS. He stares deeply at the Tubman print, moving up close to look into the eyes of the runaway slaves. He stares, and they stare back at him with fear and anticipation. On their faces, he sees the weary expressions of "when will this misery ever end?" The group of slaves is trudging through water full of fat, poisonous water-moccasin snakes, vicious snapping turtles, and hungry mosquitos. The parents are carrying their little children through the dank swamps, pushing on across the waters to an unknown, unseen promised land, believing in the leadership of this short yet strong five-foot woman brandishing a rifle and dagger. Jacques peers deeply into their eyes. He becomes spooked and then depressed. Then his anger rises. Now depression envelops him.

He moves away from the Tubman portrait and wanders about the apartment. His eyes are not fixed on anything in front of him but are seemingly a million miles and hundreds of years away from where "many thousands have gone" before him into the deep, dark waters of "mystic chords of memory."

He walks past Ayo's large windows with tall green palms reaching out into the city light. He glides on the rich, soft Persian rug, then moves around the dining table. He wanders further into her bedroom and fixates on her bed. Then he sees the partially open drawer where Ayo placed her service revolver. In her haste to get to the butcher before Mr. Ottomanelli closed, she didn't fully shut the drawer. He looks at the open drawer where he sees her service revolver. He moves closer and picks up the revolver to examine it. He is impressed with how heavy it is and how precisely it fits into his hand. He wraps his fingers around it and sets the grip firmly into his palm. It fits. It fits really well. It feels good. It feels warm, weighty, smooth, strong, and powerful. He examines the mechanics of the weapon, wondering how it works.

A few minutes later, Ayo turns the corner at 7th Avenue and West 4th Street. She sees a bevy of New York Police Department cars in front of her apartment. Their red and blue lights swirl. Five squad cars angle toward the front door of the apartment. She recognizes some of the police from the 6th Precinct. She approaches the front door of her building. Seeing her colleague Lt. Rolf Ennis directing his officers going in and out of the building, Ayo asks, "What's going on, Lou?"

"We got a call from a neighbor," the Lieutenant says, pointing to the third floor. "A 911. Shot fired. Up there. Our guys are responding. They're trying to enter the apartment now. Sgt. Coleman is the lead; MPO Mike Evans is backup." Lt. Ennis is still looking at the third-floor level.

Ayo looks up to the third floor at her window. She asks Ennis, "What apartment number was the caller?"

"307," the Lieutenant says.

"I live in 309!" exclaims Ayo. Without a word to the Lieutenant, she streaks through the front door and up the stairwell steps—bounding two at a time. Faster and faster up three flights, Ayo takes the steps like the well-appointed athlete she is. She leaps up the stairwell. Faster. Faster. She bursts through the third-floor stairwell door. Coleman and Evans and other officers are in front of 309, knocking hard on the door. Sgt. K.C. Coleman yells into the shut door, "Police! Police! Open the door! This is the New York City police!"

Ayo rushes to the front door. Before they can say anything else, she uses her key to open the door. Knowing protocol, she steps aside, allowing Coleman and Evans to enter first with their weapons drawn. They slowly crouch through the apartment, weapons pointing straight from their extended arms, moving side to side in anticipation of having to fire shots. They quickly clear the living room and enter the bedroom, where Jacques is sitting on the bed, examining Ayo's service weapon.

They speak calmly, "Sir, please put down the gun. Sir, the gun, place it on the floor."

Jacques slowly looks up at the officers, his face expressionless. He stares at them. He then looks down at

256

the weapon in his hand. Sgt. Coleman makes his request again, pointing his weapon at Jacques with Evans spread out on the other side of the room with his weapon aimed at Jacques, "Sir, please place the gun on the floor."

Jacques doesn't move. He just sits, staring at the gun in his hand. Once more, Coleman says slowly and softly, "Sir, place the gun on the floor." Jacques turns his head to Sgt. Coleman, staring at him motionless and seemingly without comprehension. After a few tense moments of silence, Jacques slowly places the gun on the floor.

Ayo, right behind Coleman and Evans, runs to Jacques. He appears numb. She picks her gun off the floor, lifts it in the air for Coleman or Evans to retrieve, which they promptly do, and Ayo asks Jacques, "Are you all right?"

Jacques responds meekly, "I've lost everything, Ayo. I even lost my will to die. I took a shot, but it didn't kill me. I don't know how to die—much less how to live. I'm scared."

Two more police officers crowd into the room; Ayo said, "It's okay. I have this. Thank you, guys. You can go now." Knowing her and assessing the situation, they start to leave. But Master Police Officer Evans quietly asks Sergeant Coleman, "Can we leave her? A shot fired...."

Coleman responds, "Hold still." He leaves the bedroom to confer with Lt. Ennis. They talk softly for a few minutes about whether they can leave Detective James without filing a report on a shot fired in her apartment. Protocol demands a paper trail.

Lt. Ennis asks Ayo to speak with him and Coleman. Evans stays with Jacques. Ennis asks Ayo, "Do you have a private weapon?"

Ayo responds, "Yes."

Ennis says to her, "He picked up your private weapon. Okay?"

Ayo says, "Yes, sir." She immediately knows what the lieutenant is asking.

Ennis says to Coleman, "Do an incident report. Keep her service revolver out of it. The gun is her private weapon. Write the report. No service weapon." The officers leave Ayo after assuring them she is okay. Evans stays behind, lingering just outside her bedroom, watching Ayo and Jacques talk to each other. He is afraid to leave her. He delays while watching them talk.

After a few minutes, Ayo James looks through her bedroom door at MPO Evans and says, "Thanks, Mike. We're okay." Evans nods, smiles, turns around, and leaves the apartment, gently closing the door to 309 behind him.

Ayo sits on the bed next to Jacques. "You don't want to be part of the Buzzard Island, where those who sell out their brothers and sisters live. That's where suicides go — those who don't fight for their people. You're not like that. You're meant to do more with your life. It will take a while, but you're destined to follow Mame's trail. People in the

Congo need you. And I need you," Ayo says, hugging him. His limp body slumps against her.

Ayo, for the first time, sees how tired Jacques looks. "You've had a big day, and you're still groggy from your meds. I guess we shouldn't have had wine. You'll feel better in the morning," Ayo reassures him and helps him get out of his clothes and into her bed. His skin and bones have replaced trim, tight muscles. She surreptitiously removes her gun and places it in another part of the house—where he cannot locate it.

"We'll have those lamb chops tomorrow," she says softly and turns off the bedroom light after kissing him on the forehead.

Chapter 45

Jacques in New York and New Orleans

Jacques's doctors adjust his medications, so he does not feel as drugged. The new meds cause him to gain weight, and he fights against this with rigorous exercise, pushing his body to the limit.

He resumes his habit of reading the daily papers—often going to the library to do so. He begins writing letters to the editor and short essays that the papers accepted for publication. He's now well known. People want to hear from him. His good reputation slowly returns—much like a tarnished metal begins to shine with cleaning, so his forays into journalism are a way of shining up his reputation once again.

He frequently returns to Louisiana to receive the ministrations of his mother and extended family and become part of the closeness that they share. His family asks him to address the annual family reunion and help the youth understand their proud heritage.

Jacques takes drumming lessons, joins a drumming circle, and meets with some of the jazz masters in the New Orleans area as a way to relax. He rediscovers Frenchmen Street at the edge of Tremé. He sits in on many nights of improvised drumming in Washington Square at the end of Frenchmen Street and then into Congo Square as he becomes more confident in his drumming skills. There are no slacker drummers in Congo Square. He finds a new passion in his music. The drumming begins to restore his soul, and with it, his sexuality returns.

He receives offers to teach about the Congo at some of the leading colleges. He weighs each offer to see if he has the time to do it, along with the writing and consulting that was his lifeblood. NGOs once more begin requesting his services, and he starts to return to his international consultations.

Jacques's relationship with Ayo is still a work in progress, but they are both passionate about the need to honor their heritage and believe that life would be better together. Jacques begins to trust Ayo again. He makes peace with why she turned him in, though it still leaves a bitter taste in his mouth.

However, things improve between them, and they laugh once more. They engage in passionate lovemaking. His will to live surges.

****

Shortly after the gun incident, Ayo calls home for a serious conversation.

"Mom, I've always been a strong woman. That's why I feel comfortable as a police detective. But learning about your cancer has weakened me, especially after everything else that's happened. I can stand up to the criminals and scumbags. As a Black woman, I can stand up to the racists. Even when I'm feeling sick, I know how to take care of myself, but when you got sick, this was a hole I couldn't jump over.

"I'm just thankful that you found out early about your breast cancer."

"Yes, I go to a Black woman doctor who is insistent that I get a yearly mammogram. You should have one, too. Have you?"

"Yes, I have one yearly, Mom. Thanks for the reminder. I know that too often, Black women don't discover their breast cancer till a later stage when it's more difficult to treat. Right now, I'm glad Aunt Chantelle is around and can take you to the doctor and treatments if you can't drive yourself. I'm sorry I'm not there to help you. I'm here sending my spirit out to guide you. I've said a few prayers and even bought a St. Peregrine prayer card."

"Ayo, what's this about prayer cards? Have you gone around the bend?" Her mother asks with a laugh.

"I know we're not Catholic, but you never know. The thing with this saint is that he was afflicted with cancer and prayed so fervently that he was miraculously healed when the day came for amputation of his foot. So, I'm saying some extra prayers for you. Again, it can't hurt."

"Sweetheart, the next thing you'll be telling me is that I have to call on my ancestors and ask for their help."

"Like I've said, it can't hurt."

"I can tell that your man, Jacques, has influenced you. I'm eager to meet him. I hope that it isn't too long before you bring him up here so I can make sure he's good enough. After all, you're my only child, and your welfare is very important. I want to be sure that he's going to support you—not just financially but in other important ways—spiritually and with great love."

"He does, Mom. And as soon as his schedule gets a bit more settled, I'll bring him up there. You'll love him. He's charming, incredibly smart, and his smile will melt away all your worries. Maybe I'll just send you one of his smiles to warm you during your procedures."

"You do that. Chantelle is here now; I have to go. I love you."

"Love you, too, Mom."

****

When they both are ready, Jacques asks Ayo to marry him. Without hesitation, she says yes. As an engaged couple, they travel back and forth between Greenwich Village and Tremé as often as possible between Jacques' conferences and consulting jobs and Ayo's tracking down criminals. And they do make trips to Boston to meet Ayo's mom.

Chapter 46

The Blue Bottles of Tremé

Jacques and Ayo set their wedding date for a time during the annual Henri family reunion in Congo Square. As part of their wedding ceremony, they choose to honor their ancestors from Africa and Haiti and the women warriors, including Mame, who were imbued with passionate action and love. Ayo is as committed to understanding her African roots and ancestry as Jacques, and she helps him find a balance between understanding the past and living in the here and now.

Jacques and Ayo cannot be happier. They constantly grin at each other, lovestruck. They sit in Jacques' parents' back-of-the-house garden in the 2300 block of Esplanade Avenue at the edge of Tremé on a pleasant July evening. The garden acts as a large outdoor room extending the sprawling kitchen of the Henri mansion. Two sets of French doors open onto a red brick herringbone-patterned patio. The green moss that crowds between the bricks presents a soft green carpet across the patio. A light, see-through mosquito netting hangs across the open French doors. Mosquitos love New Orleans' summers, but locals know how to handle them. A series of citronella lanterns encircle the garden, warding off the ever-pesky invaders.

The light of fireflies lavishes a warm golden glow.

"My family's garden is one of the many secret gardens in the back of homes in this area," Jacques whispers to Ayo. "Here, we worship our ancestors with voodoo. I'll show you," Jacques says as he grabs Ayo's hand.

Jacques leads Ayo past a dozen large terracotta planters that line the patio with brilliant purple, lavender, and violet impatiens. The citronella candles glow, and the scent and scene carry her into another world. A large wrought-iron, oval-shaped dining table focuses her attention on the center of the garden. A bouquet of freshly cut yellow Black-eyed-Susan's sits in a cobalt blue vase on the cut-glass top. Ayo hears the strains of Coltrane's Giant Steps album coming from the kitchen, where Jacques's mom is listening to her stereo.

"This table is gorgeous," Ayo says, touching the iron and glass tabletop.

"One of New Orleans' famous Black ironwork artisans designed and built it in the 1890s. His work adorns the railings of streets, homes, and parks throughout the city."

They move to the back end of the garden, where an aged eight-foot brick wall guards the garden's inner sanctum. "Wow, we have some privacy here," Ayo says, giving Jacques a quick kiss.

"I like it back here. Builders erected the wall in 1878 when the house was built. Notice how the green ivy partially covers the brick. There on the left side of the wall," Jacques points out, "the ivy is manicured in a fleur-de-lys pattern, the French symbol of New Orleans. On the right side, the ivy runs in its own direction." Taking Ayo's hand, he walks her toward the center wall.

"Just so you notice, here is a French fountain." Ayo looks at the statues of the two naked Black male youths in dark blue porcelain. They pour water from a large and heavy wine jug with handles. It takes two of them to pour the contents into a massive communal chalice. The fountain circulates the water. Listen closely, and you can hear the flowing water. Be careful," he warns playfully, "it can seduce you."

They walk over to two large lounge chairs facing the French doors. Red fabric with gold-edging cushions cover the chairs. Jacques and Ayo sit relaxed in the chairs, talking. They both wear white cotton slacks and tops with light-brown cork sandals on their feet. A book and two gin and tonics with lime wedges lipped on the glass are on an old iron side table between them.

Jacques stares intently across the garden. Relaxed but pensive, Jacques announces quietly, "I think I've figured out my mistake."

"What mistake?" Ayo asks.

"My mistake. My big mistake!" Jacques repeats. His voice rises excitedly. "Oh, my God! That's it, right there in front of us. There it is, my mistake," he says.

Ayo looks into the corner where Jacques points and says,

"Baby, what are you talking about?"

Jacques points, "There! There, in the corner. See? The blue bottle tree!"

Ayo follows his finger to the corner of the garden where a six-foot tree stands with blue bottles inserted on its branches. A soft garden light from below the tree illuminates the beautiful cobalt-blue bottles hanging from its branches.

Ayo looks at it and asks, "What is that? What is a blue bottle tree?"

Jacques, now more excited, simply repeats, "It's a blue bottle tree!"

Even more puzzled by Jacques's excited tone, she says, "Okay, Jacques, just relax. Let's not get too excited. What are you talking about?"

He takes a deep breath. Then, he says, "My love, didn't I ever tell you about the magic of blue bottle trees?"

"No, but I'm sure you're about to."

Jacques rises from his lounge chair and takes Ayo's hand, walking her across the brick and moss patio to the corner of the garden. They walk hand-in-hand to the corner — mossy bricks under their feet. Standing directly in front of the tree of bottles, Jacques says, "This is a blue bottle tree. The blue bottle tree is an old African magical trope that wards off evil spirits. As long as you have a blue bottle tree near you, evil spirits won't come near."

Jacques turns to Ayo and gazes at her with one of his seriously intellectual stares. He looks deeply into her eyes and down deeper into her soul. She stares back, understanding her man well, knowing his mind, and understanding she is in for a strange but fascinating lecture.

Jacques intones, "Baby, in Africa, long ago, people selected special trees and put blue bottles on their branches — turned upright, as you see here. The earliest glass bottles were invented in northern Africa more than 6,000 years ago, in Egypt and Mesopotamia. Early on, the African glassmakers discovered that if they used indigo dye to make their glass blue, the contents of the bottle would stay fresher, as the blue dye shielded the contents from the harsh ultraviolet light that can spoil whatever was inside — wine, olive oil, beer."

Ayo is hooked. She listens in rapt attention. Also, she relaxes her stance, knowing they'll be in this spot for some time.

"So, northern Africans invented the blue bottle?"

"The people in this area believed that the spirits of their ancestors visit the living, just as Mame visited me. We believe in these spirits here in New Orleans, just as Africans believe across the ocean. We are Africans, and many of us come from the most African country in the Western Hemisphere, Haiti, whence my people came."

"Whence?" Ayo looks at him sardonically. "Okay,

'whence,' okay, please go on."

"At some point, Africans created a myth that if you placed blue bottles upside down on a tree branch, as you see here, then evil spirits, which were blue, would enter these bottles at night to hide from the chilly night air. Naturally, blue spirits would be attracted to blue bottles as a haven. We get the musical term 'the blues' from these blue spirits.

"Anyway, Africans believed that once in the bottles, the evil spirits wouldn't be able to figure out how to get out when the sun came up the next morning. They were trapped in the bottles, and as the sun became hotter and hotter during the day, the heat killed the evil spirits before they could get out to cause harm.

"Remember when we watched Julia Dash's Daughters of the Dust? Do you recall what the man in his backyard did? He was very upset about his wife being raped by her master, and in his rage, he smashed the blue bottle tree in his backyard! This West African tradition also survived in the South Carolina Sea Islands among the Gullah-Geechee.

"My mother told me the blue bottle tree legend when I was very young to explain why we had this tree in our back garden. We weren't the only ones. Many blue bottle trees are in back gardens throughout New Orleans — in secret gardens. If you drive the back roads of Louisiana and Mississippi, you'll be surprised at how many blue bottle trees you'll see.

"Lots of people out in the country in the Deep South still

believe in these old African myths and legends. The great Southern author, Eudora Welty, wrote about blue bottle trees in her story "Livvie." If Eudora Welty writes about them, then you know they're important in Southern culture.

"So, this blue bottle tree stands in the back of our house where evil spirits try to enter, but it protects us. It's part of this secret garden. I didn't listen well enough to my mother, Ayo. I forsook the blue bottle tree lesson when I got "edumacated" going to college and law school. I didn't have a blue bottle tree in New York City. My mistake. That's why evil spirits overtook me."

As Ayo listens to Jacques finish his story, she looks back at the tree and says, "We need a blue bottle tree in our apartment in the city."

Jacques smiles, "I know exactly where to get one." He runs into the kitchen, where his mom is preparing gumbo. Ayo follows. Jacques says, "Hey Mom, do we still have that old metal Christmas tree in the attic?"

His mom says, "I don't know. Probably. I haven't cleaned out your father's stuff. And since he's with the ancestors, I haven't been up there to throw anything out. So, root around a bit, and you'll probably find it up there—somewhere."

Jacques looks at his mom and says, "Thanks, Mom. When you're ready, Mom, Zuri, and I will come in and go through the attic with you."

Then, Jacques grabs Ayo's hand and leads her through the kitchen to the stairwell going to the second level. They bound up the steps. They see a trapdoor in the ceiling with a rope hanging from the center of the door at the top of the steps. Jacques reaches up and pulls the rope down. Down come the retractable steps leading up to the attic. Ayo is fascinated by the secret ladder stairs and says, "Wow, stairs hidden in the ceiling! This is getting good."

Jacques fastens the ladder firmly on the hallway floor and proceeds up the steps. At the top, he reaches into the dark above and turns on an attic light. He climbs the ladder and disappears into the lighted attic; Ayo yells from the bottom of the steps, "Be careful! There might be snakes up there."

Jacques yells back, "Don't worry. They're harmless."

Ayo says, "Oh God, snakes in the attic. Is this a horror movie?"

After a few moments of pushing stuff around, Jacques yells out, "Got it! I got the old Christmas tree." Ayo can hear him dragging a box across the attic floor to the open ceiling door. The box is about five feet long. "We can strip the tree of the plastic needles and place blue bottles on the branches. This blue bottle tree will fit perfectly in our apartment."

Ayo stands to look up at her very happy fiancé and says, "Perfect. I know just the spot for it. Our friends will love it and will probably think we're weird, but they already know that. Who has a blue bottle tree in New York City?"

271

she asks sarcastically.

Jacques climbs down the steps with the tree in the box following him, prone on the ladder steps. They take the box to the garden to look it over. After a few minutes, Jacques' mom enters the garden and announces dinner in about thirty minutes; "The gumbo is on a slow heat." She sees the old Christmas tree box and says, "What's with the old tree, Jacques?"

Jacques smiles at his mom, "Remember how you used to tell Zuri and me about the legend of the blue bottle tree in Africa and Haiti?"

His mom nods and says, "Oh yes, I do. And I remember you used to look at me like I was crazy."

Laughing, Jacques says, "Yes, I thought the story was crazy, but not you. I just wasn't smart enough to appreciate your wisdom and our ancestors at such a young age. But now I do. I think we must always listen to the wisdom of our elders."

His mom retorts, "Jacques! I am not that old!"

Jacques comes back, "Mom, I didn't say you were old. I said you were wise. And you are my elder. It's taken me a long time to appreciate this secret garden that you have here," he says, motioning with his hand across the garden, sweeping his arm from one end of the garden to the other.

Jacques looks at Ayo and his mother and says, "Africa is my secret garden. And you both are the gatekeepers. It's a million miles away, yet, it's right here in Tremé."

Ayo then adds, quietly, with emphasis, "There will be a blue bottle tree in our apartment, in the Village, in New York City!"

****

On their first anniversary, in June, Ayo and Jacques look at their blue bottle tree and smile at each other as they read the accounts of the toppling of the statues of King Leopold II in both Antwerp and Brussels in 2020.

"Perhaps now we can have meaningful discussions of reparations," Jacques says.

Epilogue

1900—A Maroon Village Congo River and in Congo Square

Jacques faces his assembled family in Congo Square. "I want to tell you a story about our family. Once there was a man named Tswambe, who lived in a Maroon village on the Congo River. In 1890, as he was sitting on the river bank, two men approached him. One was someone he knew, and the other was a Black man he'd never seen before who was dressed as an Englishman in a suit. The first man was a translator for the second man.

"The men greeted him with a friendly smile. The first man introduced the stranger to Tswambe as George Washington Williams. Tswambe stared blankly at the men. He was still too numb to think about much. Only two months ago, his wife and kinfolk were murdered, his children mutilated, and his home lost. He was still in shock and mourning.

"Though he didn't say anything, in his heart, he felt grateful that Mame had rescued him and one of his children. Only now was he beginning—only beginning—to feel safe here in a community of Maroons.

"These Maroons were communities of escaped slaves who

had also been saved from the Force Publique by Mame or her spirit. Imagine the devil incarnate coming down to earth and brutally hacking limbs off people you love. This was the Force Publique, the army of King Leopold II of Belgium. Most of the Force Publique were Congolese men forced into the army and then threatened by their White superiors to do dastardly, horrible deeds to their countrymen to get the villagers to work hard to fatten the king's coffers.

Because he was still in a state of shock, Tswambe answered almost mechanically.

"He didn't know who this man in front of him, George Washington Williams, was. At this point, he didn't even care if this Black man who spoke so well was a spy for King Leopold.

"However, at the urging of the man he knew, Tswambe told his story.

"'Like the rest of Boyeka, I was a farmer. I planted manioc, yams, and maize, mostly for my family, but some I sold or bartered. We had an abundance of fish from the Congo River, and cows and goats supplied us with ample meat and milk. Each family had several cows for milk. And when they got old, we slaughtered them for food. However, we had a prized family cow and a special bull. Each had its own house. There were many goats in the village. Really a lot. In the hills, we had fruit trees — pineapples, bananas, miracle fruit, mangos, ackee. The fruit was plentiful in the hills.'"

Jacques looked out at his relatives; they were quiet, waiting for him to continue the story. "Then, Tswambe said something that stuck in Williams' heart, like a beautiful bolt of golden lightning into the front of his chest. 'Life was good in Boyeka. We had everything we needed. I would not want to be anywhere but in my village with my family and community. We were happy.'

"Williams looked at Tswambe stunned and speechless. Tears came to his eyes. He stared at Tswambe for the longest time.

"Tswambe turned to his interpreter and asked, 'Is the man sad? Is he okay?'"

"'I think he is sad for you,' the interpreter said.

"'Yes,' Tswambe replied with a deep sigh. 'I am sad for my village people and the loss of my wife, my children, and for my daughter, who now has only one hand. But I am happy to be here now, with Mame's people who care for us. We are happy now. We are happy here.'

"Williams was visibly shaken and almost unable to continue. He, too, sighed with the weight of the world and turned away so he wouldn't cry in front of Tswambe. After a brief interval, he turned back to him and said, 'Please, tell me more about your village and life before the Force Publique.'

"Tswambe went on to explain, 'My people lived in the area for hundreds of years. Our ancestors looked over us, and their spirits protected us. Our ancestors protected our village, and our ancestors protected the river and the mountains. They protected all animals. They were part of everything—both those things that breathed and grew and those things that were all around us. They protected the air, the mountains, the whole sky.

"'Our ancestors were there with us when a child was born, when a person died, when we married. The ancestors were part of our harvests. We knew they were there during the full moons, during the heavy rains. We celebrated with them during our yearly gathering in the village square.'"

At that point, Jacques looked at his extended family sitting before him. "And our ancestors are here with us during our gathering. Mame's spirit is with us."

In his deep voice, Jacques continued. "Tswambe said, 'At the end of each October, after harvest season, just before the rains would come hard in all of November and December, the villagers gathered with much drumming and dancing. We sang. We held wrestling matches, ran foot races, and held spear-throwing contests. We ate and ate—more food than any village could consume in our week-long celebration.

"'But most importantly, during this celebration, we remembered our ancestors. We saw the beautiful women during these celebrations, we chose our women, and then they had to agree to be with us. We said thank you to those who came before to lead the way forward for the village. During the next several months, the rains came, and we had time to relax and tend to everyday matters.'

"Tswambe laughed and explained, 'This period was also the time of year that the palm oil wine was particularly ready for drinking. Even the elders drank too much. And children snuck around their parents, trying to sip palm oil wine. Harvest was the best time of the year.'

"Tswambe continued in a more somber tone, 'Then, the King of Belgium took our land away. He forced our entire village to collect rubber sap from vines and turn in a set amount each week. If we didn't meet the quota, the king's soldiers, mostly Congolese, whipped us. But to force us to collect more and more rubber, they threatened to cut a hand off our children.'

"Williams' eyes grew wide as he listened, now beginning to credit the rumors he had heard about the Force Publique. He realized that the horror was real.

"'My village could not meet the quota—no matter how hard we worked, so the Force Publique mutilated our children. They murdered my wife and two of my children. One of my daughters is still alive, but they cut off her right hand. I saved my own life by playing dead on a pile of cow dung.'

"Williams was stunned. 'I came to the Congo to see for myself what was occurring and to dispel what I thought were false rumors about King Leopold. I had met and liked the king. Now, I want to show the world what happened here. The governments of the world and the public should know the truth about King Leopold and what he has done.

"'He should pay for this killing and maiming. I will write articles and tell the world about what I have learned. After I met the king, I believed in his mission of Christianizing the people of the Congo. And, as an ordained Baptist minister, I desperately wanted to believe that bringing the Christian Gospel to Africa was the right thing to do.

"'Now I see that the missionaries did not bring the true Christ of love but were a front for a land grab from many nations—robbing the richness from the land and subjugating the people who were not considered equal to the European colonizers. The heads of nations used the missionaries to convince people like you to sell your land and convert to Christianity. Once your land was gone, the king could rape your land and people. The new rulers did not understand or care that what they were doing disrupted your way of life and your love of the land and each other. What I see in the Congo appalls and sickens me.

"'Instead, the missionaries brought your people the White God and Jesus, his White son. I see now that the missionaries taught the people to hate everything African—to view themselves as barbaric and uncivilized. They forced the Africans to enter a new order that alienated them from who they were—including their ancestors. Often the missionaries negotiated treaties that opened up the way for losing their land and their rights. They paved the way for King Leopold's plundering.

"'I am going to let the world know about this horror.'

279

Williams then set up his photographic equipment. It took a while; he squeezed the bulb, and a puff of smoke went up from the camera. The photo Williams took of Tswambe's maimed daughter was printed in newspapers worldwide and became an enduring image of Leopold's cruelty. His words, 'Crimes against humanity,' resonated with the public.

"Over a hundred years later, I have a copy of this photo on my bookcase in my apartment in Greenwich Village. I look at it every day and feel reenergized in the fight to help all of the people in the Congo to get repaid for the cruelty to tens of millions of our ancestors."

Jacques's audience fidgeted but wanted to hear more. Jacques continued, "I was determined to find out more about this George Washington Williams. He's one of our ancestors — someone else we can be proud of. He fought with the Union Army in the Civil War, with the Republicans in Mexico against the French, then with the U.S. Army. Williams, an acclaimed historian, was one of the first to write stories about the role of African-Americans in building America. He was the first African-American elected to the Ohio state legislature. In 1882, he wrote The History of the Negro Race in the United States, 1619-1880, the first official history book about African-Americans.

"Williams pleaded with the international community to help stop the cruelty in the Congo, to make restitution to the Africans whose land was taken away from them, and to bring to justice those responsible for the slaughter of so many innocent lives. Williams wrote personal letters to King Leopold and the U.S. Congress, making one of the first appeals for what we call 'reparations.'

"Williams supported '40 Acres and a Mule' for emancipated Blacks after the Civil War, but Lincoln's assassination ended that promise of restitution, justice, and reparations.

Williams said reparations was the right thing to do in the eyes of God and warned that if it were not done, the African people would someday rise up against the Europeans. George Washington Williams never met Mame. But he met her spirit in the Congo in 1890.

"And what about the Force Publique soldiers who carried out the work of the White leadership?" Jacques asked the group of his relatives. "They were forced into their inhumanity with threats to their lives and the lives of their families if they didn't carry out orders. The henchmen of King Leopold established a system whereby each bullet had to be accompanied by a cut-off hand. Otherwise, the army commanders feared that the men would use the bullets for hunting animals. Many Congolese men deserted the ranks of Force Publique and fled into Mame's Maroon camps. The Belgian king's army murdered nearly 10 million Congolese.

"Williams, unbeknownst to himself when writing the history of African-Americans in 1880, wrote about Mame's spirit. Williams was inspired by the Haitian Revolution of

August 14, 1791, in Bois Caiman (Bwa Kayiman), northern Haiti, and was nominated to be an ambassador to Haiti, though he never served.

"For the next thirteen years, the enslaved Africans in the French colony of Haiti fought against their enslavers, overthrowing them in 1803 to establish the first independent Black Republic in the history of the world—Haiti. Those voodoo spirits were the spirits of Mame, straight out of Africa, to Haiti, then to New Orleans, and now in my heart—and perhaps in yours.

"While Williams believed in Christ, he understood that many believed in the voodoo spirits. To the Christian, Jesus. To the Haitian, Ezili Dantor. Whatever a culture calls them, they inspire mortals to make the impossible possible. They continue to rise in some of the most unlikely places, from sugar fields in Louisiana to swampy rice farms in South Carolina to segregated rough-hewn pine pews in a rickety cedar church in the slums on the Black side of town.

"Williams in his historical writings credited the Haitian Revolution—Ezili Dantor—with inspiring the U.S. rebellions, revolts, and runaway slaves and their rebellions—of Gabriel Prosser in 1800, Charles Deslondes in 1811, Denmark Vesey in 1822, Nat Turner in 1831, Frederick Douglass in 1838, Harriet Tubman in 1849, and John Brown in 1859. The result was the American Civil War and the end of slavery.

"After six months, Williams left the Congo to return to the

United States by way of England to continue his campaign for reparations. He contracted tuberculosis in Africa, died in Blackpool, England, in 1891, and is buried there in Layton Cemetery.

"The spirit of Mame lives here, in New Orleans, New York City, Haiti, Paris, London, Brussels, and yes, even Antwerp, Belgium. Mame is there when the U.S. Congress debates reparations. Mame is there when Georgetown University pays reparations."

Jacques's voice became a whisper, and the crowd inched forward to hear him. "You can't see Mame unless you try. Yeah, you must open your heart, your mind, and, indeed, all your senses. Sometimes Mame is loud and dances with the drummers. Sometimes, she's quiet and pensive while reading a book.

"Mame is now rejoicing. Just before our gathering, the work of Mame became a reality. At the end of June 2020, Belgium's King Philippe expressed regret for his nation's and his ancestors' brutal colonization of the Congo. I think it was the Black Lives Matter protest in Brussels and the growing realization of what colonization meant that tipped the scales. The King announced a truth and reconciliation commission to examine the past. 'I would like to express my sincere and deepest regrets for these injustices of the past, the pain of which is now given new life by the discrimination still too present in our society,' the king said.

"The current head of the Congo said, 'I believe it necessary that our common history with Belgium and its people should be told to our children in the Democratic Republic of the Congo as well as those in Belgium.'

"Mame will not rest until we wipe out all the vestiges of colonialism. She will not be idle while there are inferior schools for Black children all across the globe. Mame will not be still until we work to improve the health and medical treatment of all Black people. Yes, she's part of the Black Lives Matter movement because a long time ago, she realized that Black Lives Matter!

Jacques concluded, "To capture a glimpse of Mame, let the bright sunshine into the hidden corners of your heart. It is up to you to find Mame. She's here now and in all important moments of your life as well as in the small moments—when you're walking home from school alone, bopping with headphones on in the subway, plaiting your girlfriend's hair, shooting hoops, and skipping Double-Dutch in front of your mom's house. She is everywhere. She leads not into the heart of darkness but into an immense light."

The end.

Or just the beginning...

Afterword by CMZ Blackwell

Dedicated to Four Reparations' Sheroes

Belinda Royal (1713-1793). Belinda was stolen from Africa in 1713, enslaved to the Royal family in Massachusetts until her "owner" fled America to Nova Scotia at the beginning of the American Revolution, leaving sixty-three of his enslaved people behind. She sued for a pension from his estate in 1782 for the forty years she worked for free but had nothing to show for her labor. Her lawsuit demanded $21.00 per year for the rest of her life. She wanted reparations, and she won.

Callie House (1861-1928). In the 1890s, Callie House established the National Ex-Slave Mutual Relief, Bounty and Pension Association with ex-slaves traveling the South encouraging other former slaves to build an organization seeking redress and reparations from state and federal governments for the theft of billions of dollars during slavery. In 1915, she estimated that Black people were owed $68,073,388.99 for the cotton they picked without pay during slavery. She and her organization kept reparations alive.

Queen Mother Audley Moore (1898-1997). She was born in New Iberia, Louisiana, and in 1898, migrated to New York City to join Marcus Garvey's UNIA, becoming an organizer and leader in the civil rights movement. In the early 1950s, she founded the Universal Association of Ethiopian Women and the Committee for Reparations for Descendants of U.S. Slaves. Queen Mother Moore was a major force for reparations, influencing world leaders to embrace reparations.

Nkechi Taifa (1955-present). She is a graduate of Howard University and George Washington University Law School, a leader and prominent spokesperson for N'COBRA, The National Coalition of Blacks for Reparations in America. She is the founder of the Taifa Group, advocating for social justice and racial equity worldwide. She also is the author of a memoir, *Black Power, Black Lawyer: My Audacious Quest for Justice* and a Senior Fellow for the Center for Social Justice at Columbia Law School, author of two Afro-Centric children's books and a major advocate for criminal justice reform with reparations at the center of her discourse and legal work.

****

Who am I? And while I'm at it, who are you? You may see me or not, but I am alive and well in the bosom of Bernie. You may read my full-bio on the *Mame's Spirit* website - mamespirit.com.

ALERT from CMZ. Remember, I am a muse. I am not of your world, but I am. The ancestors speak to me, and they are wise; then, I speak to you. Actually, or paradoxically, the ancestors are not really from the past. They are from the future, hence, Afro-Futurism. From their knowledge and wisdom of the past, they can predict the future. Here's the bad news, we have a very short window of opportunity to reverse the madness derived from poison we have ingested for 400 years.

CMZ grew out of revolutions. The revolutions of 1776 (U.S.), 1789 (France), 1791 (Haiti), 1861, (US Civil War), 1917 (Russia), 1949 (China), 1954 (Vietnam and Iran), 1955 (Ghana), 1959 (Cuba), 1962 (Algeria), 1968 (U.S.), and 1989 (South Africa) have called the question: How and why did the people who initiated, propelled, and dared to start those uprisings come about? Who were Sojourner Truth, Harriet Tubman, Ida B. Wells, Althea Gibson, Fanny Lou Hamer, and, yes, Unita Z. Blackwell?

I, CMZ, am the spirit of those revolutions and revolutionaries—my ancestors. They live within me. Do my ancestors' spirits just die and go away? If I were raised in their spirit, filled with compassion, anger, hopes, trauma, vision, tears, dreams, and joys, how could that spirituality just die with them? It does not. Their spirit is passed from one generation to another and never dies. It evolves. It assumes new vessels of expression.

As a popular proverb states: "We stand on the shoulders of the giants who came before us."

My collaboration with Bernard "Bernie" Demczuk goes back at least 400 years, maybe more. Not just the beginnings of the Atlantic Slave Trade when the invading English trod on the peaceful marshlands of Southeast

Virginia in 1619, disturbing the Great Blue Heron, yaupon hollies, nesting turtles, and wetlands. Native Americans for thousands of years cultivated this calm coastline, thanking the Great Sky Mother for an abundance of life-giving natural wonders. A few decades after the English arrived, they forced the natives off their ancestral lands and killed them by European disease and murder. A pattern began here. The year 1619 is just a convenient time to start a conversation about White supremacy and its resultant institutional and structural racism, perpetrating violence against people of color. So, we'll start but not stop there.

Bernie told me a story long ago in one of his classes that became my birthright, too. He said:

"The main reason I am standing in front of you as a professor and a person privileged to lead a good life is that two very strong souls were courageous enough to walk off a frozen potato plantation, one in Lviv, Ukraine and the other in Krakow, Poland in the middle of a war-torn famine in 1915 filled with revolution and poverty. These teenagers walked south 595 miles through Slovakia, Hungary, and Croatia in the dark winter with no food, money, or a ticket to America. They walked and walked, determined to flee the atrocities of WWI, trying to save themselves. While they walked, tens of thousands perished from starvation, red-hot shrapnel, or froze to death. But miraculously, they survived the trek to the Mediterranean Sea, stowed away on a merchant marine ship, making its way to England, then to America. They arrived in 1916 at an illegal Baltimore port, Turner Station, near the booming Bethlehem Steel Company. America was at war and needed steel to build ships, planes, bombs, guns, tanks, and artillery. Americans were in Europe fighting. The blast furnaces needed workers to mold the war machine.

Upon arriving in Baltimore unwashed and unkept but alive and nourished with sailors' war rations, they walked off the ship and into the mills. At the start of their journey in a foreign land, they could not read or write Polish or Ukrainian, let alone English, but they had a strong will to survive in a New World — America. They married in 1916 and had children. Those children, too, suffered the impact of war twenty-two years after the Great War.

Bernie explained, 'My mother was sixteen years old when she became a 'Rosie-the-Riveter' in the same steel mill during WW II, and my father was twenty-one when he enlisted in the Navy, serving in the South Pacific. He suffered a broken back and burned body when a Kamikaze plane hit the deck of his aircraft carrier. After the war, back in the same illegal shipping port that brought them together in 1916, Turner Station in East Baltimore, they married and became my mother and father in 1947.'

'After the war, they both worked in Baltimore factories on assembly lines for over 35 years. They only had a ninth-grade education. But their factory jobs with a strong union gave them good wages, benefits, and time off to raise their children decently. And here I stand in front of you because of my ancestors. Who am I?'

Then he said to each of us in class, "Who are you? Your assignment is to go home, research your family history this week and tell us next week *who you are because you are not just you. That is much too arrogant. Who are you, really? Where did you come from? And, why are you fortunate enough to study at this great university and enjoy the privileges of an American?"*

Mame's story is my birthright, and I have a right to be here. I am CMZ Blackwell. You may see me or not, but I am alive and well in the bosom, brains and brawn of Bernie. You may read my full-bio on the *Mame's Spirit* website - mamespirit.com.

You may call me muse, spirit, role-model, mentor, idol, exemplar or life coach. You may call me ancestor. But I'm here with you all the time, if only you will open your eyes, ears, heart, soul, mind and imagination. Where does that tickling feeling come from when listening to your favorite music? When you have those deepest thoughts watching a sunset, where does that clarity come from? What is that rush of adrenaline from seeing an impossible move to the hoop by Michael Jordan? That feeling, clarity, and rush are coming together after years, decades, and even centuries of those spirits who came before. Of course, those sensations come from within you, but how did you get here? You stand on the shoulders of your ancestors, and they swirl within you alive as you are now.

Now back to 400 years ago. The Polish and Ukrainian

peoples of Eastern Europe were peasants toiling under slavery and serfdom from the Middle Ages (5th - 12th C.) to the Renaissance (12th - 16th C.). They broke out of their bondage in The Age of Enlightenment (16th-17th C.). The people challenged the king and the all-powerful church doctrine that kept them tied to a false authority; they demanded land, bread, freedom, and self-determination. The king did not give it to them, they took it. Power concedes to no one. It never did and never will. It can only be shared if taken by force from those who will deny sharing the bounty. I'm paraphrasing Fredrick Douglass, of course.

Long before Europe's colonization of Africa, long before the scramble for Africa's riches and labor power, long before Africa's partition by European powers at the 1884 Berlin Conference that designated King Leopold II the sole owner of the land occupied by the Kongo people since 1200 CE, great African kingdoms reigned, ruled, conquered, and gave the world civilization starting in 4000 BCE.

The KiKongo (Congolese) were the first foragers in Central Africa 90,000 years ago. They were the organized civilizations in the region 3,000 years ago, developing the Bantu language, family, and community-oriented structures, religion, art, agriculture, ironworks, civil society rules and laws while Europeans were still living in caves killing each other with clubs and rocks. "Pardon the interruption," but where did those pyramids come from in North Africa 4,500 years ago? Who first smelted iron or first irrigated land so it could make the desert bloom? Who gave the world written language, art, sciences, astronomy, and medicine? Where did the concept of democracy originate? Sorry Greece and Rome, not you.

Even the KiKongo people more than 2,000 years ago were electing their tribal and nation-leaders by debate and vote. I do give you credit, though, after you appropriated the riches, knowledge, arts, culture and technologies of Africa, you were smart enough, let's say slick and diabolical enough, to wipe out all historic traces of Africa's greatness, erase their dynamic culture, and propagandize them as modern-day savages with your Tarzan images and lies. Today's engineers and mathematicians are still trying to figure out how my ancestors built the Pyramids of Giza four millennia ago.

But what's all of this have to do with Mame's spirit in the second millennia?

Culture makes history, not the other way around. Culture is socially constructed knowledge acquired over generations of ancestors contributing to their children, family, community, and tribe. In America, our culture was founded, cultivated, and formed over centuries of intense and often violent confrontations with different peoples, races, languages, classes, traditions, and migrations out of necessity and survival.

All cultural knowledge is acquired from the material conditions in which people struggle to live, survive, strive and thrive. When they are hungry, they revolt and steal food. When they are cold, they break into warm spaces. When they are disrespected, they fight back. The ancestors did not leave us in death; they stayed and shaped our present and marched into our future. History is not the past. History is the culture of people in the present, shaping the future.

But we cannot start nor stop at 400 years ago. Long before the English arrived on the shores of Virginia and Jamaica, Queen Khalifa was a Muslim warrior woman, leading her people in battles against the European colonizers. Overcome by the power of Portuguese guns, she was captured, enslaved, and forced to go to Brazil. Cunning, strong and smart, she escaped up the Amazon River, the same river that runs through the Congo, when the world was one continent, Pangea. She knew the river. The Portuguese did not. She established Maroon villages, eventually making her way into Central America and then lower California. Say her name, Khalifa, Anglicized to Califa, now known as California. California is named after an African warrior woman. Does the California school system teach this history? Why not? Mame is the spirit of Queen Khalifa, Queen N'Zinga, Queen Nanny of the Maroons, and Queen Harriet Tubman.

Many people believe there is an over-reaching one-God intelligent order to the universe (the natural order of the cosmos). Still, many spiritual gods help us find our way and offer advice and guidance moving forward. How many times have you heard your mother talk about the qualities of your grandmother or grandfather that enabled

293

you to come so far on your journey toward self-determination and the pursuit of happiness? The ancestors are alive within us if we are willing to open our ears and minds to listen to them. They intervene in our lives if we are willing to accept their wisdom. "Be like Mike." Be like Fanny Lou. Be like Harriet. Be like_____, fill in the blank with your own spiritual advisor.

I am from the Delta of Mississippi, from southern Poland. I am from Baltimore's Turner Station, from the Kongo. I am Treme. I fought for my freedom in Haiti, and I am still in Haiti, helping to support elementary school students in Le Cap Haitian. I drummed in Congo Square in the 1830s and again in 2019. I am D.C., don't mute me.

I caught touchdowns in College Park, studied in Paris and Nice. I raced motocross in Carlsbad. I picked coffee in Leon, Nicaragua. I was attacked working for Harold Washington in Chicago and Jesse in Alabama. I hunkered down in libraries far and wide. I fished on the Choptank and grooved in Washington Square Park.

Who am I? And who are you? Who will you become?

Frantz Fanon said:

"In the world through which I travel, I am endlessly creating myself." He said further, "And the white man, however intelligent he may be, he is incapable of understanding Louis Armstrong or songs from the Congo. I am Black not because I am cursed, but because my skin has captured all the cosmic effluvia. I am truly a drop of sun under the earth. I am in total fusion with the world, in sympathetic affinity with the earth, losing my id in the heart of the cosmos."

When Fanon explains who he is, he is talking about the future. The past is now, and now is the future. Colonialism and White supremacy tried to erase Black history, culture and the very soul of Black folks. As such, Black people always had to look to the future – Afro-Futurism. In describing himself, I thought he was describing Mame or Harriet Tubman or Queen Khalifa.

Europeans understood Fanon's crushing insight into genetics, sociology, anthropology, geography, science, culture, military conquest, and economics. Besides their unbridled hunger for wealth, domination and power, the Europeans quickly saw the African as a superior people "in total fusion with the world," who could only be stopped by violence and trickery. Violence was the way to create and maintain White supremacy. Violence defined White supremacy then and today. The Proud Boys, Oath Keepers, Boogaloo, and The Base are the new KKK dressed up in camo and tattoos, carrying AR-15s and tiki torches.

First the Africans, then the Native Americans, then the Mexicans, then the Irish, Chinese, Japanese, Italians, and Jews. Those darker-hued Europeans joined the Western Europeans becoming White by collaborating with suppressing the Indians and the Africans. For the Irishman and Italian to join White Americans, they joined police forces with the WASPs to crush the aspirations of African

Americans after the emancipation of 1865 and cleared the West of Natives for the Iron Horse. If the Natives refused to give up prime real estate at the intersection of great rivers, they were killed. Their scalps, called *Redskins,* were turned into the U.S. Army for a $10.00 bounty. Might this be the reason Native Americans wanted to change the name of the Washington football team?

Dr. Martin Luther King, Jr. said that the United States is the world's most prevalent purveyor of violence. He said the bombs dropping in Vietnam are exploding in the streets of Detroit. How many massacres can you count?

Fort Pillow in 1864, 255 dead.
Opelousas, Louisiana, in 1868, 225 dead.
Colfax, Arkansas, in 1873, 237 dead.
Wilmington, NC, in 1898, 175 dead.
Atlanta, Georgia, in 1906, 100 dead.
Elaine, Arkansas, in 1919, 200 dead.
Red Summer of 1919 in 30 cities, 550 dead.
Tulsa, Oklahoma, in 1921, 300 dead.
Rosewood, Florida, in 1923, 150 dead.
Between 1868 – 1968, 4,743 lynched. Why? To maintain White supremacy. The science, culture, and migration of melanin is the White supremacist's greatest fear.

George Floyd is the modern-day Emmett Till. Stacey Abrams is the modern-day Sojourner Truth. There's no going back, again. That young lady, Darnella Frazier, carrying a Steve Jobs invention, screwed up the old arrangement. She videotaped the murder of George Floyd for 9 minutes, 29 seconds, showing the world what White supremacy looks like. She exposed the "heart of darkness" in the "heart of the cosmos," and stuff went viral, or as Frantz Fanon said, "it saturated the total infusion of the world," and the rest is history but now called 'culture.'" "No justice, no peace."

No! No, it is not about better police training, although that is necessary. No, it is not about pumping more money into inner-city schools, although that is necessary. No, it is not about stopping voter suppression, although that is necessary, too. No, it is not about getting ten million electric cars on the streets, although necessary. All necessary. Not sufficient.

What is necessary and sufficient? Reparations. But let's pause here and not get too far ahead of ourselves.

This Era of George Floyd has ushered in a New Black Arts Movement, but guerrilla-art taggers are not the only ones painting "Black Lives Matter." Mayors and local government officials are doing it too on public streets and in public squares of America. A corporate consciousness never before known is growing—Delta Air opposing Georgia's voter suppression laws. Average, everyday young White Americans vote to elect Black-East Indian women and Black and Jewish men into the highest offices in America, including Georgia. White, Black, and Brown kids are holding hands, kissing in public and marrying. Trans-people are getting elected to office and excelling in the military. NASCAR bans Confederate flags and encourages "Black Lives Matter" to be embossed on race cars. No turning back this cultural tsunami initiated by Hip-Hop in 1979 when The Sugarhill Gang unloaded *Rappers Delight.*

At the same time, in 1979, Lee Atwater and Ronald Reagan saw a wedge issue into the body politic based on race and racism. They tried to convince poor Whites that Blacks aspiring to the American dream were why White insecurity, not politicians, would shut down steel mills, auto and textile plants and mines to secure higher profits overseas with cheaper non-union wages and benefits. And the labor union bosses like George Meany and Lane Kirkland fell right in line, blaming Blacks and women and the democratic aspiring Vietnamese for White workers' woes.

These politicians fueled their racist, White supremacist base, driven out-of-their-minds ever since the Supreme Court desegregated schools in 1954. Oh My God! My Pure White children might date Black and Brown kids. OH NO! The world is coming to an end. We must fight them with sticks and stones, guns, beat them, and throw them in jail. Re-fly the Confederate flag, again. Heaven and Jesus forbid White and colored children from dating and loving each other! Stop them with violence, if necessary!

The *Browning of America* will be official between 2042-2045, with Queen California, New Mexico, Hawaii, Nevada, Texas, and Washington, DC, already majority-minority. And what is the response of the right-wing Republican

Party? In 2016 they elected a racist enabled by bodyguards wearing camo and Neo-Nazi tattoos, strapping AR-15s. Might they look a little ridiculous as throwbacks to Neanderthal comic images? Yes, but take them seriously. They are dangerous domestic terrorists. Get ready. Remember what I said earlier? White supremacy can only be maintained with violence.

Remember the torture and murder of Emmett Till? Remember the murder of SNCC organizers Andrew Goodman, Michael Schwerner, and James Chaney. Remember the four little girls bombed to death in the church at Bible study in Birmingham? Remember the attacks on the Selma bridge. Remember the Confederate flag-waving racist who murdered nine people at Bible study in Charleston? Remember the murder of Jewish worshippers in the Tree of Life synagogue in Pittsburgh. "Jews, they will not replace us!" was the chant by tiki torch-carrying White supremacists in Charlottesville while the Racist-in-Chief called them "very fine people."

Who were those "patriots" who stormed the U.S. Capitol killing five people while carrying Confederate flags and erecting a hangman's gallows with a noose on January 6, 2021? Do your think they were All-American Boy Scouts? Maybe they were when they were twelve years old, but their twisted, angry and violent "patriotism" has molded them into killers. They will not be stopped with nice words and appeals to moral suasion. They have become mentally ill with the poison of institutional and structural racism embedded into American White culture for 400 years.

Racism started in the early 1600s, with British laws legalizing Africans and other people of color as less than the White Englishmen. Those BIG LIES became embedded into laws and created White supremacy, a very big lie.

After 246 years (1619-1865) of the laws of slavery, they then embedded another 103 years (1865-1968) with more BIG LIE-laws, establishing Black Codes, the convict-lease system, Jim Crow, lynching, red-lining, and mass incarceration. These legal structures became embedded into our institutions, creating a culture of White is right and superior, and Black is wrong and inferior. The system *was* founded on the BIG LIE of White supremacy. Their M.O. is domestic terrorism today, just as it was in the Post-Reconstruction era and during slavery.

For a 500-year historical overview of White supremacy, watch Raoul Peck's series "Exterminate All the Brutes."[1] Peck examines the origins of White supremacy, racism, and colonialism in a series streaming on HBO MAX. The docudrama, an illustrated lecture, provides a film essay on the history of White supremacy. The title comes from the line spoken by Kurtz's character in Joseph Conrad's novel *The Heart of Darkness*, 1899, detailing the "crimes against humanity" committed against the people of the Congo.

The poison of racism is tearing us apart from within. History is clear on this point. All great empires collapsed from within, not from outside assault. Racism and White

---

[1] https://www.hbo.com/exterminate-all-the-brutes

supremacy are tearing us apart. White men and infected White women (47 percent of white women voted for Trump) are going crazy, trying to stop Black and Brown people from organically and legally becoming the majority. They are insane with a pandemic of racism, hurling us toward a second American Civil War. If we do not reverse this downward spiral, our American Empire is over. Finished. China, Russia, India, Germany, and the African continent's combined countries qua Africa, are next in line to become the next superpowers. The more we tear each other down, the stronger our competitors get.

If we do not understand how White supremacy maintains a stranglehold with violence and if we are not prepared to stop the White supremacists, then we do not understand the war they started when a Black man and a Black woman lived in the White House for eight years. They are winning the war by making us weak from within first.

But here's the good news. I do think we have time to reverse this downward trend. And here's how: American exceptionalism. Yes, I believe we are exceptional in many ways. Our organic diversity is our secret strength and also our exceptionalism. The more eyes and minds on a problem from different perspectives, the quicker and better we can solve the problem. But White supremacists want only their viewpoint and knowledge base. They cannot possibly solve problems judiciously and fully without employing violence. Our eyes did not lie when we watched the George Floyd video. We saw a murder. And finally, the jury saw what we saw.

Our eyes did not lie on January 6, 2021. We saw White supremacists waving Confederate flags storm the U.S. Capitol; they killed five people and erected gallows, chanting, hang Nancy Pelosi and Mike Pence. They are domestic terrorists. Today, they have slithered back into the woods in the Great White Upper North, the hills of Appalachia, the suburbs of Dallas, cattle ranges in Wyoming, and practice rapid-fire gun practice on the Eastern Shore Maryland, where I hear them shooting every night after work. Their Congressman, Andy "New Jim Crow" Harris, voted several times to overturn the election of Biden and Harris fully supported by his right-wing militiamen dressed in camo. I count three Confederate flags in my local area when I drive just fifteen miles from Easton to Denton, Maryland. Believe your eyes! Those wavers of the Confederate flag support violence against people of color. The Second American Civil War is on. Domestic terrorism is on the rise. If we do not win the second American Civil War, The American Empire is over.

We rose out of severe adversity before: The 1776 revolution, the War of 1812, the Civil War, the Great Depression, the Civil Rights Movement, the Vietnam War, and the Great Recession of 2008, and now the pandemic and a further recession. We came back each time, and we were stronger and better for it. We can do it again. Here's how:

1. Stop the White supremacists and their domestic terrorism by any means necessary. Use the power of the courts, the legislatures, the media, the Justice

Department, the schools, and society to stop their terror. If necessary, use violence to stop their violence. Fine them to the point of bankrupting them as we did to the KKK in the 1990s.

2. The federal government must transfer trillions of dollars from waging constant war and funding the industrial-war-military-police complex. Tax the super-rich and corporations that pay zero income tax and pump those trillions into struggling White, Black, and Brown communities in massive debt who struggle from paycheck to paycheck—on the verge of bankruptcy and homelessness. We spent 6.4 trillion dollars in Middle East wars since 2001, and what do we have to show for it? Spend those trillions of dollars on jobs, job training, affordable housing, public works, infrastructure, health care, daycare, better schools, climate and environmental justice, free community college, and criminal justice reform. We must take the initiative and the care to improve the lives of the bitter and disillusioned White workers; they blame people of color for their woes and turn to White supremacy rather than understand that the super-rich employ White supremacy to blame the poor and people of color.

3. Both White workers and people of color are interested in the rich paying their fair share and ending the cycle of constant, costly war. Each state and local jurisdiction needs a New Federal Works Project Administration to fund billions of dollars

into arts, cultural and history programs locally to drive economic development and revenues into state and local coffers and put artists, teachers, historians, and cultural workers to work.

4. The federal government must create a Domestic Peace Corps, similar to the CCC camps (Civilian Conservation Corps) in the Great Depression that put hundreds of thousands of youth to work improving parks, playgrounds, schools, rural and urban recreation centers, green spaces, and mandating that every high school graduate devotes at least two years to the domestic peace corps or volunteer two years to work abroad, assisting developing countries in need of peaceful works projects.

5. The U.S. Department of Education must create truth-based Critical Race Theory (CRT) education, which will enable our children to learn honest American history and culture, teach us how to celebrate all races and cultures, and increase proficiency in other languages to appreciate other people worldwide and people of color in the United States. CRT does not divide races nor run-down America's past. It tells the truth about our history to begin the process of healing the harms of the past. The purpose of history is not to make you feel good. Its purpose is grappling with the past to improve the future.

6. Along with our children, we must study the history and theory of reparations in schools and hold creative local debates to figure out how to repair the harms done over the last 400 years and heal the pain between the races so that we never again have to fear violent White supremacists and their domestic terrorism agenda.

Reparations. What does it mean? According to the National Coalition of Blacks for Reparations in America (N'COBRA), reparations is "Payment for a debt owed; the act of repairing a wrong or injury; to atone for wrongdoings; to make amends; to make one whole again; the payment of damages to repair a nation; compensation in money, land, or, materials for damages." In America today, we have numerous creative forms of reparations, reflecting this definition. For example:

1. The city of Manhattan Beach in Los Angeles County, California, passed legislation in 2021 returning prime waterfront property to the Charles and Willa Bruce family who owned the waterfront resort, Bruce's Beach, enjoyed by African Americans during Jim Crow, but stolen from them by the city in 1924 after years of KKK harassment. The descendants of the Bruces will have the prime waterfront property returned to them with $70 million worth of equity from wages, business profits, and waterfront land value taken from them since 1924.

2. Georgetown University students in November 2019 voted to assess themselves additional tuition costs to establish a $400,000 fund for reparations to the descendants of 272 enslaved African Americans who were owned by the university Jesuits and sold "Down the River" (the Mississippi River) from the university in 1838. The enslaved were sold into Louisiana sugar cane slavery, the worse form of slavery in America. The life-expectancy rate was five-to-seven years due to harsh slave labor conditions, heat, humidity and malaria. The university sold the enslaved men, women and children to satisfy the university's debt. The university will now admit with a full scholarship any descendant of those enslaved and sold by the university.

3. Evanston, Illinois, passed legislation in March 2021 to pay reparations to any African-American family that was "harmed by discriminatory housing policies, practices and inaction on the city's part" during the Jim Crow era from the early 1900s to the 1970s. The city council voted 8-1 to set aside a start-up fund of $400,000 for down payments for new homes or home repairs, offering $25,000 per Black family. The city said the legacy of harm caused by slavery, Jim Crow, White supremacy, redlining and racism must be alleviated and the pain of past wrongs healed.

These are but three modern-day forms of reparations that

local Americans have agreed to pay for past wrongs saying, "We harmed, we are sorry, and we want to make amends, help to heal the pain, and move us to a better place and a better America."

Many local jurisdictions in American now grapple with ideas and methods of reparations to their local Black community to heal the pain for past harms. In Washington, DC, the city council passed a law to study reparations and commission a team of experts to find ways to correct the harm done to African Americans in our Nation's Capital. D.C., founded in 1791, was a jurisdiction where slavery was a way of life and where enslaved people built the U.S. Capitol, the White House, and virtually the entire city without reward or compensation. Today, in D.C., African Americans die from diabetes five times the rate of Whites; they die from COVID-19 three times the rate of Whites, and where White household wealth in D.C. is $284,000, it is only $3,500 for Blacks—the legacy of slavery and White supremacy. These are the "stubborn facts" we are trying to reverse and repair.

When the Nation's Capital ended slavery on April 16, 1862, nine months before the general Emancipation Proclamation that went into effect on January 1, 1863, former slave owners in D.C. received compensation of $300 for each of their enslaved property that they set free. In other words, the slave owners were paid reparations!

Reparations are not some wild, made-up, crazy idea that a bunch of angry people dreamed up to upset White people.

It's a fairly conservative idea. Writing in the Sunday Op. Ed. section of *The Washington Post* on April 25, 2021, Gary Abernathy, a conservative Republican, penned "Why I support reparations — and why all conservatives should."

Abernathy said, "Like most conservatives, I scoffed at the idea of reparations. I did not enslave anyone, so why would I support my tax dollars for reparations or an apology?" When Mr. Abernathy began studying wealth, health care, housing, education, and criminal justice disparities between Blacks and Whites after reading *From Here to Equality: Reparations in the Twenty-First Century* by William A. Darity, Jr., Abernathy wrote, "Black household net worth averages $17,600 — a little more than one-tenth of median White net worth" at $171,000."

Abernathy quoted Darity saying, "White parents, on an average, can provide their children with wealth-related intergenerational advantages at a far greater degree than Black parents. When parents offer gifts to help their children buy a home, avoid student debt, or start a business, those children can retain and build wealth over their lifetimes."

Abernathy ended by saying, "It is a tenet of conservatism that a level playing field is all we should guarantee. But that's meaningless if one starts with an insurmountable lead before the play even begins. It's not necessary to experience 'White guilt' or buy into the notion of 'White privilege,' a pejorative that to me suggests Whites possess something they should lose, when in fact, such benefits should extend to all. Supporting reparations requires a universal agreement to work toward righting that wrong."

American sportswriter Ralph Wiley was fond of using sports analogies when describing reparations. If a White woman sprinter in the 100-meter dash starts thirty-five meters ahead of a Black woman sprinter, who do you think will win the race regardless of who is faster? He may have said it best when he wrote:

"Give me the free labor of one Black person for one year; I would be a rich man.

Give me the free labor of a dozen Black people for one year; I would be a very rich man.

Give me the free labor of millions of Black people for 250 years; I would be America!"

But raise the specter of reparations to White supremacists, and they will accuse you of being a Communist-demon who wants to crush the White race and populate American with all Black, Brown Muslims, Mexicans, Gays, Trans-people, and Socialists to wipe out the White race. These notions of "The Other" plotting to take over the United States is very old and tiresome. It is wrong; it is the same paranoia that we have heard for hundreds of years. But the alt-right believes it, and they are dangerous.

The threat is real; domestic terrorists are here, now and increasing. Domestic terrorism has soared under the Racist-in-Chief Donald Trump, with White supremacy incidents rising 123 percent from 2018 to 2019 with 1,214 to 2,713 activities. It then rose again another 90 percent in 2020 to 3,566 incidences. According to the Southern Poverty Law Center, White hate groups increased 128 percent from 1999-2018, with the biggest rise since Barack Obama entered the White House. The Proud Boys, Oath Keepers, Boogaloo, and other like-minded camo-wearing, Neo-KKK members plot a violent overthrow of the U.S. government, trying to start a race war. They are training every day in war-games-camps in rural country sides. On December 8, 2020, Maryland District Court Judge Theodore D. Chuang sentenced a resident from the Eastern Shore of Maryland, William Bilbrough IV, to five years in prison for participating in The Base, a domestic terror group training in Georgia, plotting to start a race war to kill Jews and African Americans. If he were not in prison on January 6, 2021, he would have been storming the U.S. Capitol.

I believe in passing legislation, lobbying, letter-writing, voting, petitioning the government, waging peaceful protests, and non-violent direct action to solve social injustice and racial inequality issues. However, I am violently non-violent. Why are camo-clad Neo-Nazis, strapped in AR-15s strutting around State Court Houses plotting to kidnap governors and kill them? How do you protect yourself against a rattlesnake that refuses to back up? Cut his head off.

Question: Why did Reconstruction fail after 1877? It's simple. The federal government removed armed Union troops stationed throughout the South to protect African-

American enfranchisement and freedoms to work, worship, travel, build businesses, own land, build schools, publish newspapers, and elect Black officials. The Union troops needed guns to protect the four million Black people newly emancipated in 1865.

In 1876, presidential candidate Rutherford B. Hayes agreed to withdraw these protective troops in exchange for southern votes to secure the presidency. With the removal of an armed force protecting African Americans, the KKK, the White League, the Knights of the White Camellia, Red Shirts, and the White Citizens Councils organized to terrorize African Americans to keep them from voting, owning land, building businesses and their communities for the next 100 years. They killed, lynched, burned out, raped, mutilated, and terrorized Blacks with guns and violence to stop them from voting. And why did the insurrectionists storm the U.S. Capitol? To reverse the huge Black vote-turnout in Atlanta, Philadelphia and Milwaukee that gave Biden the victory. Deja vu.

In addition, President Andrew Johnson, a slave owner, who became president when a White supremacist assassinated Abraham Lincoln, pardoned all the slave-owning Confederate officers. These officers organized the anti-Black KKK terrorist groups, establishing the Black Codes, the convict-lease system, Jim Crow, and aided and abetted lynching. Over 4,700 lynchings occurred from 1868-1968, sending a clear message to Black Americans that they will be killed if they dare to question White supremacy.

311

A rabbi once asked me, "Do you know the mistake we made during the 19th and 20th centuries?" The rabbi said in a low and gentle voice, "We did not master the gun." Zahkor![2] Never, ever forget who the Nazis and White supremacists are. They will murder us and anyone else who does not look like good-ole-boys in camo.

Ida B. Wells once said, "In every Negro household, there should be a place of honor above the mantle for a repeater Winchester to protect us from what the law will not." No, I am not violent. But I am violently non-violent. The White supremacists are coming and getting closer. Be like Mame, like Khalifa, like Harriet. Be ready.

Stop with the accusations. I am non-violent. Period. But I study history. Historically, only after direct action, that sometimes turns violent from White supremacists trying to stop civil liberties, has social change happened: the American Revolution; the end of slavery; women suffrage; the signing of the 64, '65, and '68 civil rights acts; the pullout from Vietnam; and police reform in the Era of George Floyd. Why is it so hard to do the right thing?

Some White people view themselves as a public enemy walking the streets. Some are on the defensive and scared. They perceive that America's history, social, cultural, economic, and political march is not their friend. They feel pressure. Insecure. Erasure. Black and Brown culture

---

[2] Zahkor (You shall remember) is historical thinking of a very high order—mature speculation based on massive scholarship invented by the Jews of Mali.

impacts the news media, sports, entertainment, film, primetime T.V., the fashion industry, vernacular language, the criminal justice system, religion, cuisine, and education. These things are happening worldwide, from K-Pop to South African Be-Bop to some of the best baseball in the world in the Dominion Republic, Cuba, Puerto Rico, Japan, Korea, and Venezuela. One of America's greatest examples of *exceptionalism* is our export of extraordinary Black culture. It's a multi-trillion-dollar industry where everyone, to a degree, benefits and enjoys.

However, the more that White people feel they are the enemy (in the case of White Nationalism, they are) of American progress, the more they strike back and delay the inevitable march toward an America that rewards young people for their skills and the "content of their character" rather than the good-ole-boy network.

There is no need to turn against White people where White, Black and Brown are making amends and getting along better. James Baldwin said, "It is not necessary to tear down the White man to uplift the Black man."

Or, as the conservative Republican Gary Abernathy said above, it's not the intent of reparations to take from White people and give to Black people. The intent is to right past wrongs, repair damage done, heal the psyche, and heal the land. White working-class people are in economic peril and dislocation in this highly charged technological economy that seems to be passing them by. They need financial support and programs from the government,

313

bringing promise and progress to their lives, families, and communities. West Virginia miners are not the enemy. They need support and a massive infusion of government programs in health care, education, job training, and public works projects jump-starting new industry, tourism, and commerce in their beautiful environment. The more we care for each other, the less we turn against each other.

Who am I? I am CMZ. I am Ayo. I am you.

Nice to meet you. Let's try to get along.

CMZ Blackwell

For a full bio on CMZ, go to: **mamespirit.com**

Bibliography and Resources

Website: www.mamespirit.com. Please visit and leave your comments.

Mame's Spirit is a novel but built on the work of many notable individuals. If you would like to read about the spirit of Mame or other topics discussed in this novel, I recommend the following books and other resources.

We Are All Africans:

Alex, Bridget. "We Are All Africans," *Discover Magazine.com*, December 21, 2016. We Are All Africans | Discover Magazine

Mascarelli, Amanda. "Climate Swings Drove Early Humans Out of Africa (and Back Again)," September 21, 2016. *Sapiens.org.* out of Africa theory - Climate Swings Drove Early Humans Out of Africa - SAPIENS

Reparations:

Abernathy, Gary. "Why I support reparations and why all conservatives should." April 22, 2021. Op-Ed. *Washington Post.* Opinion | Why I support reparations — and all conservatives should - The Washington Post

Araujo, Ana Lucia. *Reparations for Slavery and the Slave Trade: A Transnational and Comparative History*, 2017.

Bloomsbury Academic.

Berry, Mary Frances. *My Face is Black is True: Callie House and Her Struggle Ex-Slave Reparations*, 20006. Vintage Reprint.

Bittker, Boris. *The Case for Black Reparations*, 2nd Ed. 2003. Beacon Press.

Blakemore, Erin. "The Thorny History of Reparations in The United States," Updated August 29, 2019. History.com. The Thorny History of Reparations in the United States - HISTORY

Brooks, Roy L. *Atonement and Forgiveness: A New Model of Black Reparations*, 2004. University of California Press.

Brophy, Alfred. *Reparations: Pro and Con*, 2006. Oxford University Press.

Coates, Ta-Nehisi. "The Case for Reparations," *The Atlantic*, May 22, 2014. https://www.theatlantic.com/magazine/archive/2014/

Ekiyor, Henry A. Making a Case for Reparations, The Journal of Pan African Studies1:9, August 2007. Reparations1.9.doc (jpanafrican.org)

Feagin, Joe R. *Racist America: Roots, Current Realties and Future Reparations*, 2000. Routledge.

Franke, Katherine. *Repair: Redeeming the Promise of Abolition.* 2019. Haymarket Books.

Henry, Charles P. *Long Overdue: The Politics of Racial*

Reparations, 2009, NYU Press.

Horowitz, David. *Uncivil Wars: The Controversy Over Reparations for Slavery*, 2003. Encounter Books.

Peck, Raoul "Exterminate All the Brutes." Series streaming on HBO Max. https://www.hbo.com/exterminate-all-the-brutes.

Robinson, Randall and Lisa Jewell. *The Debt: What America Owes Blacks*, 2001. Plume.

Shriver, Don. *Honest Patriots: Loving a Country Enough to Honor its Misdeeds*, 2008. Oxford University Press.

Taifa, Nkechi Taifa. Black Power, Black Lawyer: My Audacious Quest for Justice. 2020. House of Songhay.

Taylor, Flint. "Were Chicago's Police Torture Reparations From 5 Years Ago Implemented?" *Popular Resistance.org*, 2020. https://popularresistance.org/were-chicagos-police-torture-reparations-from-5-years-ago-implemented/

Torpey, John. *Making Whole What Has Been Smashed: Reparations Politics*, 2007. Rutgers University Press.

Winbush, Raymond. *Should America Pay: The Raging Case for Reparations*, 2003. Amistad.

The Congo:

Butcher, Tim. *Blood River*, 2008. Vintage Books.

Conrad, Joseph. *Heart of Darkness*, [originally published as a book, 1902] Red Globe Press. 1998.

De Witte, Ludo. *The Assassination of Lumumba*, 2nd Ed. 2003. Verso.

Devlin, Larry. *Chief of Station Congo: Fighting the Cold War in a Hot Zone*. 2008. Public Affairs.

Donelson, Dave. *Heart of Diamonds: A Novel of Scandal, Love and Death in the Congo*. 2009. CreateSpace.

Franklin, John Hope. *George Washington Williams: A Biography*, 2008. Duke University Press.

Guevarra, Che. *Che in Africa: Che Guevarra's African Diary*, 1999. Ocean Press.

Hochschild, Adam. *King Leopold's Ghost: A Story of Greed, Terror, and Heroism in Colonial Africa.* 1999. Houghton Mifflin.

Kingsolver, Barbara *The Poisonwood Bible*, 2013. Faber and Faber.

LaGamm, Alisa. *Kongo: Power and Majesty*, 2015. Metropolitan Museum of Art.

Lumumba, Patrice. *Congo My Country*, 1962. Praeger.

Meredith, Martin. *The Fate of Africa: A History of the Continent Since Independence.* 2011. Public Affairs.

Mudimbe, V. Y. *Before the Birth of the Moon*, 1989. Simon & Schuster.

Nest, Michael. *Coltan*, 2011. Polity.

Newkirk, Pamela. *Spectacle: The Astounding Life of Ota Benga*, 2016. Amistad.

Nkrumah, Kwame. *The Challenge of the Congo*, 1967. Panaf.

Nzongola-Natalaja, Georges. *Patrice Lumumba*, 1964. Ohio University Press.

Nzongola-Natalaja, Georges. *The Congo: From Leopold to Kabila, A People's History*, 2002. Zed Books.

Rutz, Michael A. *King Leopold's Congo and the Scramble for Africa*, 2018. Hackett Publishing,

Stearns, Jason. *Dancing in the Glory of Monsters: The Collapse of the Congo*, 2012. Public Affairs.

Turnbull, Colin M. *The Forest People*, 1987. Touchstone.

Twain, Mark. *King Leopold's Soliloquy: A Defense of His Congo Rule*. [originally published 1905]. 2018. CreateSpace.

Van Reybrouck, David. *Congo: The Epic History of a People*, 2010. Ecco.

Williams, Susan *Who Killed Hammarskjold: The UN Cold War and White Supremacy in Africa*, 2014. Oxford University Press.

Wrong, Michela. *In the Footsteps of Mr. Kurtz: Living on the Brink of Disaster in Mobutu's Congo*. 2002. Harper Perennial.

West African Spirituality:

Alvarado, Denise. *Hoodoo & Conjure Quarterly: A Journal of Magical Arts with a Focus on New Orleans Voodoo, Hoodoo, Magic and Folklore*, 2011. Create Space

Assan-Anu, Hru Yuya T., *Grasping the Root of Divine Power*, 2011. Create Space

Clarke, Austin *The Polished Hoe*, 2004. Amistad.

Correal, Tobe Morela. *Finding Soul on the Path to Orisa: West African Spiritual Tradition*, 2003. Crossing Press.

Doumbia, Adama. *The Way of the Elders: West African Spirituality and Tradition*, 2004. Llewellyn.

Ephirim-Donkor, Anthony *African Spirituality: On Becoming Ancestors*, Revised Ed., 2011. Upa.

Gebmudu, Ife. *West African Spirituality in Social Work Practice*, 2004. Authorhouse.

Hochschild, Adam. *King Leopold's Ghost: A Story of Greed, Terror, and Heroism*, 1999, Houghton Mifflin.

James, Marlon. *Black Leopold, Red Wolf*, 2019. Random House.

Joiner, Monique. *Seven African Powers: The Orishas*, 2016. Oshun Publications, LLC.

Olajubu, Oyeronka. *Women in the Yoruba Religious Sphere*, 2003. State University of New York.

Olupona, Jacob. *African Spirituality: Forms, Meanings, and*

Expressions, 2001. Herder & Herder.

Opulona, Jacob *Beyond Primitivism: Indigenous Religions and Modernity*, 2003. Routledge.

Some, Malidoma Patrice. *Ritual: Power, Healing and Community*, 1993. Swan Raven and Co.

Some, Malidoma Patrice. *Of Water and the Spirit: Ritual, Magic and Initiation in the Life of an Ancient Shaman*, 1995. Penguin Books.

Some, Malidoma Patrice. *The Healing Wisdom of Africa: Finding Life Purpose Through Nature, Ritual and Community*, 1998. Tarcher Perigree.

Some, Sobonfu E. *The Spirit of Intimacy: Ancient Teaching in the Ways of Relationships*, 2000. William Morrow.

Thompson, Robert Ferris. *Black Gods and Kings, Yoruba Art at UCLA*, 1976. Indiana University Press.

West, Elizabeth J. *African Powers in Women's Fiction: Threaded Visions of Memory, Community, Nature and Being.* 2011. Lexington Books.

Williams, George Washington *The History of the Negro Race in the United States, 1619-1880*, 2016. Create Space.

Algeria:

Algerian War of Independence, *World Atlas*. https://www.worldatlas.com/feature/the-algerian-war-of-independence.html.

Champagne, Duane. "Assimilation, Integration, and Colonization." February 7, 2016. *Indian Country Today*. https://indiancountrytoday.com/archive/assimilation-integration-and-colonization-7wy5Jkji8k-drES-ocFfwA.

Cobban, Helena. "Between our life and our mother Algeria, we chose our mother: Excerpt from *Inside the Battle of Algiers: Memoir of a Woman Freedom Fighter*. 2017. Mondoweiss. https://mondoweiss.net/2017/09/between-excerpt-freedom/

Drif, Zora. *Inside the Battle of Algiers: Memoir of a Woman Freedom Fighter.* Just World Books, 2017. English translator Andrew Farrand.

Haffaf, Melyssa. "Algerian women have waited 57 years for equality. Now it's time for action." *International Journal of Francophone Studies*, 21(3-4). 2018. Intellect Ltd Article. English language. DOI: 10.1386/ijfs.21.3&4.233_1.

https://www.washingtonpost.com/opinions/2019/04/04/.

Moussa, Nedjib Sidi. "Algerian Feminism and the Long Struggle for Women's Equality. The Conversation." October 4, 2016. https://theconversation.com/algerian-feminism-and-the-long-struggle-for-womens-equality-65130.

Rountree, Kathryn. "Catholic missionaries in Africa: The White Fathers in the Belgian Congo 1950-1955." 2009. LSU Master's Thesis. 3278. https://digitalcommons.lsu.edu/gradschool_theses/327 8. September 26, 2017.

Shatz, Adam. *The Torture of Algiers. The New York Review of Books.* www.nybooks.com/articles/2002/11/21/the-torture-of-algiers/.

Wilson, Siona. "Severed images: Women, the Algerian War of Independence and the mobile documentary idea." City University of New York. https://www.gc.cuny.edu/CUNY_GC/media/Handboo ks/Wilson_SeveredImages.pdf.

About The Author

Bernard Demczuk, Ph.D., is a professor of African American history and culture living in Washington, DC and the Eastern Shore of Maryland. An avid traveler in the Deep South, he searches for blue bottle trees and their stories in South Carolina, Mississippi, Louisiana, and the secret gardens of New Orleans's Treme, French Quarter, and the Lower 9th Ward communities.

He spends considerable time in the Mississippi Delta, attracted to its landscape, history, culture, but mostly its people: humble, funny, smart, and tough. He gives civil rights tours of the Mississippi Delta and New Orleans and is obsessed with Emmett Till, Ella Baker, and Congo Square. And Jimmy Morrison. Toni, too. He likes to say, "One cannot understand America without understanding Mississippi first." He loves Memphis dry-rub BBQ and fried Delta catfish—throw in cold beer and the Blues at a Delta juke joint festival—he's in heaven.

He likes frogs, swamps, bayous, bass-fishing, and sunsets. He enjoys sweating in his gardens when it's 95 degrees. Hot weather makes him happy. Danger too. He likes to walk in the woods naked during snowstorms at night with only a flashlight leading the way. When violent July storms approach with the "speed of summer lighting" across cornfields and wetlands, he likes to stand on his river pier in the stinging rain and wind, naked again.

For his 70th birthday, he climbed *and summited* Mt. Kilimanjaro in Africa. It almost killed him. He did so not only to reach "The Roof of Africa" but to go through the roof experiencing the spirituality of the origins of

325

humanoids in the East African Rift Valley: "We are all Africans," he says. "We all come from Africa. That's why it's called 'Mother Africa.'"

He's a good cook, wears a "chef's hat" stirring up omelets with lots of butter and herbs de Provence from his garden. He can make a good rosemary-roasted chicken ala Julia Child - butter under the skin. He loves to cook for friends and banter during dinner, telling stories of which some are true. Yes, he did play professional football with the Philadelphia Eagles farm team, *The Firebirds,* the 1970 Atlantic Coast Conference Champions as a wide receiver. And yes, in 1974, he raced motorcycles across the USA with Robert Pastrana (Travis Pastrana's father). Yes, he almost died a few times doing so. And yes, he has been arrested twenty-three times for civil, human rights, and anti-war activities.

He went to the University of Maryland on a football scholarship, participating in the Student Nonviolent Coordinating Committee (SNCC) in Cambridge, Maryland, '64-'66. Stokely Carmichael kicked him and other White students out of SNCC in '67, but he understood why and agreed with Stokely. Now, he thinks it was a mistake.

Bernie was born in 1947 in a small Polish-Ukrainian community in Turner Station in Baltimore surrounded by a large and successful Black community. His very smart and kind parents only had 9th-grade educations but worked hard in factories.

His family doctor was the famous Dr. Joseph Thomas, a Black man in Turner Station, Bernie's first hero. His second was Jackie Robinson. The community where he grew up was overwhelmingly Black, where stars like Congressman Kweisi Mfume, Henrietta Lacks, Kevin Clash, Astronaut Robert Curbeam, and NFL player Calvin Hill lived. He played baseball there daily and swam in the Turner Station Park Beach with Black kids. They didn't discriminate.

He was a trusted confidante and senior advisor to Jesse Jackson, Sr., Mayor Marion Barry, Congressman Mike Espy, and Mayoral candidate Harold Washington. That explains his affinity for Black culture. He was often the only White guy in the room. He sometimes spells the name of his country: AmeriKKKA, and until it rids itself of the New-KKK wearing camouflage-hunting gear and toting AR-15s, he will continue. Do something US Justice Department—Stop Domestic Terrorism!

A blues and be-bop enthusiast, he would rather listen to Sun House and Coltrane mixed with Mozart. He's an art collector. He dug his own wine cellar along with Josh Lasky. His friends stock it—it's their tariff when visiting his four-one-half acre garden on the Eastern Shore possessing the only exact replica of Monet's Japanese Footbridge in the world. True! His country house, *GivernyWest on the Choptank,* is dedicated to Claude Monet and local residents Harriet Tubman and Frederick Douglass. His library in the woods, *The Growlery,* is a nod to Charles Dickens's and Frederick Douglass's libraries.

He believes in violent-non-violence and possesses many firearms. His favorite quote is from Ida B. Wells, "In every Negro's home above the mantel should be a place of honor for a Winchester rifle to protect them from what the law will not." He only hates Neo-Nazis and Neo-KKKers like Proud Boys, Oath Keepers, the Boogaloo and their violent ilk.

He's happy watching sunsets on the Choptank River, writing poetry, listening to *Love's Supreme* and Mozart arias competing with mating frogs in summer. He catches catfish and blue crabs off his pier, watching and waving at a myriad of waterfowl.

He lived in Paris in 1989 not to return, until Jesse called him to come home and work for him. In Pere La Chaise Cemetery, he often visited Jimmy Morrison and Edith Piaf's graves and *Le Mur des Federes*, placing red carnations. Bernie travels easily to exotic places but would rather be in LA with his son, Che Marley Demczuk, at a Dodgers versus Nats game, chowing down on a ballpark spicy-mustard hotdog, drinking an IPA with his glove ready to catch a foul ball that never comes his way. Still, he hopes, glove at ready.

329

He can be reached at <u>bdemczuk@gwu.edu</u>. See his full bio at <u>mamespirit.com</u>.

About CMZ Blackwell

CMZ Blackwell is a part-time farmer, poet, history teacher, agro-ecologist, raconteur, and aspiring actor living on a Delta farm collective in Issaquena County, Mississippi. But most importantly, CMZ is Bernie's muse. She/he is an international traveler fluent in French, struggling to learn Creole. CMZ is often in Clarksdale in the Delta listening to the Blues at Reds Lounge juke joint yet as comfortable in Provence reading Frantz Fanon in cafes or drumming in Congo Square, NOLA, and Washington Square Park in The Village.

 CMZ studied French and Africana Studies at Tougaloo College in Jackson, Mississippi, then in the South of France at Aix-Marseilles University. She/he worked in French-speaking West Africa in the US Peace Corps, experiencing out-of-body moments during two civil wars that altered her/his consciousness. CMZ's experiences in war-torn Africa reminding her/him that "There is always something new out of Africa." (Pliny the Elder) She/he is

331

an Afro-Futurist, and says – the past is not history, it is the future if we know how to envision a world without White supremacy, greed and what our ancestors dreamed for their children.

Strangely, CMZ is a New Yankees fan obsessed with Derek Jeter and can rattle off all his stats. She/he loves a NY hotdog with ballpark mustard at Yankee Stadium in the Bronx. Although often unseen, yet everywhere, she/he will read your handwritten letters and cards with sketches of flowers, birds, animals, cotton fields, sunsets, rivers, and humanoids. Write to CMZ at PO Box 509, Mayersville, MS 39113. See CMZ's full bio at mamespirit.com.

Made in the USA
Monee, IL
31 December 2021

3d9bb255-0c10-4440-963e-ac35c4d89b4dR01